THE MECHANICS' INSTITUTE REVIEW

ISSUE 1 AUTUMN 2004

The first Mechanics' Institute in London was founded in 1823 by George Birkbeck. 'Mechanics' then meant skilled artisans, and the purpose of the Institute was to instruct them in the principles behind their craft. As Birkbeck College the Institute became part of London University in 1920 but still maintains one foot in the academy and one in the real world.

This issue is dedicated to Sophie Warne

1974 – 2004

Birkbeck
UNIVERSITY OF LONDON

The Mechanics' Institute Review
Issue 1 Autumn 2004

The Mechanics' Institute Review is published by MA Creative Writing, School of English and Humanities, Birkbeck, Malet Street, Bloomsbury, London WC1E 7HX.

ISBN 0-9547933-0-7

Project Director: Julia Bell

The Mechanics' Institute Review was brought to you by: Lamya Al-Khraisha, Sally Hinchcliffe, Alessandra Sartore, Amanda Schiff, Sue Tyley, Cathy Wasson, Rachel Wright.

The team would like to thank Lisa Abraham, Anne-Marie Whiting, Wendy Brandmark, Sally Ledger and Laurel Brake for making this project possible both financially and practically. Also an extra special thank you to Sue Tyley for keeping us all so meticulously organized.

For further copies or information, please contact Anne-Marie Whiting, MA Creative Writing, School of English and Humanities, Birkbeck, Malet Street, Bloomsbury, London WC1E 7HX. Tel: 020 7631 6000. Email: a.whiting@bbk.ac.uk.

Website: www.bbk.ac.uk/mir

Printed and bound by Antony Rowe Ltd., Bumpers Farm, Chippenham, Wiltshire.

The Mechanics' Institute Review is typeset in Garamond.

FOREWORD

RUSSELL CELYN JONES
MA CREATIVE WRITING COURSE DIRECTOR

I N AN AGE WHERE A GROWING NUMBER OF UNIVERSITIES ARE PLAYING
host to creative writing, it's worth pointing out what distinguishes
Birkbeck from the rest. Its London location draws from the city's
heterogeneous population, but also attracts students from countries as
diverse as Jordan, Greece, Italy, Canada, Nigeria and the USA. All
classes are held in the evening to accommodate those students who
need to continue with their jobs while studying. This turns out to be
our good fortune. An inalienable truth about fiction is that its
characters tend to have jobs – the prism through which narrative voice
passes – and you will find these stories and novel extracts informed by
worlds such as casinos, the health industry, restaurants and journalism
in various milieux around the globe. Fiction is not like life, but has to
have life and its authors need to be close observers of where this life
occurs. The writers introduced here not only have a great deal of
experience of work and society, they also have the craft and
imagination to transform that raw material into works of art. Teaching
writing is a very intimate business, because fiction tends to begin –
but doesn't end – with autobiography and our methods are tailor-
made to individual students, geared to help them find their form. This
anthology is the evidence of that live game we play.

The writing workshop, on another level, is a new and innovative
way of learning. By engaging in original fiction students discover what
it's like to live inside the novel or short story, which complements
rather than contradicts the exterior view offered by academics.
Writing students are taught by both writers and academics and the
dual approach deepens their understanding of literature and helps
them find their place in contemporary literary developments. The
success of this enterprise depends heavily on the quality of teaching,
and I have been fortunate to have as colleagues world-class academics,
as well as the novelist and publisher Julia Bell and the novelist and
playwright Deborah Levy as co-tutors. Two writers with proven
intellectual and creative integrity in an aggressive market, they are also
experienced and gifted teachers.

Launched in 2003, the MA Creative Writing builds upon the
established Certificate Programme at Birkbeck and this anthology
includes entries selected from Certificate students. Managed by staff
and edited by a team of MA students, the magazine demonstrates the
wide range of styles from over twenty contributors. University writing

courses are often assessed in terms of the number and quality of published authors they produce and no doubt we will be judged by the same criteria in the future. But in the meantime, I invite you to enjoy this first issue of *The Mechanics' Institute Review* as a preview of who may be joining the next generation of bold new voices.

TABLE OF CONTENTS

INTRODUCTION
JONATHAN COE

THERE ARE THREE QUESTIONS THAT WRITERS DISLIKE INTENSELY: 'Where do you get your ideas from?', 'Do you write with a pen or use a computer?' and, 'Why do you write?'

Actually, perhaps it's only the last of these that we really dislike. The first couple are a shoo-in, a good opportunity for a few minutes' light relief at the dreaded question-and-answer sessions at the end of a reading, before the crazy-looking guy with the bushman's beard and the plastic carrier bag full of empty milk cartons and old sci-fi magazines can lob you some scary question about mythopoeic strategies and intertextuality.

'Why do you write?', however, is – to put it mildly – a rather more difficult one to crack. Sometimes it comes up from journalists (particularly French and Italian journalists, I've found) as well as festival audiences. Some people might think it's such a big question that it is, literally, unanswerable, and therefore not worth asking, but I would disagree. Unanswerable questions are the only really interesting ones. I've got a standard answer, in any case, one that I've been trotting out for a few years now, and it usually seems to do the trick (or at least fill the silence): viz., 'Because I'm unhappy when I'm not writing.'

In some ways, of course, that only raises more questions; but at least they're ones that the interviewer will – with any luck – be too polite to pursue. Anyway, I've decided that I'm not going to give that answer any more. I think there's a better way of responding, which is to turn the enquiry back on the questioner, and ask: 'Why do you read?'

It's just as important a question, after all. I always feel there's something vaguely accusatory about the 'Why do you write?' line of enquiry, as if I'm being ticked off for some act of unspeakable presumption. But if writing is a presumptuous, self-proclaiming act, the act of reading – certainly reading *fiction* – is open to charges, at the very least, of being time-wasting and delusional. Perhaps this only occurs to me because I am so fresh from my work on B. S. Johnson – a novelist who eccentrically insisted that 'telling stories is telling lies', and that writers who *invented things*, as opposed to writing up their own personal histories in faithful detail, were all immoral charlatans. Even he had to admit, however, that there was a public *appetite* for fiction, although it was something he deplored.

I suppose the point I'm trying to make is that we are all of us – writers and readers (to say nothing of publishers, booksellers and creative writing tutors) – involved in a highly dubious game of mutual double-dealing and deception, a story-telling conspiracy the moral legitimacy and purpose of which it can be fatal to question too closely. Meanwhile those outside the circle can have very little sense of what it's like to be inside: how raw and urgent and life-and-death everything feels in there. If you don't know what it is to want to write, to *need* to write, you will find it hard to imagine what a valuable public service Birkbeck is currently offering with its writing programme. I don't think I've ever seen such a happy or relieved set of faces as I saw at the start-of-year party last September, as it began to dawn on the assembled students that for a whole year – two, in most cases – they weren't going to have to fight, any more, for the right to snatch a few guilty hours at their desks: for those precious months, writing was going to be the top priority, the activity that everything else (work, family and all that other distracting nonsense) would have to slot itself around.

This simple but profound inversion of the writer's universe is perhaps the most important benefit that the Birkbeck course can offer its lucky intake. It is an incredible luxury and judging from the prose pieces now collected in this anthology, the writers concerned have taken every advantage of it. I find this heartening because, more than anything else, you need to be driven, nowadays, if you are going to make any headway as a writer. While newspapers may occasionally regale us with stories of a single mum on a council estate who has just been paid ninety million pounds by Steven Spielberg for a story she wrote on the back of her old P45s, or an eighteen-year-old Oxford undergraduate who only this morning had an idea in the bath which has already been translated into forty-seven languages, this will not be the experience of most aspiring authors. There is a reason stories like this become headline news, and it's because they hardly ever happen.

Instead, for most of us, you need a solid core of self-belief – which is not the same as self-confidence, incidentally. (The former is intrinsic, the latter superficial.) The kind of self-belief a writer needs is childlike in its intensity and impermeability. In fact many children have it as a matter of course – I see it in my older daughter, Matilda, as she crouches over the kitchen table writing stories using the words she has only just learned to form. The idea that this might be anything other than a valuable way to use one's time has yet to occur to her. And I suppose I must have been like that, too, at the age of eight or so when I spent an absurd number of sunlit hours cooped up indoors writing a long mock-Victorian detective story called *The Castle of*

Mystery, full of cliff-hanger chapter endings and bizarre historical detail. (It contained, I remember, the unlikely sentence, 'In a flash he had drawn his blunderbuss.')

Since I have strayed into autobiography I shall add this anecdote. When I was twenty-two my grandfather became terminally ill with prostate cancer. For me, it was probably the most upsetting episode in a life which (so far) has been almost magically free of emotional or physical pain. He was always the family member I felt closest to. Humour was how we bonded, most of all: he had a deep vein of warm, ironic humour that ran through his whole being like words through a stick of rock. We would watch programmes like *The Fall and Rise of Reginald Perrin* together through tears of laughter. I'm not sure how well-read he was but he loved Wodehouse (which I don't) and the Sherlock Holmes stories (which I do) and he would gamely have a try at some of the contemporary novels down at the local library, usually returning them half-read with a baffled, disappointed shake of his wise old head.

I remember him looking over my shoulder once as – preposterously – I sat under the awning of our caravan in North Wales one summer, bashing out a novel on the typewriter my parents had bought me. I must have been about fifteen. 'That's very implausible,' he said, noticing that my central character was said to be drinking red wine out of a pint glass. He was quite right. But I ignored him anyway. Seven years later, when the disease had really taken hold of him – to the point where he was having trouble talking – I can remember telling him how my latest novel had come home in its Jiffy bag again, rejection slip attached, and he spoke, firmly but indistinctly, some words I have never forgotten: 'Listen, Jon. Get yourself a good job teaching in a university.' (I had just graduated from Cambridge.) 'I shouldn't think any more about writing for a long, long time.'

Again, he was quite right. And again, I ignored him anyway. It was perfectly good advice, on one level, sanely and compassionately offered. But I'm glad I didn't take it. Sometimes, when I am also feeling sane and compassionate, I think of all the people up and down the country hunched in front of their Macs and PCs, spilling their souls onto paper – and then sending their books (as Muriel Spark put it so beautifully in *A Far Cry from Kensington*) out to sea in a sieve – and I feel like giving them the same advice. Maybe after a few drinks, I would even give it to the students on the Birkbeck writing course. But the point is, I wouldn't want them to take it; and on the evidence of the pieces contained in this book, I don't think that any of them would.

INTERNMENT

RACHEL WRIGHT

WEEK 1

Wear black heels and a smile that says 'I'm confident'.

When you meet the deputy editor, Simon, a slight man with rheumy, bulbous eyes, note the ink stains around the edge of his left pocket. He's poring over a chart with tiny columns of numbers when you interrupt his train of thought. Explain that you're the intern.

Because he doesn't know you were meant to begin work today, shake his hand especially emphatically. Say: 'I have the date written down in my purse. Would you like me to confirm it?' as if you could think of nothing less necessary, but you're willing to indulge him. 'No,' he sighs, and turns his back to lead you down a corridor. Fish frantically for that scrap of paper anyway. Dig beneath the sedimentary layer of unfamiliar coins that's settled on the vast ocean floor of your purse, forgotten. When you find it, the folds are already soft with a morning of checking and double-checking.

Simon takes you around the perimeter of the building. The entire floor is open-plan with honeycombs of cubicles at half height so neighbours can peek over the partitions. He nearly runs down a girl with bleached-blond spikes for hair and bluebird eye-shadow. 'Whoa, mate,' she says, and Simon manages an apology, but not an introduction. Instead, he brings you into a small conference room with glass walls on two sides.

'I'm sorry Michael, the editor, isn't here to greet you. Normally, he handles this sort of thing,' Simon says, gesturing towards the chair across from him. 'He's an American, too. From Manhattan,' Simon continues, dropping his pen on to the table so that the space between you seems to widen. Nod vigorously. Nod like you're pretty sure you grew up just one stoop over from good ol' Mike, somewhere on the Lower East Side, or maybe it was Queens – though you've never actually been to Queens. 'He's on holiday this month, but I know he'll be thrilled to see a compatriot around the office.'

Offer: 'Someone to celebrate the fourth of July with.'

Simon's smile is wan. 'A bit like that,' he says. 'Do you know much about *Sage Money*?'

'Not really.' Before he even blinks, you know this is the wrong answer. You're practically a summa-cum-laude student, unaccustomed to false starts or failure. Fidget with your faux pearls – your mother wanted to give you the real thing, you wanted London instead – and try to explain: 'I didn't get my placement until I arrived last week and then I tried to find it on the news-stands but –'

'It's all right,' he interrupts, 'it's not *Marie Claire* is it? I don't think my wife reads the magazine and we've a free subscription.'

Exhale. Note the space between rib and lung. It's a space for breath, for manoeuvre.

Simon asks, 'Are you particularly interested in financial journalism?'

Say: 'I'm an English major', like it's an excuse, an apology.

Simon shuffles a couple of papers and clears his throat with a cough. Finally he leans across the table. 'So, why have you come here?' he asks.

Bite your lower lip. Inspect your ragged nails. The truth – the secret truth, the one you haven't admitted to your parents or your friends or yourself – is this: you have come to London to chase after a boy, to wear him down and make him love you. But this boy has planned to spend the summer in Berlin.

Look Simon straight in the eye and say: 'I'm here because I want to write.'

WEEK 2

Write labels on several file folders and put them – still empty – in the cabinet near your cubicle. Write your computer password on your hand. Write addresses on forty-three preprinted postcards to *Sage Money* readers including one to a Mr James P. Brook in Gloucestershire who forgot to include his postcode. Write an email to your mother, like the kind that kids send from camp, the ones that say 'having a great time; don't wish you were here', when what they really mean is that they're counting the seconds until the familiar blue stationwagon comes to whisk them back to a land without swimming tests or macramé keychains. Write, erase, rewrite a text message to this boy – this beautiful, blue-eyed artist boy – that you want; suggest meeting up tonight or this weekend or any time. Write him before it's too late.

Wait at your desk.

The three-man advertising department sits on the other side of your cubicle. They make a series of quick phone calls: 'Yes I know the markets are down, but people are beginning to talk recovery' and 'Hugo, even the Americans are past all that and I have every confidence that our readers are more forward thinking than those cowboys. The magazine is called *Sage Money*, isn't it?' Ian lets out a belching laugh when he puts down the receiver. He thinks the next issue is sorted, inserts and all. Though the other two haven't had as much luck, they discuss the chances of a large commission in July. Perhaps a holiday in Bali, the renovation of an en-suite bath, a new computer for the wife. It's a long shot, but they're hopeful.

Wait at your desk.

A buzz – an embarrassing, attention-seeking buzz – of your mobile and the boy has finally called back. No time for you today, he says, but soon.

The pressure off, all three men from the sales department huddle around Ian's computer – just across the partition from yours – to watch the first-round matches at Wimbledon in something near real time. At first, they're quiet, tight-lipped as Americans and Aussies advance. Then Tim Henman takes to the grass and they curse each missed opportunity and cheer every point. Ian's a real enthusiast, a gifted amateur, he brags, patting his round belly – well, once upon a time, anyway. Still, he's got tickets for a semi-final match and he'd love to tell his grandchildren that he saw an Englishman win at home. It's a long shot, all right, but he's still hopeful.

WEEK 3

Fourteen minutes late, search for your building pass. Decide that when Simon asks, you'll say: 'There was a signal failure on my tube line' instead of 'I overslept because it's Monday and because I hit the snooze button three times and because every day I look forward to coming to work only so I can go home again and concentrate on the things that matter in my real life.'

Already you have plans for the evening. You'll leave the office at half past five and meet the boy – your boy – in the lobby. You'll go for drinks. When you try to pay, he won't hear of it and, instead, he'll offer you a second just to cement his own generosity. Warm and tipsy, you'll take the edge of his sleeve as you step back into the evening light, your strides only half the length of his. He'll lead you down a footpath, past docks and dinghies and towards a place where the river widens and London expands against its banks. Quietly, he'll chat with you – catch you up – about work and study plans and flight schedules. He'll say it's good to see you again and too bad he can't stay longer. Have a good summer and take care of his city. Write, if you get a chance. Before you know it, you'll be standing in the grey and mossy alcove of an ancient building – Westminster, maybe – and he'll lean towards you and just when you think that you might bubble over with that secret hope that you've harboured for two semesters from across the sea, he'll hand you a slice of orange from the one he's peeling. And it will be the brightest orange you've ever seen and it will be the best you've ever tasted and you'll close your mouth around its flesh without another word.

By the time you get to your desk, you're a whopping nineteen minutes late. Keep your eyes low over your keyboard while you log in to the system. Duck behind the wall of your cubicle when you sort the mail. Wait for Simon – for someone – to reprimand you. No one does.

Deliver Simon's letters. Deliver letters to the ad team. Deliver letters to the writers and designers and artists. When you hand a small brown envelope to Hannah Berry – the one with golden quills for hair – she smiles. 'I'm sorry, but do you work here?'

'Sort of, just over there,' you say, nodding towards your desk.

'Yes, I've seen you come in.' She tugs absently at the silver 'H' around her neck and then drops it on to somewhat exposed cleavage. Her nails are painted bright as a robin's egg. 'But no one ever introduced you, so I thought you worked for one of the other groups. There are loads, you know,' and pointing around the huge room, she mentions five or six other magazines, every one more interesting than *Sage Money*. Leaning closer, she lowers her voice. 'Really I should have guessed that Simon would be rubbish at anything to do with people and Michael is *completely* useless.'

'Oh,' you say, expectantly.

But she only winks and giggles, picking up a sheaf of layouts ready for Simon's approval. 'Well, if you need anything . . .' she says, pushing past you.

Return to your desk. Keep the letters to the editor, unless they're marked 'private and confidential'. Those are Michael's credit card bills. They go directly to his office. They're the only ones he sees. The rest are from readers who want free financial advice or a free copy of the book featured in last month's issue or advertising space for a start-up business – free. Or else they want a refund, in which case you forward the letter on to another anonymous intern in Swindon or Norwich where it sits in a heap on someone else's desk.

Regardless, open each envelope deliberately. Mr James P. Brook from Gloucestershire has written a second letter and a third, plus a postcard cut from the back of an emptied muesli box. When he stresses that he requires a swift answer to his mortgage question, rewrite this in your head. Pretend these are letters from home. Make it your mother's voice in each plaintive question: 'Have you eaten this week? Have you even got enough money to eat? Can I trust you to take care of yourself?'

Mr Brook, on the other hand, suggests that he has always trusted the columnists and pros employed by the magazine. He hopes his trust has not been abused. Begin to draft a response: 'Dear Reader, As the editor of *Sage Money*, I appreciate your patience . . .'

Better to fool him if you have to.

WEEK 4

Wear khaki trousers – not pants, not in this country – and a grim expression that says 'I'm competent'.

Sort the papers. This is the news: the Americans bomb again. They inquire into the largest case of corporate fraud in their history and now there are questions about every company in every country. They bring world markets to another five-year low. The Americans have lost control.

Michael's back in his corner office and it seems he's catching up with the staff individually. Through the glass panel in his door, you spot the back of Simon's head, nodding. A short man with curly black hair and wire-rims, Michael paces behind the broad desk, waving his fist in a gesture of defiance or victory. Simon takes note. He scribbles furiously and then stands to go.

Race back to your desk. Your cubicle is darker than usual, the light more blue. The clouds hang low in the sky, level with the office windows and they cast a shadow over the whole floor.

Ian doesn't watch Wimbledon, even in these final days. Perhaps the grounds are already too wet in south west London. Perhaps he's gone off tennis – the precision of it and the chance. He's on the phone most of the morning. By lunchtime, he's lost his appetite. 'Mates, I've got nothing,' Ian says to his team, 'not even a strong maybe and the way the wind is blowing today, I don't even know who to ring.' The two younger men nod. They've had more of the same.

Michael saunters down the corridor and, like a principal rounding up the rowdies, double-checks his list. He calls out to Ian. Ten minutes later, Ian returns red-faced and muttering. 'Not my fault if things aren't going so well' and 'New people come in here and think they can turn it all upside down.' Note the highway of purple veins that criss-cross Ian's face, the way he steadies a shaking hand on the edge of the partition.

'Well, Abbie Greene,' Michael says. Jump at the sound of his voice. Jump at the sound of your name. 'I've been wondering about you. Have they kept you busy?'

Glance down at the neatly stacked postcards ready to be mailed, the pile of fax confirmation sheets, the office supplies unused. 'Oh yes,' you say.

Michael's eyes follow your own. 'Why don't we talk about that in my office?' he asks. 'And then we can get to know each other a little bit better.'

Walk down the hallway beside him. Try – fail – to match his stride.

He swivels back and forth in his chair, arms behind his head. 'Tell me about yourself.' His accent is New York clipped and efficient, strange after a month in sing-song England. Still, it's a comfort of sorts and you feel your stomach muscles relax for the first time in weeks – if only momentarily. Explain: 'I used to work in a law office, so I've faxed and copied and stuff but I guess I'm a little bit concerned –'

'I'm sorry.' The corners of Michael's mouth curl. 'I meant tell me about you.' He leans closer. Retreat into your chair. 'Where do you go to college again?' Watch his hands. Keep them in your sights. His knuckles are the hairiest you've ever seen.

'Bryn Mawr, it's –'

It's a bunch of crazy girls running through the halls in the middle of the night. It's your parents' life savings, your grandparents' too, for that matter. It's you, digging in your heels at seventeen and hitting the books at twenty-one. It's standing in the kitchen in pink pyjama bottoms, the big white envelope in your hands, the one that says you're in and it's the catch in your throat when your father brags and your mother cries.

'Oh yeah, I know Bryn Mawr, Katharine Hepburn's alma mater – women's college, society girls and all that.' Michael leans back again, puts his huge feet on the desk. The sole of one Italian leather loafer is pocked with an ancient wad of gum. 'Can I ask you how much a place like that sets you – or your parents, I guess – back these days?'

Smile your most polite, small-town girl smile. 'The tuition's about $35,000 a year.'

Michael whistles, stretches his arms over his head.

'Not so sage, I guess,' you say. He laughs a rough bark of a laugh, an I-like-you-kid-really-I-do kind of laugh. You hate that laugh.

'Friend of mine,' he says, 'a Princeton man used to go down to Bryn Mawr for the parties once in a while. He told some wild stories. Said the girls were cute but crazy. And more than half were lesbos.'

'I beg your pardon.' Cotton-mouthed, your lips stick to your gums before sliding closed. For a moment, your teeth are bared.

Michael misunderstands. 'Lesbians,' he mouths. 'Women with women, you know.'

'I think you're right,' you say. 'It's a tolerant place.'

'And how did a nice girl like you end up there?'

You fell in love with the thought of dull green leaves transformed, made bright by nature and then spent, fallen under schoolgirl shoes. You dreamed yourself into a room of your own with a fireplace and a wide wooden window seat. 'I wanted an East Coast education,' you say. 'I liked the tradition of it and I wanted to live with other women. It's the kind of experiment that I'd only get to try once.'

Michael smirks. 'Well, I hope you'll feel the same way about your time at *Sage Money*.'

Return the smirk. Lob it back to him. Say: 'I'm sure I will.'

At your own desk again, Simon tells you that a man – a Mr Brook – called for you twice. He left voice messages both times, but you don't know how to retrieve them. The lines are all busy anyway.

Ian is speaking in low tones to his daughter. 'Well, all in all, how did you like your first tennis lesson, Soph?' He's expectant. 'No, I'm sure that you'll learn to like it, darling. In fact I know you will.' He hangs up the phone with force.

Across the room, a writer for another publication yells into his own phone. 'I'll do it. I think I can handle it, Harry. I'm not from the sticks, you know. I'm from New Jersey, for God's sake.'

Ian shoots the man a look and says under his breath, 'Shut your mouth with that bloody stupid American accent.' When you peek over the low wall between your cubicles, he's holding his head in two hammy hands.

At the end of the day, sort your emails. This is the news: he has written, the boy in Berlin. He's written to friends and relatives. He's written to you. The city's made him think about so many things. He'd love visitors.

Don't write back yet. You don't want to seem desperate.

You don't want to jump to conclusions.

WEEK 5

On the tube, read the free newspaper and watch a boy who reminds you of your boy. With his messy hair and brown corduroy jacket – stained at the lapels – he looks like Holden Caulfield. He looks like he could use a little care.

But as the train lurches, he steps expertly. He dips and bobs and balances himself. He stands right when you nearly fall.

At lunchtime, hang back at your desk to consult an old issue of the magazine. Hang back to calculate your current bank balance, to check the cost of the air fare from London to Berlin.

Hannah spots you behind the partition, hunched over a copy of

Sage Money. 'Oh,' she says, 'you must be bored if you've had to resort to that for recreational reading.'

'I'm just doing a little extra research for –'

'Then Michael has gotten to you, has he?'

Protest: 'No, it's for –'

'It's all right. No one would blame you. You're young,' Hannah says. Ignore the patronizing tone. Ignore the Playboy bunny T-shirt she's worn to work, only half disguised by a thready cardigan. 'And at one time or another we all want that.'

Shake your head. 'But I don't want that – whatever it is.'

'Oh, come to lunch,' she laughs, grabbing the magazine from you. 'Come on then and we can have a proper chat.'

Scrape the bottom of your purse for a rogue two-pound coin – every penny counts – and then sit quietly with your steaming baked potato while Hannah chirps and nibbles her way through two tuna sandwiches and her entire sexual history. She says, 'And if I'd known,' glancing around uneasily, 'that it could be this good with a married man, well, I would have done it a long time ago.'

Shift in your seat.

'I don't fancy myself an adulterer or a serial mistress or anything, but married men – they know things other men don't.' Hannah dabs at the corners of her mouth. 'Have I shocked you?'

'Oh no,' you say. 'Not at all.'

She shrugs and gulps back her Diet Coke. Still, you suspect that she's disappointed. 'In fact, I'm thinking I might leave him soon, too much bother and all with the lying and sneaking, which isn't really my concern, but I'm constantly having to plan – and I don't believe in looking two days ahead – and then he wants me to change my plans to be more available and last week I went clubbing and met this South African who –'

'I have been in love, you know.' The words escape – loosened from behind the sternum and caught in the throat – like a hiccup, unexpected and a little painful.

Hannah arches a single over-plucked eyebrow. 'Have you now?' she asks.

Yes, you say, yes. You have been in love with a boy who's gone to Berlin, a British boy with a beautiful accent and the best smile – the smile of all smiles, the smile worthy of this second trip to Europe and a summer's work.

'So you're going to Berlin?' Hannah taps her aubergine nails on the table.

It's *the* question.

'As soon as I finish my time here,' you say. You are succinct, surprised. 'I'm booking the trip this afternoon.' But you won't have a chance to speak to your father until this evening. You'll have to remind him of the opportunity to live the history, to live. You'll have to beg.

Hannah looks at her watch and gathering her trash onto a tray, she says, 'You are a funny one, you know.'

Week 6

Run in from the rain. Strip off the scarf around your head. Strip off the raincoat. (Check your email.) Hang them both to dry from the back of your chair. Walk in wide circles around the office to warm up. (Check your email.) Slip into the kitchen and pour a cup of coffee – too burnt and bitter. Tip it down the sink and begin again. You like it best when it's sweet, sweet, sweet. Drink the coffee in swigs and gulps at your desk. (Check your email.)

Shiver. It's the fingers and the toes, still cold. It's the caffeine, too. It's the boy.

You wrote him with details – London Heathrow to Berlin Tegel and all that. You wrote him with your details and he hasn't written back. Though you think – you're sure – there are plenty of explanations, he hasn't been the most predictable friend and now something is frozen inside you and won't melt. There is a block of ice in your gut, and you feel like a Sunday-dinner turkey waiting, undefrosted on Saturday night. You are plucked clean and full of fear and deadly purpose.

Hannah isn't at her desk. Edited page designs spill onto the floor before anyone else notices and then Simon says that someone should ring her up. 'Something may have happened to her and these pages have to go to the publisher on Friday, with or without her.'

'Maybe she's committed suicide,' Ian says.

Simon is contemplative, bending to pick up the layouts. 'Yes, maybe.'

Try her house line. Try her mobile. Leave messages at each, long ones with all the office extensions, as if the numbers were the problem, the big unknown. Try not to imagine her holed up somewhere, rearranging decorative pillows and making herself available to the married man. Try not to imagine the alternative.

When the phone finally sounds, answer after the first ring. 'Hello, Hannah,' you say. Pretend to be as calm as a British Telecom operator. Intone: 'Will you be coming in today?'

'Excuse me. I must have the wrong number.' The voice is male, deep and tight. 'I was trying to contact *Sage Money Magazine*, but it appears that – as with so much of their supposed information – they have provided a false number.'

Apologize: 'I'm sorry. I thought you were someone else.'

He says, 'You don't know who I am.' A question? A statement. 'In that case, I'm calling for Michael Brown, the editor.'

Michael says he gets too many calls. Michael says that it's the burden of being in charge. 'He's unavailable right now. Can I take a message?'

'You have a lovely accent, darling,' the man says. 'How long have you lived in London?'

'A month, this time,' you say, 'and a whole term last year.'

'My son's a student, too – well, he's about to finish the sixth form and then I expect that he'll be off to one of the Oxbridge colleges. He's very bright.' The man sighs and it sounds like static on the other end of the line. 'And quite a looker, too, like his father.' He pauses for your laughter. There is none. 'If my son could hear you, I think there'd certainly be a boy in Gloucestershire begging for a ticket to London or, I dare say, America.'

Be coy: 'A ticket to the States is very expensive.'

Michael struts past you with Hannah's substitute. When he realizes that both you and Ian are on the phone, Michael puts his hairy hand over his mouth. His platinum wedding band shines under the fluorescent lights.

'And that is precisely why I'm calling your fine publication, Miss. Miss . . . Miss – I'm sorry, I don't know your name.'

'Abbie.'

'Yes, well, Miss Abbie, I'm having a bit of financial difficulty and I would really like to speak to Michael Brown, who is, if I'm not mistaken in my reading, an American, too, although I'm willing to wager that he's not as beautiful as you.'

The line between you crackles and pops.

Lie: 'I'm sorry, sir, he's out of the office right now but I can take a message if you –'

'Yes, you can,' he says. 'You can tell him, you can tell him,' he gears up, like a preacher, like a rusty engine. 'Tell him that I've never been so disappointed with any one man in my entire life.' His voice shakes and strains, climbing a register closer to hysteria. 'I thought that I could count on you – tell him that. Yes, you promised advice, but I've gotten none of that. You promised me answers, but I'm still here – all alone.' The line goes dead.

Shiver. (Check your email.)

WEEK 7

Wear your silver-plated watch and a certain serenity about the eyes that says 'I'm complete'.

Bring a thank-you card for Michael. Leave it on his desk with the bills. Bring a black backpack, your passport, the ticket to Berlin. Bring a toothbrush and all your secret hopes for the blue-eyed boy.

Simon invites you for a farewell lunch. Michael would do the honours but he's gone to Leeds for a conference. Simon orders starters. 'You've really been a tremendous addition to our team,' he says. He pours the wine, takes several gulps. 'You stepped up to the challenge.' He insists you have dessert. 'You should be proud of the work you've done. You'll be a writer someday. I can see it.' He drinks his coffee black. 'If you need a recommendation for anything . . .' he says, without looking at you. He pushes away his empty cup and saucer. 'I've got to get back, you see,' he apologizes. Simon searches for one waiter in the crowd, his bulbous eyes bulging.

Offer: 'Yes, I need to get back and finish a few things up, too.'

He blinks. You like to think he's grateful.

At your desk, rearrange the paper clips and the pencils for old times' sake. Leave notes on the computer and fax. Write a long letter to the next intern with instructions about filing and post and all the important dates.

Don't leave instructions for the telephone. Don't mention voice mail retrieval. There's no point. You still have no answers for Mr James P. Brook, in Gloucestershire or anywhere.

He can call day and night. He can call you by name, call you terrible names. You'll be gone.

Now, you're only minutes and hours away. Soon the plane will be on the tarmac. You'll find your seat and you'll be shown safety measures – in English and German, and the voice will be foreign, pleasing, calm – and the plane will lift you up and touch you down again and while you collect your things you'll imagine him there – your boy – waiting just beyond the door, waiting to call out to you, to loosen the heavy bag from your shoulder, to take up the weight himself.

Walk down the gangplank towards him.

Run.

TEST DRIVE

PAUL DALY

I KNOW FINE FUCKING AND AS I SLIDE INTO THE GLEAMING roadster, that's just how it feels. It's the soundless entry, the receiving and enveloping by the interior, the cosseting, the luxurious squeezing. The climax is the twist of the ignition (they should take more care of those keys) and as the engine sings its road-lust I feel like I've slipped into a dream that at fifteen you wake from with the jizz clammy on your thigh.

'Nothing like that sound.' The sales-pussy peers through the window. Her lips are blood red against bleach-white teeth; teeth like that would never touch the cock on the way down the shaft. Such blowjob impropriety would be unthinkable for teeth that expensive.

'You're not wrong.' I give her the smile. She blushes and I know I've got her. I'm a handsome man: trustworthy air, devilish twinkle (Gucci shaded), tousled hair, chiselled jaw, smartly tailored shirt under rakish linen suit. I'm not young any more but sometimes that helps, the touch of silver at the temples. I've been through a lot of pussy and I can feel the fuck-current running strong today: she was flirting when I walked in the showroom and she's giving me doe-eyes now.

Her perfume wafts in as she places delicate fingers on the window sill. Big rock, expensive-looking band.

We do introductions. Amy and John. Pleased to meet you. Lovely day.

'Can I take it out for a spin?' I ask.

'It' is a BMW Z8. You could strap the engine under an airplane wing: three-ninety-eight brake horsepower with torque that could spin a vault door off. Tail end is a slavering quad-exhaust: you can hear rainforests choking when you rev it up; idling in traffic makes Arabs happy. If power corrupts, this car would shame a Venezuelan junta.

I press on. 'Someone take care of the Merc for me?' The Merc is parked out front. She looks uncertain and glances at it: low spec but collateral enough to prove I'm a player. It's a reasonable car but I've not had the chance to form an attachment. She nods and I toss her the keys.

She slides into the car and when she closes the door I can feel the *thunk* in my balls.

'Let's go,' she tells me and it's almost like we're on a date. Me with the shades and the swept-back hair, her with the red two-piece suit to match her lips and glossy brunette bob. Except no date of mine would say 'Let's go'. My dates tend to be the quieter type, more sure of their place in the relationship.

A loser assistant opens the showroom doors and I pull out fast onto the street.

'Careful with the power,' she tells me, watching my smile closely and then is quiet for a moment. Maybe she's wondering if my bridgework is more expensive than hers. 'I could drive if you like.'

I tell her I'm used to handling power and she seems to relax as we shuttle between the traffic lights in town. 'Let's stretch its legs,' she says eventually, gesturing towards the slip road for the M32 and reaching for the roof toggle. 'I'll take the top down.'

Talk of taking tops down makes me glance at her tits. A good set. She sees me looking and angles her body away from me, pretending to check something in the wing mirror. I can see she's smiling a little, enjoying the attention. I slot into the motorway flow and feel the pressure of my piece against my waistband and I know we're going to have a good time.

I make short work of the runty M32 and she nods when I point to the M4 junction. 'So what do you do?' she asks, half shouting, looking over at me.

'Now that's just lazy,' I say, keen for some sport. I ease up to a ton and slip by a couple of affordable runabouts in the middle lane. Fucking things shouldn't be on motorways in the first place.

'Pardon me?'

I spare her a glance. 'Why don't you form your own opinion of me.'

'What? I was just being polite.'

'Polite. Lazy. Letting society's preconceptions take the place of really getting to know me. Hang on.' A white van is blocking the outside lane. I duck in and out of the middle lane, flipping the bird at the scrote trio occupying the van's front seat as we hammer by.

'Politeness,' I say as I reclaim the fast lane, the white van's lights punching out the impotent rage of the poor in my rear mirror, 'politeness is us happy with our pigeon-holes.'

'What?' Her hair is streaming in the wind. It's well cared for, sleek. Hubby must love looking up at that hair being thrown around as she bounces on his dick.

'If I said I was a bond trader, you'd treat me differently than if I said I was, say, a convict.'

I can see her eyeing me. 'You ever been in jail?' She's laughing.

'Never been caught.'

'Well then that's just fine. I never understood those shares and stock market things.' She looks at me sidelong, flirty. You could stun cattle with this fuck-current.

I don't know whether to feel disappointed. 'It's very complex,' I say and turn the stereo on loud, for a break in conversation. Classical music blasts us, and I feel like I'm in a film, music swelling, informing me what to feel. It makes me feel magnanimous and after a minute I offer her another chance at conversation.

'What do *you* do?' I shout.

She shouts something I can't hear. She turns the stereo down and I am reminded this is no date of mine. On my dates the volume gets left where I put it.

'What do you mean, "What do I do?" I sell cars.'

'No you don't.'

'I'm pretty sure that I do.' She frowns. Maybe she's getting the first scent of it, the underlying whiff masked by the deodorant of assumption. Unfortunately for her, for all of them, you have to get up close to smell the real me.

I can feel my piece hard in my pants. 'You being there helps sell cars, but *you* don't sell them.' I look at her and grin. 'Men buy cars because other men tell them they will be able to fuck girls like you when they have one.' There, I've said it now, I've crossed the line.

'I don't think that's appropriate,' she says in a Daddy's-a-lawyer voice.

'Strange,' I say. 'From where I'm sitting it is.'

'Stop the car.' She's frightened, can sense danger, but not shitting it yet.

'Let's have the roof up,' I tell her and flip the toggle. Behind me the top unfolds, whistling in the wind, enclosing us with a mournful sigh.

'Stop the car.' Now I can hear the tremor in her voice. 'Stop it right now or I'm calling the police.'

'Give me your phone,' I say.

'I'm serious. If you don't pull over I'm going –'

'I said give me the phone.' I pull out my piece and point it at her thighs, keeping it low, out of the sight of the other cars. *Now* she starts shitting it. 'I shoot and you spend the rest of your life in a wheelchair pissing through a tube.'

She reaches into her bag and offers me the phone, never taking her eye from the gun. It's a Kimber forty-five and a mean looking little blue-steel fucker.

'Toss it out.' I motion with the pistol. She opens the window a little and pushes the phone through the crack and I see it explode-bounce in the mirror.

'What do you want?' Some of her hair has fallen over her eyes.

'I want you to ask me what I do again.' I'm getting hard; I glance down and the speedo says one-twenty and my cock's saying *Let's party*.

'What do you do?' Except it doesn't sound exactly like that: there's a lot more gulping.

'No. You look at me when you say it.' She's hiding behind her hair and that's just rude. 'Look at me and say it!' I take off my sunglasses for full effect and stare at her in the mirror. My eyes freak them out for some reason; perhaps they can see the purpose.

'What . . . what . . . is it you do?' She looks at me with nervous flicks.

'To pretty ones like you? Anything I can get away with.' I laugh and make it nasty. It feels good to fuck with them in the head before the real fucking begins.

She looks like she's going to blubber. That's the problem with these rich girls slumming it in the world of work: no backbone, no driving necessity to toughen them up. She starts sucking in huge breaths of air and then she starts to cry.

Still, it's time to stop playing: junction 22 is coming. I decide to take it up a notch, just for the hell of it, make car and pussy sing.

'Look at me,' I tell her. She doesn't and I poke her in the thigh with my piece. 'Look at me!' She's terrified now. I think I can smell the acrid tang of piss. One-thirty on the speedo.

'Don't hurt me.' It comes out breathy, like we're lying next to each other in bed. Her eyes are big and welling with tears. I bet hubby loves those eyes.

'Ask me again,' I tell her, 'and this time I'll really tell you. I'll really *show* you.' One-forty; everything else is just a blur.

She looks at me and asks in a tiny broken voice, knowing that she doesn't want to know the answer.

I nod and spotting a three-lane window I swing one-handed across the carriageway and slam on the anchors, sending up a great wail of beeping behind us. We come to a halt on the hard shoulder and cars blat past, horns dopplering away.

We rock with the passage of the thundering traffic. I reach over and unclip her belt, and lean into her, breathing her perfume, brushing the lobe of her ear with my lips. 'I "do" stealing cars,' I whisper. 'Expensive ones. To order.' I nibble her lobe and a little shriek escapes her. 'Keep the Merc. The owners will come looking for it soon enough. Get the fuck out.'

She cannons away from me and scratches for the handle. She falls out of the car, legs splayed, and I get a glimpse of white knickers on tanned legs. I point the gun at her and make a little *pow* noise. I smile as she scrabbles back and I lean over to close the door before accelerating out into a gap in the traffic.

She's on all fours as the car lifts off like an earth-slung rocket. If she ran, she could get to an emergency phone in a minute or so, but by the time the filth arrive I'll be gone. Off junction 22 on the Avonmouth industrial estate, the crew's waiting with a van big enough to take a Beemer and by the weekend this cock-buggy will be shipped, chopped and on the continent and I'll be nuts deep in something somewhere while it all calms down. Amsterdam probably.

I tuck my piece away and indicate for the junction. There's the definite reek of piss mixing in with the smell of the new leather, but I don't mind; it's the scent of victory. My erection's aching. Maybe I'll snare some foolhardy party-pussy in Amsterdam that looks like her, now a mere speck in the rear-view mirror. And this next one, well, it won't be a test drive.

FALLING

SOPHIE WARNE

G ILL ENDS THE CALL AND PULLS A FACE AT THE STEERING WHEEL. 'Bastard HQ,' he sighs.

Nicole has learnt not to react, but beside her on the double passenger seat James clears his throat and leans forward eagerly. He's been on the team less than a week and doesn't know the way of things yet.

'We only got today to do these windows,' Gill elaborates, 'or they'll have our balls off with a blunt spoon.'

They sit in a row in the cab of the van and contemplate the hotel through the windscreen. It's a bland building, its smooth face of ochre cement studded with blank squares of greenish glass. No drooping gutters, no squiggly drainpipes, not even an open window to mar the lines or hint at forms of life. Everything neat and symmetrical, like a building in a toy town. Except that at full size the effect is vaguely sinister. Nicole cranes her neck to see the top of the building. She counts six storeys, each with fifteen windows.

'Front and rear,' she says. It is more of a statement than a question.

Gill nods sadly. He's a sensitive psychopath. It upsets his karma when Head Office issues impossible objectives.

'Fifteen drops of six each side,' she calculates, 'makes thirty times six . . . so . . . er . . . 180 windows.'

They consider this information. It's going to be a long Friday.

'Where *is* that South African fucker?'

The passenger door of the van opens as if in answer to Gill's question. Roach stands there, his fist full of sandwich.

'Good mornin' all!' He grins, revealing half-chewed food and ketchup-covered teeth. As usual he's dressed in jeans and trainers, even though they're supposed to arrive on site in overalls. A policy designed to communicate 'efficiency and professionalism' to the clients.

'Was when we got here,' Gill retorts. Nicole waits for him to mention Roach's clothes, but the warm smell of bacon wafting into the van apparently distracts him.

'D'you have to eat pig right under my nose?' he barks. 'Infringement of site regs!'

With that he jumps out of the van and strides round to open the rear doors. James immediately follows. He leaps out so fast it's a miracle his gangly legs don't tangle up and trip him. Nicole quite envies his enthusiasm though. It's not a state she's very familiar with.

Roach winks at her, holding out the last of the sandwich. She eats slowly, watching as he up-ends his bag onto the tarmac. The newspaper, the toothbrush, the wallet and the Tupperware he stows back in the bag; the faded blue overalls he drags on over his clothes, taking care that his jeans don't snag and ride up, and gripping the cuffs of his fleece as he passes his arms through the overall sleeves. Then he attempts to iron the crumpled material against his body with flat palms, a look of mild disappointment on his face. He is completely absorbed and unrushed. There is, Nicole realizes, something rather intimate about watching a person dress, even when it is their second set of clothes.

The van rocks beneath her as James gambols about in the rear in response to Gill's directions to pass out various items of equipment. Rope bags. Buckets. Window-cleaning gear. Harnesses. Hard hats. Nicole doesn't move, except to tighten her overalls at the neck. A sneaky wind is cutting through the van now that the doors are open. According to some – specifically her mother – 'it's definitely spring at last', but of course *she's* never up at this bleak hour.

If ever anyone asks Nicole what she does – which they do, all the time – she sometimes says she's a plumber. Or a lap dancer. Other times, she tells the truth: 'Rope access technician.' She likes the way it sounds – the weight and mystery of it – and its implied lifestyle choice. Blue-collar, hard-working, honest in the old-fashioned sense. Wasn't this what they used to mean by gainful employment? She even likes getting her hands dirty. What she doesn't like is feeling obliged to explain herself. But she can, if the conversation requires it, go into greater detail.

'What do I *do*? Well, let's see . . . In a 168-hour week I spend on average fifty-six hours asleep, about forty hours hanging off ropes. Probably three hours swimming . . . five hours watching television, five hours eating – there might be an overlap there . . . What are we at now? About 110-ish? Between two and six hours having sex – also possibly an overlap, ha ha, don't tell David . . . up to an hour on the phone to my mother, if we're speaking . . .'

It riles David, this habit of hers – 'Do you have to be so . . . so *prickly*?' – but then he's one of the ones on the other side. The smug professionals, the I-am-what-I-do types.

Gill raps his clipboard on the side panel of the van.

'Look lively!' he shouts.

The four of them heft the equipment on to their shoulders and follow Gill across the car park towards a green door with a diamond-shaped window. As they approach, the door opens and a large man in a checked shirt appears, his hands wedged deep in the pockets of his oversized jeans. He is bald, but has a passable beard, as if the hair on his head has grown downwards to sprout out of his chin.

'Morning!' he shouts.

'Morning,' Nicole mumbles along with the others.

'Here for the windows?' His eyes flick from the buckets to Gill's straggly, headbanger hair, before resting on Nicole. He is nonplussed. Evidently he isn't used to seeing blondes look so good in blue.

'I'm Gill Tibbitts,' says Gill. 'Site super. These the stairs to the roof?'

'From Vertical Access Limited?' the man persists. He might as well have added, '*You* motley lot?'

Nicole and Roach exchange glances. The company name is emblazoned all over the van and down both sleeves of their overalls, although admittedly only James's overalls are new enough for the writing to be legible.

'Yup!' affirms Gill.

'Righto.' He chuckles into his beard. 'Well, welcome to the Quality Hotel!' Nicole shuffles impatiently, the straps of the rope bags digging into her collarbones. 'Better let you get on then.' He steps aside to let them pass, hands still in his pockets.

Nicole walks with her head down, watching her boots disappear and reappear on the steps, listening to the growing thickness of her breath and the crash of the buckets as they swing against the banisters. By the sixth flight, her collarbones are chafed and burning, but as soon as she steps onto the roof she experiences the familiar lift of being in the open.

This is her favourite part of London. The rooftops. A whitish sky spirals into the far distance, patched with blue and scattered with downy, benign-looking clouds. She sucks in the bracing air, relishing the way it jolts the dregs of sleep from her body in a cleansing shiver.

'Front elevation first!' Gill hollers above the roar of the wind. It's his preferred strategy: Do the Worst First. The windows at the front will be dirtier thanks to the main road.

The rigging is straightforward – all these modern hotels have purpose-built steel eye-beams – and within twenty minutes she's standing on the ledge. Ahead, at eye level, is a cluster of yellow cranes, their necks fixed at a sickening tilt, and above, vertiginous glass-and-steel towers overtake the roof of the Quality Hotel and keep climbing. In most of London, the buildings are so closely packed it's as if they are holding each other up, but in the Docklands the towers are free-standing, supported by an edgeless, hollow sky. Her belly tightens. She spins the safety catch on her karabiner as far as it will go. For the first time, it doesn't seem natural to be climbing into the void.

She turns her back on the stolid cranes and clambers over, wrenching her hands from the ledge. The slack rope catches her weight almost immediately. She squats on the taut rope, knees braced against the smooth concrete, grateful for the way she is sheltered from the slapping wind.

By the last window of her first drop, the knot in the base of her stomach is loosening. The rhythm is soothing. Descend, lock off, dolly, squeegee, descend, lock off, dolly, squeegee. The pull in her shoulder and upper back muscles is fluid, not yet tainted by fatigue. The wan spring sunlight warms her back; the cleaned glass gleams.

To her left Roach's movements mirror her own. He is close enough for them to talk but it is their unspoken etiquette not to in the mornings. He is singing under his breath. On her other side is the missed drop – they skip every third drop or they'd never finish – and beyond are Gill and James. This is James's first window clean and he is lagging behind, showing the soles of his boots.

The windows belong to bedrooms. All of them the same; all of them unoccupied. At each bedroom, she hopes the door to the corridor – or worse, the bathroom – won't open and she will be caught prying, suspended in mid air with nowhere to hide.

The three of them touch their feet to the ground almost simultaneously, leaving James above, a full window behind. They unclip their harnesses and plod back up to the roof. Nicole re-rigs for the second drop and swings herself over the ledge. Nothing. Her reluctance before was nothing but a silly aberration, like falling prey to stage fright after the final curtain has come down. Flush with relief, she pushes her boots hard against the wall, lowering herself down level with the first window in increasingly wide, optimistic bounces.

When she locks off at the fourth window, she sees they have arrived at a function room full of people. Their arrival – for Roach's window gives onto the same room – inevitably causes a stir. The trick, Nicole knows from experience, is not to make eye contact. She corrects the depth of her gaze, so that she sees no further than the glass and the window frame and the foamy head of the washer. Even so, she is aware of people straightening their necks to look up at her, spread-eagled in the window, blocking their sunlight. Voices exclaim in surprise. Arms are raised in mock salute.

She sweeps the dolly over the smooth glass, top left to right to left to bottom right in an inverted 'S'. The room and its occupants disappear behind a soapy film. Through the white soap bubbles, she can glimpse bits of what's inside. A half-finished jigsaw puzzle. Fleshy moving mouths, a biscuit in a manicured hand, the curve of a saucer. She drops the dolly into the bucket and picks up the squeegee. It glides along the top section of the window, wiping away the soap to unveil a broad, sparkling strip of the room.

As she twists the squeegee back on itself something tugs at her retina, forcing her to focus on what lies on the other side of the glass, in the strange cut-out of sunlight between her raised shadow-arm and her bowed shadow-legs. The briefest glimpse of a face. Broad nose, thick eyebrows, a mole. An altered face, but a face so familiar and so real that her sense of well-being splinters. The face turns to her, squinting, but all too quickly it moves away. She leans out on the rope and scrambles her feet along the sill, struggling to follow it as it drifts out of her line of vision into the shadow beyond the edge of the window frame. Swaying giddily, she snaps her gaze back to the point where she first focused. Her feet lose their grip, pedal air. For a sickening moment she feels as if she is falling. Everything solid has been blown away.

To one side of the turmoil, a tiny part of her brain is still functioning as it should. It is directing her fumbling fingers and her sluggish limbs; because of it she squeezes the stop and feeds the rope fast. At the first touch of tarmac, she is unlocking the safety catch of her karabiner, releasing her harness from the rope. She is dashing over to the door and up the stairs, this time stopping at the second floor.

As soon as she steps into the corridor she can hear the drone of voices and see the open door. 'The Falcon Room' is stamped on the wood in curly gold letters. It is the same room, and yet not the same. As a reflex, she glances to the windows. Two glistening windows, each one bisected by a taut rope, the third window untouched. Roach has disappeared, and uninterrupted patches of sunlight spill over people and bleed onto the conference table and the floor.

She is aware of the conversation dipping, of the men – because there are no women – looking askance at her hard hat, her grubby Marigolds, and her big boots tramping on the fleur-de-lys carpet. Her heart is racing but her mind can't keep up. The men are too young. They are wearing suits. She scans the faces again, waiting. Finally, a figure detaches himself from a group and scurries over in a proprietorial manner, ushering her out with two firm fingers pinched to her elbow. The door clicks closed.

She lurches to the bottom of the stairs, desperate for air, and bumps into Roach.

'Nicole?' He smiles, perplexed. 'What's up? You missed . . .' His face is fuzzy at the edges and his voice comes from very far away.

My father is returned from the dead, she thinks, turning to spit a gob of bitter-tasting saliva into the gutter.

'Falling' is an extract from the novel *John Angel*

AFTER NOAH

SALLY HINCHCLIFFE

S IX A.M. ON A SUMMER'S MORNING AND I WAS RUNNING LATE AGAIN.
From my fourth-floor perspective I could see Noah's parents,
setting up their daily picket line, folding their leaflets. Around me, the
shelter was already beginning to stagger into life. The building
vibrated with the hum of poorly maintained pipes as the second-floor
men – the ones with jobs – got up to face the day. Some of the first-
floor men – the ones without jobs – were still straggling back in from
the night before. Noah's parents didn't bother to hand them a leaflet.
The men had seen them already; you couldn't go a yard into the
shelter without finding one of them, by now faded and blurred by
repeated photocopyings. *Our son has been kidnapped by a cult! This
building houses a dangerous cult! Stop this evil now!*

The air conditioning started up suddenly, adding its note to the
background harmony of pipes and the growing roar of the Washington
traffic outside. Two day volunteers, middle-aged Georgetown matrons
dressed down in slacks for a day of slumming it, approached the
doorway, faltering at the sight of Noah's parents. I didn't recognize
them; our day volunteers had a way of not coming back for more than
one day. Maybe it was Tyrone's teasing them, asking them who their
parole officer was. Maybe it was the general craziness. Maybe it was the
two specific crazies handing out their leaflets at the door. It must be
difficult to turn up for a day's do-gooding at your local homeless shelter
and be told you're entering the next best thing to the Moonies. One of
them wasn't fazed. She marched straight past, city-trained blinkered eyes
seeing nothing. The second, slower, paused, made enough eye contact
to be caught, took a leaflet and, as she followed her friend into the
building, looked back nervously for a second before she disappeared.

Celeste materialized beside me on her tiny silent French feet. She'd
barely woken up but I knew she would be immaculate in ten minutes
while I, who'd been up for half an hour, was still looking for a clean
shirt.

'What's up? Oh, them.' She did one of her perfect Gallic shrugs,
the kind they teach them in primary school over there. 'Why they
think this is a cult I will never know.'

'I don't know,' I said, 'one minute you're raising a little lawyer,
halfway through Harvard, the next he's spending his days cooking
pork and beans for a thousand men. If that isn't the work of a cult,
what is?'

'Me, I blame the parents.'

Jessie and Hina turned over in their bunks and muttered at us to shut up. They worked on the political campaigns for the organization and their day didn't start until eight. It was what I'd come over for that summer, halfway through my politics degree: two months' practical experience, a line on the CV. But this was the dying end of the eighties: greed was good, the Republicans were in the White House, ketchup was a vegetable. The campaign office stuffed envelopes, organized marches, achieved nothing. The kitchen fed the men. I'd drifted down there to help out one morning and never left. Just as Noah had done a year earlier, and he'd ended up running it. Now my two months were almost up. My bunk was scattered with my stuff, half-written letters, postcards on the wall. My best friend, Inter-Railing her way round Europe, sent me markers of her progress. Paris, Brussels, Amsterdam. I'd meant to travel round the States a bit before going home, had never managed to see more than a few blocks round the shelter.

By the time I got down, the day volunteers were already sitting in the meeting room, Celeste neatly at their side. Jerry, I noticed, had been putting them at their ease which was not a good thing. Jerry's neurones had long been disconnected by too much skunky weed, and he was last known to have finished a sentence some time in the seventies. They sat bolt upright, casting sidelong glances at Tyrone who sprawled in his chair, his legs apart, and at Jerry, who smiled gently at nothing. Noah sat at the front, a pale young man, tall, soft-bodied, his hair sticking up in patches where he clutched at it while thinking. His clothes hung off him, relics of a more substantial frame.

'Glad you could join us, Suzy,' he said, mildly. Technically he wasn't in charge. The rules of the community that ran the shelter were few. Nobody was any more important than anyone else. No illegal substances. No hate speech. We broke them all, but the first one only subtly, deviously. All decisions were taken by consensus. But in the heat and pressure of a kitchen that fed a thousand men from the table scraps of the city, somebody had to be in charge, and only one person cared enough to take on that burden. Noah.

'Suzy, can you take Marianne and Betty?' The two day volunteers smiled at me nervously.

'Marianne and Betty, yeah,' said Jerry. He kept track of complicated conversations by repeating the last thing anyone said to him.

'What's the veg?'

'Cabbage.'

I groaned. No one could ever remember a day volunteer that came back more than once. But on cabbage days if they made it through the morning we were doing well.

'Cabbage, yeah.'

'Tyrone and I will do the meat,' Noah continued.

'Meat is murder, yeah.'

'Jerry, can you go pick up the stuff from the dairy? Take Celeste?'

'Celeste, yeah.'

I never did work out which egalitarian principle it was that determined that the staff member with the attention span of a goldfish was the one named on the insurance of the shelter's one remaining pickup truck. Tyrone tried to explain it to me once but every time he got to the bit about 'responsibility breeding responsibility' he'd start laughing so hard he simply couldn't finish the sentence. Just one of those little details of communal life we all had to live with. Like holding hands in a circle before meals, and taking turns to pick up the mail, and always stealing the last of the milk when everyone else's back was turned.

Just as we were about to start work, Leroy and Jimmy shuffled in. I hadn't thought it possible for Marianne and Betty to get any tenser, but they managed it. Leroy and Jimmy looked every inch the tramps, from their taped shoes to their wild dreadlocked hair.

'Gentlemen, there's nothing left for you to do but the dishes.'

'That figures. Always down to the coloured folks, the dishes.'

'Dishes, yeah.'

Leading them over to the salad area I tried to sort out Betty and Marianne in my mind. Usually I don't pay much attention to the day volunteers, stick them under the heading of 'life's too short', like trying to follow Jerry's conversation or understand what brings Leroy and Jimmy down to the kitchen every morning. But we were short-handed at the moment. The summer influx of college students had waned and the year-long interns had not yet started. The men still needed to be fed and these two, however unpromising, were all the help I was going to get today. Celeste was already skipping out to the truck, blowing kisses. Betty, it seemed, was the hard one, the one who'd walked straight past Noah's parents. Marianne looked less definite, softer, pleating the leaflet between her fingers. Noah's photo showed a plump boy, his hair slicked down, teeth freshly released from their braces. He'd smiled for the photographer, freckled and all-American. Tyrone used the leaflets for darts practice, upstairs in the staff room. We had all idly sat in meetings one time or another and blacked out one or more of Noah's teeth, adorned him with glasses, a moustache, an eye patch. He littered the place. I'd long since stopped associating the grinning cipher in the picture with the shadow who haunted the kitchen, forever checking stock levels, three floors of hungry men on his shoulders.

I smiled in a way that I hoped was as un-brainwashed as possible. I silently cursed the God who decreed that, whatever else was in short supply, cabbage was always plentiful. I handed each of them a sharp knife and a large, clean apron.

'Cabbage,' I said, 'has a habit of rotting in a particularly unpleasant way.'

My little introductory spiel was supposed to forewarn them but Betty still took an involuntary step backwards when I brought the first bag out. There are twelve cabbages in a standard bag, too heavy for me to lift other than by hugging it like a child and staggering from the walk-in cooler to the salad table, flinging it down before it takes me with it. This meant my front was smeared with the snot-like slime that cabbage turns into when it rots. I had a sudden vision of these women's homes: thick, white, sculptured carpet with the vacuuming marks still on it, low cream couches, matching towels and flannels and soaps.

'Who wants to wash, and who wants to chop?'

It seemed they didn't want to do either.

'This is a great way to relieve tension,' I suggested, ripping through the netting of the bag with my knife and pulling out one of the heads. As I slammed it stem down on the counter I saw Betty flinch but Marianne smiled. 'Pretend it's someone you hate.'

I showed them how, stripped of its outer leaves, the inner heart of the cabbage is usually sound. Wiping the worst of the slime off my hands onto my face, I transferred the disembowelled cabbage on to a chopping board and sliced it open.

'The rest is pretty easy.'

'I could do with some of that stress relief.' It was Marianne who spoke up. I think it was the first time either one of them had opened their mouths. She picked up the second cabbage with a will and slammed it down. I wondered who she had in mind when she smiled like that. Betty chopped, stopped to sigh, chopped again. Pretty soon Marianne had a pile of stripped and cleaned cabbage and Betty had a backlog. Without being asked Marianne took up a knife and started alternating, chopping and slamming. I began to see how the day might not work out to be a disaster.

Noah drifted in, silently. I was busy with the tomatoes, teasing slices out of collapsing ruins, adding their seeds to the cabbage slime in my hair.

'We'll need that cabbage soon.'

'Almost ready,' Marianne piped up. Betty sighed again. She'd been out for three cigarettes already, plus one cup of coffee. I saw Noah with Marianne's eyes, wondered if she saw one of her own sons. In true American fashion we'd seen her entire family already, pulled out of her purse. They gleamed toothily in the sunshine: a handsome man, two handsome boys, a handsome dog. They pursued various outdoor sports all of which seemed to require expensive equipment, dead animals and no women.

'Where are you?'

'I just take the pictures.'

Noah leant against the wall as though holding it up were also one of his responsibilities.

'How's it going?'

He shrugged. He'd never been known to take a day off in the year he'd been here. It was beginning to show.

Tyrone bounced in. 'Yo, Noah, pan's boiling over again.'

Noah closed his eyes. 'Turn the heat down.'

'Oh, yeah.'

'And this is the man who wants to be a chef.' Betty laughed, a cynical laugh. Marianne shushed her.

Marianne and I carried in the cabbage while Betty went out for another cigarette. In the heat near the stoves, Tyrone was stripped to the waist, stirring and tasting, his dark torso dancing through a cloud of steam. Noah opened the convection ovens, pulled out trays of pork chops and poked them with an impervious finger. Taking one side each of its giant vat, Marianne and I levered the cabbage up onto the stove. There was a roaring from the ovens, shouts, the background clanking of the dishwasher conveyor belt. Marianne said something but I couldn't hear her. Noah ticked things off his list, frowned at the stock figures. Dinner was coming together. Another daily miracle.

'Why don't you leave?' I'd asked Noah when I'd first seen the leaflet. I had my air ticket home tucked into my bag. I had another year at university waiting for me. 'Go back to college, finish your degree?'

'Why don't *you* stay?'

This was the big question. Why not stay? What could I possibly do that was more worthwhile than this?

'You'll be dead in a year.'

Noah shrugged. 'Fifteen men froze to death last winter. Here in the heart of government. Their bodies were never claimed.' I knew this. Their cremated ashes decorated the campaign office in Perspex boxes. Most had only a first name. There were already two Jimmys, one Leroy. No Noahs.

Betty's last cigarette took so long Marianne went to see what was up. She came back shaking her head. Gone. 'You can take off too, if you like,' I offered, 'we're kind of winding down here.' This was a lie. The worst part, the clearing up, still remained. And the sorting of tomorrow's produce, in from the farmers' markets and the dairy. Celeste and Jerry were back with the milk that had been returned from the supermarkets unsold.

'How was it?'

Celeste rolled her eyes. 'We got lost.'

'On the way to the *dairy*?'

'Worse. On the way *back*.' Celeste had a nice line in Gallic contempt.

'Lost, yeah.'

In the walk-in cooler I showed Marianne how to sort through the milk.

'Don't open it, and don't worry about the sell by date.'

'It all went off today.'

'It will last at least a week after that, as long as the cold chain is preserved.' I tried not to think about Jerry lost in the freeway system round Washington, the milk cooking in the back of the uninsulated truck.

'Just discard anything that's bulging really badly, or leaks.' I turned one gallon jug upside down to demonstrate and it started dripping down my hand.

Marianne held up another container.

'Or anything that's actively green,' I agreed.

I sorted through the older milk discarding anything more than a week old. I had to stop and think what the date was for a minute. One of these days, I thought, I'll wake up and realize I've missed my flight home.

The day really was winding down now. I stood and wiped my face with a cloth, warming my fingers up after half an hour in the cooler, watching Tyrone and Celeste having a water fight with the dish sprayer. Marianne caught a stray jet as she unwisely crossed their path, trailing a mop and bucket. Tyrone and Celeste froze with their hands clapped to their mouths like naughty children. Marianne froze too. Her neatly coiffed hair hung down in rat-tails and I noticed that her carefully applied make-up had pretty much all gone. Dripping and dishevelled, only her apron now marked her out as a day tripper. Carefully she picked up a mop, and swirled it in the gritty grey water of the bucket. Celeste and Tyrone stood uncomprehending until the very moment when the mop head flicked its filthy spray straight in their faces.

Leroy whistled. 'You go girl!' and even Jerry took up the chorus of cheers.

Marianne bowed, replaced the mop, took up a pair of trash bags and exited with dignity. Only Noah was silent. He walked into his little office, shaking his head and muttering at the childishness of it all.

Outside, by the dumpsters, Marianne asked, 'Do your parents know you are here?' I had the impression she'd been nerving herself up to ask the question all day.

I heaved a black bag up onto the pile. 'Kind of.' They knew where I was, what I was doing. They didn't see me up to my ears in cabbage, their little girl. They didn't see how easy it would be to stay.

She threw up a bag of her own. It threatened to roll back down the pile, engulf us in a shower of rotting cabbage leaves. Someone was going to have to climb up, tamp it down a bit. I decided that, for once, that someone wasn't going to be me.

'And are you going back to them?'

'Them, school, life, my career.'

'My kids . . .' she started, but stopped, changed tack. 'The oldest's a junior at Swarthmore. The other's starting college next year.'

'Hardly kids.'

'You know, Suzy, they're always your kids.'

I asked Noah the same question. 'Are you ever going back?'

'Who would take over if I did?' Tyrone was running up and down the kitchen chasing Celeste with a mop. 'Jerry?'

'Jerry, yeah,' I said, but Noah didn't laugh. 'How about me?'

He looked at me for a minute, as though he were considering it. That was when he laughed. 'You'd have to stay, then, wouldn't you? And that would never do.'

We all sat on the steps outside the shelter watching the craziness wind up for the evening. Tyrone had mysteriously got hold of beer.

'It's Friday, after all.'

'Is it?' I had lost track. 'Praise the Lord and pass the ammunition.'

He passed a beer instead. 'Another day older.'

Jimmy's deep baritone started up, '*Load sixteen tons and what do you get?*' and in a moment we were all singing. Even Marianne, perched neatly to the side of the steps on a milk crate, raised up a sweet soprano. All singing in harmony, except that I was singing, too, light-headed with tiredness and beer. The weariness seeped up from my limbs, addictive as a drug. I leant back against the sun-warmed wall and tried to imagine leaving.

'Guys, this time next week I'll be gone.' Saying it made it real.

'Everyone leaves,' Tyrone said. 'Everyone but me and Noah.'

'I'm staying, yeah,' Jerry said, suddenly coherent.

'Only cause you ain't got your shit together to leave.'

Noah said quietly, so only I could hear, 'And that goes for all of us.'

On Thursday night I packed my backpack with the faded remnants of my clothes and sat on my bunk for a long time looking at my tickets. I turned over the latest postcard from my friend. Still in Holland. 'What's the point of travelling when you've found what you're looking for? In my case – Jan . . . Can't wait for you to meet him!' Turned it back and looked at the picture. The little Dutch boy, with his finger in the dyke, holding back the tide. A pedantic note in small print on the back said that this was merely a legend, and that nothing could prevent the sea from dissolving a dyke once it had started to crumble. In the picture the little boy had a worried expression on his face, as though he realized the futility of his action. His plump finger was thrust into the bank, and his eyes stared fixedly out of the frame, waiting for the salvation that never came, the vast grey weight of the North Sea behind him.

Noah and I spent the evening sitting on the roof in the warm summer night, drinking beer. One of his parents' leaflets lay discarded at his feet. I took it for a souvenir, folding it up carefully. We sat side by side, in silence, nothing to say, leaning back against the parapet. In profile he seemed younger, seemed his age. His face still had the soft curves of a child, full-lipped, and when he closed his eyes the long lashes rested on his cheek. He finished the beer he was technically too young to drink and crushed the can, lobbing it over the parapet down onto the street. Someone cried out, an incoherent shriek of rage.

'Goodbye to cabbage,' I said.

'Hello, career.'

'There are worse things.'

'Like people dying in the streets.'

'They died while you were here.'

'Not the point.'

'There is no point.'

He took my beer can too and crushed it.

'I hadn't finished.'

'No. You hadn't.'

I sat on my bunk and argued with Noah in my head. He always won. In the end, I got my mother to argue with him instead, lay down and tried to sleep.

Friday, my last morning. Marianne came back, to a chorus of surprise.

'You came back.'

'I came back.' She took a little bow. 'Where's the cabbage?'

I was leaving halfway through the day. Celeste was doing the vegetables. I wandered round the kitchen, touching things, people. Tyrone said if I patted his ass one more time he was going to do me for sexual harassment. I just wanted to remember he was real. Noah sat in his little office and didn't come out. When Marianne and I went in he was hunched busily over a sheet of paper. I repeated my question.

'Er, just do ten bags of the potatoes.'

'You said twelve, yesterday.'

'Ten . . . twelve.'

'Twelve, yeah,' said Jerry, passing. Noah turned his attention back to the paper and I could see now it was one of his leaflets. Slowly, carefully, he was blacking out his own features one by one. When he had finished, he lifted his head and stared at the wall, as though waiting for salvation.

We didn't even notice Marianne's disappearance until she reappeared, leading Noah's parents like a tour guide. Her voice preceded her, crisp and clear, making everything she said official.

'And this is where the vegetables are prepared. Food for over a thousand men comes out of this kitchen every day.'

Not once in the year had they walked in through our open door to find their son, see what he was really doing. Not once had he gone out to reassure them. They looked around, hands clasped in front of them, silent. Both of them held aspects of Noah in their faces. His father had a familiar, weary, look. Noah came out of his office.

'Mom, Dad.' He led them inside and shut the door. Through the glass window we could see their mouths moving.

Marianne said, 'I thought to myself, there's a boy who needs his mother.'

The years were dropping off Noah as we watched. His face crumpled, and we all turned away, embarrassed. Marianne put her hands on her hips.

'Right, troops, we've got a meal to prepare. Let's leave them to it.'

My cab didn't want to hang around outside the shelter while I hovered on the steps making my mind up.

'Lady, get your ass in here, while I've still got hubcaps.' He wouldn't get out, popped the trunk so I could throw my backpack in. 'I hope you got the fare.' I waved a fistful of dollar bills at him, my last remaining cash. As I stepped into the cab, there was a cry from the door. Noah and his parents came running down the steps, carrying all his worldly possessions in a holdall. They all climbed in after me, breathless.

'You're leaving?'

Noah shrugged. 'I'm taking a break. That's all.'

'A break? Who's looking after the kitchen?'

He looked at me sideways for a while, then laughed, a single, humourless bark. 'God will provide.'

His mother was holding his hand, tightly, as though he might escape again. He gently disengaged it, placed it back on her knee, patted it. Then he leant back against the seat and fell asleep. His father, in the front seat, did the same. She remained awake, watching over them both.

At the airport a Hare Krishna was chanting. His pale blue eyes and freckled nose sat oddly above the saffron robes, and his shaved head was growing in blond stubble. Somebody's son. As I rode the escalator up to my flight, looking downwards I could see Noah's mother pause, let go of Noah's hand, and dart back towards the saffron-robed figure. His chanting stopped for a minute as she grabbed him and he faltered as Noah and his father pulled her off, dragging her with them towards the domestic terminal. He didn't restart immediately and for the few moments he stood there, tambourine dangling in his hand, he looked as though he'd been abandoned. A lost boy. Then he shook his head, recalled himself, and took up the chant once more, and I rolled on upwards until he was out of sight.

THE VINES

LIZ FREMANTLE

THE PARTY WAS ONE OF THOSE GLITZY AFFAIRS WITH WHITE-jacketed waiters and people you think look familiar but you don't know where from. I recognized a singer, from the posters on my daughter's bedroom wall, encircled by a fawning ring of toadies, and there was a sushi chef slicing technicolor slabs of fish and, with an elaborate performance of sleight of hand, transforming them into polite, bite-sized offerings.

A ring of thoroughbred women swayed on the dance floor. One girl stood out; she was dark-haired, elongated and mesmerizing, with skin less golden than her friends' like the pale marble of Greek statues; her dress was plum-coloured, clung to her in places and was slit high, revealing, as her hips undulated, a livid bruise on her thigh. She danced trance-like, as though no one was watching, but somehow you could tell she knew that all the eyes in the room had rested on her greedily for more than a moment. A hopeful man meandered, half-dancing, in her direction and she took up the challenge, hanging her arms over his shoulders, gyrating with him for a while, gazing into his eyes and then walking away with a provocative look back over her shoulder.

People gathered in groups, and I wandered from room to room feeling that if I kept moving it wouldn't be noticed that I didn't belong to one of the clans. I only knew a few people there, and none of them very well: the odd face from work, a columnist, who I was trying to avoid; and an actress I'd interviewed once, babbling away and gesticulating theatrically. The hostess, Zaza, I'd only met recently, and she'd latched herself on to me, since I broke up with my girlfriend. I didn't mind at all as she was quite something, although she did go on a bit, sometimes, with a lot of new age nonsense. She'd made herself a fortune, with some kind of phone chat line, I'd been told, and liked to spend it on munificent parties.

'I have to introduce you to this friend of mine,' she said, pulling me over. 'You have the same name.'

The friend was tall and angular with a disorder of dark curls. He was dressed rather unremarkably, in his jeans, though they were vintage red tags, and a dark green T-shirt that said 'bored' in pink on the chest. But the shoes told another tale; they were snakeskin and spivvily pointed and they seemed to say, in a not too overstated way: 'I've got *it*'.

'Dominic Vine, meet Dominic Vine,' said Zaza gliding off, as if she were auditioning for an American soap, and leaving us staring at each other in that awkward cocktail party way.

He took a sip from his glass and smiled looking me right in the eye and, wanting to fill the silence, I laughed saying: 'What are the chances of that? But, actually, everybody calls me Dom.'

'They call *me* Mod.'

That was when I clicked. I should have recognized him. He'd been all over the press, a year or so ago, with his first novel. They were all calling it a 'tour de force' and banging on about 'the new voice of British fiction'. Maybe it was because of his name but I'd willed myself to hate that book, to find it pretentious, at least. It *was* good, though, and *my* half-finished manuscript still sat in a forgotten file somewhere on my hard drive.

'Actually I'd heard there was someone going about with my name,' he continued. 'And you're a writer too . . . aren't you?' He had this way of speaking, which unnerved me a bit: slow and distracted, as if there was something else, much more important, on his mind.

'A writer, yes, but not like you. I'm just a hack.'

'Ah! Journalism.' I couldn't tell from his tone if it was a put down or not. 'So what do you think of our hostess?'

Silence. I wanted to come up with something sharp and funny to make him think I was worth it. 'I don't really know her . . .'

'You should go there. Great fuck.'

That threw me. I suppose I'd been expecting him to say something else, and I was unsure how to respond, when the bewitching woman from the dance floor slid up beside us weaving her arm through his and handing him a joint. Close up she was chiselled and translucent, with inky make-up smudged around her green eyes, and I had to stop myself reaching out to touch her skin to see if it was real. There was something about the look of them together that made me take them for brother and sister.

'Darling, I've been looking for you everywhere.' Her voice was slow, and thickened by drink, and it was as if she had to concentrate very hard to keep her head straight and get the words out of her mouth. 'Who's a great fuck, Mod?' Her tone was conspiratorial and quite without accusation.

'Zaza,' Mod said.

She shut her eyes and opened them again in a kind of slow-motion blink, while an almost imperceptible smile caught itself in the corners of her mouth. 'Oooh, yes,' she emanated.

I was quite embarrassed by the effect of her, and I found myself playing with my glass and looking down at those rakish shoes.

'Will you take this for a bit?' she went on, producing a baby intercom from her bag, which she handed to Mod. Then turned to me saying, 'Baby's next door, you see. We live next door. So convenient.' Her voice slurred a little but she clipped off the ends of her sentences sharply, giving the impression of a kind of control.

They were a couple.

'Meet my namesake,' he said to her, as he took the gizmo and passed the joint on to me. 'Dom Vine,' he announced as if it were in italics, 'this is my wife, Eva.'

And pressing a long finger into the middle of my chest she oozed, 'So *you're* the naughty boy who's stolen my husband's name. I hope he gave you permission.'

I knew the moment required an Oscar Wilde-type response but I was blunted by the spliff and all I could manage, as I lifted my glass to my mouth, was a nervous laugh. Her recoiling arm knocked me, spilling a streak of red wine down the front of my white shirt.

'Oh dear,' she purred, dabbing at me with the corner of a nearby tablecloth and sending an ashtray thunking to the floor scattering its powdery load.

'Take him next door and give him one of my shirts,' Mod said.

'No, it's fine,' I protested.

'But you must.' Eva took my hand and began to pull me in the direction of the door.

'Really, it's not necessary.' I was surprised that her insistently gripping hand felt so cool.

'I want you to come with me.' Her tone had become petulant.

'Eva always gets her own way,' said Mod with a half smile, 'you may as well submit with dignity.'

Their house was one of those tall, London town houses. A magnificent wisteria clung to its front, laden with purple flowers, heavy, like bunches of grapes; its long fingers had woven themselves through the railings of the first-floor balcony as if to pull itself up from the earth. She led me straight up, flight after flight of stairs I followed her up, hypnotized by the swaying of her dress, to their bedroom on the top floor. It was a large room with an enormous abstract painting on the wall, which was clearly by *somebody*, and an arch through to a bathroom with an implausible sunken bath. Beside the bed, his side I supposed, was a small table stacked high with books, their pages marked with fluorescent Post-its, which spilled over on to the floor. A copy of *Gatsby* lay akimbo on the bed and I wondered which one of them was reading it. Opposite the bed a row of floor-to-ceiling cupboards was haemorrhaging clothes and every surface had collected a layer of detritus: make-up, jewellery, ashtrays, empty glasses, towels, underwear, baby paraphernalia and all sorts of unidentifiable miscellanea. In the corner was a cot.

'Come and look at my darling,' she whispered, stumbling slightly and righting herself on my shoulder, her scent wafting around me like incense. The baby lay on its back, with its arms spread above its head, absolutely still, apart from the occasional, minute, sucking motion of its mouth. A warm wave of nostalgia washed up images and sensations of my own child as a baby – the limpet grip of her hands, the milky smell of her head – and was swiftly followed by the, now familiar, icy flood of emptiness. But the proximity of Eva pushed all that into the background. 'There are men that would sacrifice it all for a woman like that,' I thought, as I sat down on the edge of the bed and watched her gazing into the cot, mesmerized by the thing she'd created.

She eventually pulled herself away, and lengthened herself onto the bed next to me, asking quietly, 'Do you miss your little girl?'

I was puzzled that she knew about Rosie, but then women talk, and I didn't really want to go into it because of how it would make me feel. And underneath that there was the itch of desire, and I tried to keep my eyes off the place where her dress had fallen open to reveal the curve of her breast.

'Zaza's told me all about you,' she continued, as if she had access to my thoughts.

'Has she,' I replied, wondering how much of my story had done the rounds and thinking that I should have been more circumspect, particularly with someone like Zaza who seemed to survive on a diet of chat.

'How does it feel to be left for a woman?' she murmured, stopping abruptly and covering her mouth with her hand before continuing. 'I'm sorry. I was just being wicked. Forget I ever said that.'

I was trapped in that moment of resonant silence, agitated by my lust; at last allowing myself to imagine having her.

'Come on, take it off then,' she murmured and began to unbutton my shirt. And then, rising all at once, like a charmed snake, from the bed, she went to the cupboard and started pulling things down from a high shelf. Cellophane bags crackled onto the floor slipping out, one on top of the other, each one holding a laundered and folded shirt which was ripped from its packet by her hungry hands and thrown into a pile on the bed. I was worried that the noise would wake the baby, and looked towards the cot, noticing the green light of the monitor glowing beside the oblivious child.

'Look at them all.' Her voice had a manic note to it. 'He buys them six at a time. He's never even worn most of them. Just likes to swagger around saying "I'll have one in every colour", and watch the shop girls grovel.' She stroked the fabric of one and held it up to her cheek. 'So smooth,' she whispered, 'and smell them. They smell of money.' I buried my face in the pile, inhaling, and she was right.

Then, giggling, she picked up the other half of the baby intercom and pressed her mouth to it, hissing 'Moddie,' and more insistently, 'Moddie, can you hear me? I've got a half-naked man in our bedroom.'

His reply came fizzling through the air waves. 'Put him down, darling, and come back to the party! Find him a shirt and bring him back.'

'The Vines' is an extract from the novel of the same title

WHOSE LILIES?

JONATHAN CATHERALL

The flowers, blushing in the window.
Mallinson's Free Range Eggs Medium 6.
Sainsbury's Chives 50g.

I CAUGHT HER THOUGHTFUL EXPRESSION AS SHE GLANCED UP AT ME.
She made an omelette, beating the air into it, slicing the herbs fine.
She said, 'I don't want to', but she was hungry, she had a bit from the
plate before she walked away to the table.

I smell the big yellow yolks, from the cracked shells.

Deceiving me, deceiving herself with him.

'Here,' I said. 'Why?'

She was very pale, she turned her face away. It was then I realized
he'd given them to her, how embarrassed she was about the whole
thing, when she reddened and said, 'I don't want to'.

I suppose she had to pretend to accept his interest. It was a
complicated thing but above all she must have felt guilty for what
she'd put me through.

'Don't you understand?'

She'd done that for me. I found those flowers in the rubbish later.

This is the BT voicemail service for oh-two-oh . . .

The pub is busy with regulars, pressing against each other.

'I'm telling you,' Matt says, sitting very close. *'You've got to tell her
jus' how ya feel,'* he croons. Tune of *Roxanne*. The Police. Original
release date February 1978.

Matt in his own voice: 'I'm serious, man. They like it when you're
decisive. They love it. Say it. Better still, just go ahead and do
something.'

But I'm not sure.

'Surprises, a bunch of fresh flowers . . . You know the kind of
thing.'

And she had flowers, coming back the night of the concert,
blooming red-orange lilies making the air woozy around her . . .
Whose lilies?

'It's different for you, you're already with her, but it's the same
principle, yeah? I remember a girl – cute little tarty redhead. What a
puss! It was some house party.' Matt smoothes down his leather jacket.
'I got next to her, ended up pouring wine into her glass –'

She touched her lips appreciatively to the flowers and smiled. She cradled the flowers across her body. I knew then that I didn't want to know any more about that smile. A warm evening breeze made them jostle and come to life. But whose flowers?

'. . . just the start of it. She had a boyfriend, he was actually there.' Matt chuckled into his glass. 'In the next room. One of my better days. I was showering her with praises, refilling her glass. There was still a catch: the boyfriend.'

Still a catch.

'So I lean over and say in her ear, "You've got a choice. Either we can meet upstairs in ten minutes, or I'll make a pass at you right here and now." My hand touched her arm, it was electric. I knew what was going to happen –'

I needed to know whose flowers, but I didn't ask. If I had done, she would've said triumphantly, with laughter blazing in her eyes, 'Mine!' It's what Matt was telling me. 'You're right,' I said.

'Nice one, mate,' said Matt, swinging his legs off the bar stool and straightening up. He leaned against me, breathing into my ear. 'Nice talking to you.' He drained his pint and burped and set it down firmly. He patted my arm and said, 'I've gotta go. See you around.' He walked very slowly across to the door, his steps careful, his tan leather jacket flapping as he went.

My mate Matt, listening to my problems, telling me what to do.

Your ear was tucked in against the violin, Sarah, playing so beautifully. Bartok Violin Concerto No. 2 with the London Symphony Orchestra. I wanted to reach up and brush away that curl of brown hair that always fell across your eyes when you were concentrating deeply.

Saying, it's all right now. I trust you, I forgive you.

'Don't you understand?'

A final flourish of your bow, the music ebbing away like your breath against my skin. The crowd roared around me. You put the instrument down, smiling at me, your face pale and your lips dark with make-up.

Why didn't you answer my calls? Or call me? You made me so worried. All the calls you made to him are there on the bill. You can tear it into pieces but you can't hide it from me. BT Together. There in black and white, because you were kind. Because you felt sorry for him and the accident.

You play so well, I can feel it from the strings. My fingers feel the old used strings. I can feel and hear your wonderful tone.

You play Tchaikovsky's Violin Concerto in D with the Berlin

Philharmonic. The crowd bellows and applauds. The conductor bows stiffly, squares his shoulders, takes your small hand in his and holds it up. The cameras move in. I feel so proud, so very proud of you. My sweetheart.

'You like the flowers, you know you do.'

The lamp is broken, but I can fix it for you, you don't have to throw it away. I'll take it home and fix it for you.

'Don't you understand?'

Sometimes it's necessary to take a step back from our relationship. To do my best to understand her. Sarah is everything to me, Matt, but I have to recognize the warning signs.

She is labile, prone to sudden and dramatic mood swings. In the course of an argument she could easily have smashed the lamp. She can go from moments of love to moments of extreme temper and even burning hatred.

'Thank you so much for the flowers,' she said, gathering them into her arms. 'They're lovely. These pure white lilies, they're my favourites.' She looked down at them, then looked up. 'But how did you know?' Her smile caressed me. The crowd surged around us.

All of a sudden she began to raise her voice. 'Go away! Leave me alone!' She stepped back. 'Sarah,' I said, looking around us nervously. 'Please. People might hear.'

She is such a talented musician, but so young. She is twenty-one and I am thirty. Do you think that has a bearing? She is still immature. She needs attention to sustain her self-esteem, and then, of course, she is uncertain how to deal with it. The forcing house of classical music, the pressure: it gets her confused. I'm afraid she can't always make distinctions as neatly as you or I can, Matt.

He smiled as he went up to the door with his cello. His name is David.

He came here, of all places. He rang and you let him in and kissed him. I don't understand you, Sarah. I try my best but it's difficult. I try to protect you.

I won't share you with another boy.

You closed the door and I heard music. And I watched and after another hour I saw the light disappear in her room, and I ran away. In tears. Were my tears for her or for myself? I couldn't be sure.

It turns out she smashed the lamp. She said nothing, as if it was an accident, but she must have got angry with him for trying to come between us and she threw the lamp at him in a rage.

I had to call him, of course, and tell him not to come any more. 'David,' I said, 'I've tried to be tolerant and respect her wishes. But you're confusing her. I'm sorry about your mother and father and the terrible accident, and she feels sorry too, but it's not good for her to have her emotions manipulated like that.' David tried to say something on the other end of the line, but I felt it was best to be firm. 'She wants to be kind, but . . . Do the mature thing and move on. I don't think it's a good idea for you to talk to her, even at rehearsals.'

Her home is so quiet. There's no one in the road at this time. The air is fresh, and as I turn to leave, the black rubbish bags are glistening with raindrops in the moonlight. I think of all the chances, all the lives that we throw away. That we never see again.

That's why you're so precious. Why I want to cherish you, as you are and have been and will be. Even your mistakes and the cruel things you say.

Every day I learn to see you in a new way, I make a new discovery.

Even those flowers, lying there among the rubbish.

'I'm here for you, Sarah,' I whispered. 'But I can't make decisions for you. You have to decide who you want.'

'It's you! You're the one,' she said, her lips wide.

Last night I think he may have gone in to you again. I have to see for myself. I have to know.

The path is old and rarely used and covered in winding brambles and nettles. There is a red brick wall, her wall. Small flakes of brick crumble on to my new leather jacket. Ivy runs along the wall.

The assistant at Ted Baker smiled at me. His black hair was plastered down. 'Looks good, right size on you. Yeah, neat. Tan's the hot colour this year. Ain't nothing like a good-quality skin.'

There is no one in the kitchen, but there is a subdued glow from upstairs. The lamp I fixed for her is glowing there in the half darkness.

Finally she is there, upstairs, brushing her long brown hair with a white plastic brush, drying your hair, and I watch and wait, and he is not there. You have remained faithful to me, my love. How could I have doubted you?

'What are you doing here?' The man is big-jawed, standing by his dirty gate on the other side of the path. 'Nothing,' I say, and move away. I turn around to see him still staring after me. But I'm so happy I go down the path through the nettles, not minding whether I'm stung or not.

My fears got the better of me, Sarah, but I will tell you how sorry I am, and you will tell me, and hug me and kiss me, all the nice words.

I buy white lilies from the shop, their stamens as dark as lips. I come back to the door. I straighten my new leather jacket, and brush off the hints of red dust.

All because I rang the bell.

Because I smoothed my hair back.

In my skin, my good-quality skin.

I could see her bare feet through the frosted glass, coming up to the door.

'Oh,' she blinked at me, her eyes adjusting to the light.

'I've brought some flowers,' I said simply, holding them up.

'You . . . Oh, yes,' she said, still blinking, 'You gave me some the night of that concert? The Bartok?' She smiled. 'The same ones? That's so sweet.' She moved forward to take the flowers, but she stopped suddenly. She reddened. 'But . . . how . . . how did you know I was here?'

'I saw you in the window, Sarah. It's fine now, I trust you, I forgive you –'

She looked at me. Her lips and eyes were wide. 'It's you, you're the one . . . Oh, God!'

'I love you so much,' I said, 'and I know we haven't been talking so much lately –'

Her lower lip trembled. She was very pale, she turned her face away.

'Don't you understand? I told you on the phone, I don't want to –'

'Why –'

'So many times. Please don't, please.'

'Sarah, it's all right now.' I leaned forward with the flowers. She stepped back, her eyes large and wild. She pushed the door closed. I heard her crying and shouting, horrible things.

'Sarah,' I said, looking around us nervously. 'Please. People might hear.'

She finds it hard to form attachments, Matt. Her own strong emotions terrify her. She needs time.

But she tells me I'm the one. She tells me I'm sweet.

We have all the time in the world.

VENCEREMOS

MATTHEW LOUKES

THE HOTEL INGLATERRA HAD SPANISH TILES, FRENCH WINDOWS, Arabesque arches and German guests. Everywhere you turned were wicker chairs, and hundreds of stained glass windows twinkled from behind enough slatted wood to make a Venetian start learning Braille. Ceiling fans loped lazily round to the beat of a distant conga. I couldn't see a conga player; maybe they piped it in for us dumb tourists. Lady's room had two big beds, one big bath and an overwrought iron balcony overlooking the Parque Centrale. This was not really a park, but a giant paved square that we'd walked across to get to the hotel. It was dominated by a collection of palms – either soaring above you or stretched out towards you. Cars were parked all along the road in front of the hotel, a crazy mixture of giant American vehicles from the 1950s and Eastern European tin boxes of more recent vintage. Lady nudged me to one side and pushed her way on to the balcony. She put two green cans of Cristal beer on the air-conditioning box and handed me a packet of Popular.

'Go on' – she held up a lighter – 'these will make your balls touch the floor.'

I lit one with a big drag and my eyes swam, my legs crawled and my lungs tried to take flight. I thought I saw my toenails turning brown.

'Haysoos!' I croaked. 'You're not wrong, fucking hell, give me that beer.'

'Yeah, I know.' Lady grinned and handed me the beer. 'It makes you wonder what the unpopular ones are like.'

Lady and I strolled out of the Inglaterra, across the Parque and up a decrepit and incredibly dusty street called Obispo. At the end was a bar that Hemingway had hung out in. Lady and I went in through a slatted door that leaked chill air out on to the dry hot street. Lady ordered the drinks. The *mojito* is about a half pint of white rum, smashed ice, fresh pummelled mint leaves and a two-day hangover.

'So,' I said, as we sat at a wooden table with wicker chairs round it. 'Do you want to tell me why I am here, in this bar, with you and the strongest drink I can remember?'

Lady took a sip of the *mojito*, made a little face and pushed her sunglasses up on to her head. 'Slim, I don't know now if I should have asked. I'm not sure what you'll be able to do. But it's one of the men here at the conference. He works for a child protection agency – as a policy maker or something.' She paused and chewed her lip. I wished she'd chew mine. I encouraged her by keeping quiet. For a change.

'The thing is, Slim, I think he is fucking young Cuban girls, and it's not right, and it's disgusting and I don't know what to do about it and I hate men, sometimes, and I hate asking you for help, and I hate this place where the only people drinking are the ones with US dollars and I want to kill him.'

Her words came out in an inarticulate rush. I just nodded, fighting the *mojito*'s urging to say, 'Oh, is that all?'

Lady's eyes were bright, almost wet-looking. She was warming to her theme, if not her subjects. 'Slim, you can see the men in our hotel. The middle-aged ones sitting on the terrace with these young girls, and boys. They aren't here for the culture or the salsa or the cigars. They're here to get some cheap sex for the price of a tube of *pasta dentale*. Would you want to be having sex for a squeeze of fucking Colgate? With some nebbish sweating on top of you? It's disgusting. And I am sure that Mr smoothy-pants Ambrose Coombes is one of them. I wanted to do something, and I want you to help, Slim.'

'Nebbish?' I said. 'What class of a word is that?'

Lady gave a half smile and a wave of her small hand.

'Ambrose Coombes,' I said. 'That's some name. Well. If you're sure he's up to no good and it sounds like you are, then maybe I can get to know him a bit and have a wee chat about his little peccadillo. And maybe give it a bit of surgery.'

That's what I said, anyway, but I didn't have a damn clue what to do – or even if he was doing what Lady was so burned up about.

'So, baby, tell me about old Ambrose.' I still used language that was probably inappropriate.

'He's about fifty, but he could be younger or older, and sort of handsome, in a politician kind of a way. Tanned, almost orange-coloured and quite tall.'

Lady could have been talking about half the tourists in Havana.

'Anything else?' I asked. 'Distinguishing marks, facial tattoos, missing limbs?'

She started to look a bit cross, as though I were not being serious enough, but then smiled, as if we both knew something.

'Yes.' She was almost giggling. 'Ambrose wears a wig.'

I laughed out loud.

'Darling, you have learned well. The bastard does not stand a chance.'

'I know, babe.' She looked happier now than for an hour or two. 'But it is a pretty good one. No one else at the conference has said anything. It was only the sweat on his brow and that funny way they have of touching it that made me sure.'

I was ready to blow by this point. Lady smiled again, but her eyes looked worried.

'Slim, don't make fun of this – I mean it.'

I said nothing, but lifted my hat just a little, so it hovered just above my head.

Lady said Ambrose was staying at the Nacional but spent most evenings on the terrace bar outside the Inglaterra, drinking cups of iced tea and smiling at the locals. She had seen him chatting to, and leaving with, several different girls. Lady reckoned they were aged between fifteen and eighteen. I made the point that in some countries fifteen was, legally speaking, OK. I shut up pretty damn quick when she gave me a look of scorn that Medusa would have been proud of. Holding up one hand I took it all back. It was not the legality of what he was doing, she stressed, but the immorality. The way he could use his money to make these people do as he pleased. To use them as he might a handkerchief, depositing his snot and tossing it in the laundry, where someone else could clean out the stains. I looked at Lady and wondered if there was another issue, something to do with the work they both did. I took a deep breath.

'Lady, we have got to be sure why we are doing this – why you asked me to come.' I let the air out a little as she narrowed her eyes and thumped the table, not hard, but hard enough.

'Fuck you. Yes. Part of it IS the money. The work. If Ambrose was a German tourist or an accountant from Stevenage I'd hate what he's doing, but I'd move on. I'd have told you, but not asked you to come. But he's not.' Lady looked grimly at me, her jaw set like a terrier. 'And you came, didn't you?'

'Yes, darling, I did. I always will.'

Installed on the terrace, I ordered a Cristal, pushed my hat back on my head and set about trying to read the local newspaper. I soon gave up and looked around to see what Lady was talking about. The terrace bar sat maybe a hundred and was mostly empty. A few tables were occupied by single, middle-aged European men. On the other side of some flowerpots and a brass railing was the pavement. By about six the pavement became the stroll. Women and men, or boys and girls, strolled up and down in less clothes than I ever wear. Lycra hotpants seemed to be the order of the day, accompanied by spaghetti-strapped tops that would make a good hatband, if you had a small head. I felt a bit ashamed as I eyed the Cuban youth. Maybe the reason I was here was moral, or maybe it was to give Lady some revenge on a man she didn't like. Either way, I was looking at the cathouse walk and finding that a part of me was most definitely interested. Every so often one of the guys sitting at tables would look over and make a come-hither gesture, the spider saying look at my flies. The young people, and they did look pretty young to me, would sashay over to a table and peck a cheek or shake a hand and sit down. Without ordering a drink the pairs got up and left. In the time I was there I saw one guy, with pink cheeks and a mullet haircut, get up and come back with three different friends. Must be a gregarious sort of a guy. No one who looked like Lady's description of Ambrose showed up. At eleven I got up and went to bed.

The next afternoon I sat down at my usual table and the waiter was there before my arse hit the wicker. *Buenas tardes* to you too. *Sí, Cristal por favor*. I looked around the bar; most of my fellow men were already there, filling whatever space the testosterone left with rum and Coke, all eyeing the pavement with its traffic of tax-deductible warmth. Sitting three tables away from me was a man with nice hair, smooth chops and all the appearance of having the name Ambrose Coombes. I stayed where I was and looked him over a little. Lady had been right. He was gorgeous in a morning television way. Ambrose, and I was sure it was him, wore neutral colours with no hint of a man-made fibre and butterscotch loafers with no socks. The only thing about him that was not 100 per cent kosher was the nylon guinea-pig sleeping softly on his head. As hairpieces go it was not at all bad and might have fooled a novice, or a camera. Ambrose gave the game away, as they all do, with that little nervous pat. I in turn patted the Polaroid camera in my pocket and watched for a while. While I glanced over my paper and sipped my drink, Ambrose kept what I took to be a beady eye on the sidewalk. I waited and the minutes crept by like mourners at an East End funeral. I was starting to think that I'd got the wrong rug, when he waved a linen-clad arm at a young girl. Friends greeting each other on the evening stroll. She stopped on the pavement and gave a dazzling smile. It looked real enough to me. Ambrose touched his hair and left his table, the drink still half full and the chair left pushed out behind him. It was not part of the plan, but I took off and followed.

Ambrose and his new friend took off across the Parque. It was only about seven in the evening but quite dark, and there were enough people about to not make me too conspicuous. Also, I'd been in town for a few days now, and the novelty of a short fat man was beginning to wear off. As they walked down O'Reilly, the situation changed like a malevolent traffic light. The street got darker which was a good thing, but what was not so good was that it also got a lot less busy.

Apart from Ambrose and his paramour, there was just me, bringing up the rear. But neither of them looked round and Ambrose slipped a lover's arm round the girl's bare shoulder. I played it cool and strolled as normally as I could, just an evening ramble. About halfway down the street they took a left into a very dark alleyway. I'd been down O'Reilly myself the day before and that alley led to nowhere but a parking lot, a kind of American elephants' graveyard. I crossed the narrow street to the other cracked pavement and went straight on by. Let love take its course, I said to nobody. I paused at a streetlight on O'Reilly, above a sign that gave the reason for a street in Cuba to have such a non-Hispanic name. It was more of a plaque than a sign and it talked, as far as I could make out, about 'two islands united in a common struggle for freedom'. Our day will come. Looking half at the plaque and half down the street I could just make out the alley entrance. Nobody came out. I lit a Popular and stood and smoked, and coughed, and waited. Halfway down the cigarette was about as far as I could get without an oxygen mask. I killed the butt on the pavement and walked back towards the alley.

The alley was in almost complete darkness. Many of the buildings round about were occupied, but electricity in Havana was in shorter supply than toothpaste and the only lights were feeble and wobbly. So was I, so I stood for a minute, waiting for my eyes to get some sort of grip on the gloom. I held the camera in my left hand, and pushed the button to switch it on. In a few moments I could see the shapes of the American cars, some with huge fins arching out of their backs, others more rounded and lumpy, as though they had yet to spread their wings. In the less than half light I could count about ten cars, sitting at odd angles where the tyres had given out, or been removed. But only one of them, in the far corner, was rocking on its rusted axle. Ambrose, I said to myself, you are a class act. Take the young lady for a spin in your flash wheels. Show her a good time. All for a tube of toothpaste. I spat on the ground and moved slowly past the empty dead lumps of steel and chrome, towards the car that still moved gently from side to side. As I got near I could hear a small squeak as the ancient suspension gave and took. The car was a 1955 Chevrolet. It had no bumpers and no tyres. As I reached the car itself, I could just make out a pair of feet, pressed against one window. The feet were inside butterscotch loafers and pushed against the window in front of me. I wondered if he had hung his hair from the rear-view mirror. I took a deep breath, lifted the camera to my eye and reached for the door handle. I yanked open the door. And shouted one of the few Cuban words I knew off by heart.

'*Venceremos!*' – We will win!

My voice sounded very, very loud. I pressed the shutter on the camera three times. Ambrose shouted, 'What the fuck?' or something close to it. I turned and ran on short legs.

'Say "Cheese". You piece of shit.' Lady looked at the three Polaroids I'd tossed on to the bed. In the first picture you could see Ambrose, a shocked look on his face, with his cock in the girl's mouth. One hand over the back of the big bench seat while the other, behind his head, was holding the piece in place. The girl to one side in the gap where the steering-wheel once was. His underpants, tight brief-style ones, half down his legs. In the next picture you got much the same view, but the girl's face was clearer as she had spat Ambrose out by now. The third shot showed Ambrose still with his pants down and his lad out but sat up across the bench seat. His wig a little off-centre and his face contorted. His right hand was in the act of slapping the girl across the face.

'Piece of shit.' Lady looked a little contorted, but pleased at the same time, like Ambrose before I made him watch the birdy. I didn't want to piss on Lady's bonfire but I was not exactly sure what these pictures meant. A guy, who probably ought to know better, is getting a nosh from a woman of an uncertain age. Despite that, I agreed with Lady, Ambrose was a piece of shit. He had no call to be cuffing that girl, no one ever does. Lady was sitting up in bed, wearing a blue silk nightdress, with the bed sheet folded down round her waist. In different circumstances I'd be angling to get in with her.

'So, babe,' I said. 'What do we do now?'

'Let's go and have a drink and talk.' Lady threw back the covers and rolled off the bed. 'I'll meet you in the bar on the roof in ten minutes.'

We'd been together, in one way or another, for ages. I'd seen Lady naked more times than I could count, but just now she wanted a bit of privacy. I gave it to her and walked out to the creaking brass lift that struggled up to the rooftop bar.

The bar on the roof was almost empty. A pair of tourists sat at one of the tables, both reading a guidebook and not talking to each other. Drinks came from a tired-looking man in a white dinner-jacket who leaned forward across a small bar under a canvas awning. Lady came up after twenty minutes. I was working on my second beer, and wondering where we went from here. Up there on the rooftop I'd come to the conclusion that down was probably the only way. She was wearing a black long-sleeved T-shirt cut very wide at the neck, so it sat outside her brassière straps. Her eyes were made up but looked a little red and puffy. She smiled wanly at me. The waiter slouched over, his thin neck rattling around inside his collar, like a lone umbrella in an elephant's foot stand. Lady ordered a *mojito*. I had another beer, ignoring her look of mild disapproval. Tonight was not one for cutting back on weekly units. As we waited for the drinks to arrive Lady looked out across the bar, over the roof and towards the sea. The only noise was the muffled conga that echoed round the old hotel at all hours and the thud of the barman's pestle, smashing mint leaves for the *mojito*. When the drinks arrived, Lady handed the man a few crumpled dollar bills and he shuffled back to his position, leaning on the bar waiting for an order. I knew how he felt.

Lady sipped her *mojito* and made a face.

'Slim.' She sounded bluer than Billie Holiday. 'I've been giving all this some thought. I hate it, but I think you are right. You've not come out and said it but I know what you think. You don't think it is any of our business what Ambrose does. He's not breaking any law that we know of, the Cubans don't seem to care. You think I want to blackmail him. You think that I am jealous and angry that a man can be in a position of power and behave like that. You don't think that's right. You think he's a scumbag, but you can't do anything about that and, even if you wanted to, you shouldn't sink to that level. So we try and forget Ambrose and his shitty behaviour, have a bit of a holiday and relax. That's about the height of it, isn't it?'

I checked myself for a contents page and an index.

'Darling.' I was none too pleased either. 'That is sort of it. It's not that I don't care what he does, but what about all the other men, sitting there with their bad haircuts and worse manners? We could try and put the bite on Ambrose, and he might pack it in, but won't some other nonce in a syrup slide into his loafers right away? I do hate them, and I hate what it does to you. But what do we do. Kick his head in? Send the pictures to a tabloid? Tell his mother?'

'I know. But there ought to be something we can do.' Lady looked as if she might cry. 'They shouldn't be allowed to get away with it. It just isn't right.'

I'd nothing to say to that. Hell, I agreed with everything she felt, but she was right that I didn't want to get into the blackmailing business. Not particularly because it was immoral or illegal but that I just didn't think it would work. I sipped a bit of beer, looked at Lady and came right out and said it. Again.

'My Lady.' I reached for her hand. 'Don't worry. I have a plan.'

The next morning I went out, the *mojitos* and beer having a fistfight in my head. Lady was asleep, with a note on her pillow telling her not to worry, that I'd be back soon. How often had I told her not to worry? How often had I been right? Leaving those thoughts brooding in the hotel lobby, I headed out across the square to the taxi rank on the other side. The taxi was a Lada and the driver spoke only Spanish so our conversation was limited to 'Hotel Nacional', '*Sí*' and '*Gracias*'. The Nacional was a relic of the 1930s, the days when Cuba was a destination for Americans who took advantage of lax laws on drinking, drugs, gambling and, in particular, vice to make Cuba a paradise for the thirsty, the itchy and the horny. All you needed was dollars. It seemed to me that the only difference now was that the rich visitors were Europeans. I strolled around the massive lobby, which had an inlaid marble floor and art-deco lamps hanging from a vaulted ceiling. This place had missed the decay that infected most of Havana and was full of bellboys, porters and men in elegant suits running about after guests tricked out in high-end casual clothes. This was the sort of place where you might be refused entry for being inappropriately dressed. It didn't matter if you had on a jacket and tie or not, but your shorts had better be top of the range and your sunglasses absolutely must come with a cord and a logo on the side. The staff were black- and brown-skinned, the guests all a shade somewhere between orange and buffed pine. While the desk clerks were busy booking in a man and a woman whose boat shoes probably cost more than my entire wardrobe I slid an envelope on to the counter and walked slowly out. Nobody called after me or seemed to care. If they had noticed me leaving they were probably relieved my suit was not going to spoil the look of their lovely place.

Lady was standing out on the balcony as I got back to the Inglaterra. I gave her a wave from the street below but she didn't see me. She was still out there, smoking a Popular, when I got up to the room.

'*Hola*, baby,' I said as I squeezed out onto the balcony beside her.

'How did you get on?' Lady was wrapped in a sarong and the sun had made her shoulders red.

'Good, I think. I left the photos in an envelope. It might just take the lead out of his wee pencil.'

'Don't be revolting.' Lady was serious enough in her admonishment but she seemed more pleased than the night before. 'It's not blackmail, then?'

'No, I didn't put a note in, just the holiday snaps. Who knows, he might just add them to his collection and show them as slides when he has the relations round for dinner. This way we will never know. But we do know that we tried, and he knows that somebody else knows his game. On this trip, mate, that is probably as good as we are going to get.'

'Thanks, Slim.' Lady grabbed me and hugged. We kissed and cuddled. I am pretty sure that she never felt the outline of the one Polaroid picture I had left in my breast pocket. Ambrose could keep the other two for his collection, but I wanted something to hold on to. Apart from Lady, that is.

BLIND FRIEND DATE

HEATHER WILLIAMS

MY EYELIDS SCRAPE OVER EGGSHELLS AND ALCOHOL SEEPS FROM my pores. Touching my throbbing forehead, I notice a black crescent under my thumbnail. I close my eyes again.

Where was I last night?

There'd been a mirror: my face a pale smudge against a jigsaw of shoulders and the backs of heads. I was early, perched on a stool, scratching my name with a fingernail into the sticky counter-top grime. A man with green dreadlocks and a silver grommet in his tongue drained the foam from his glass, poked the grommet out, and belched. 'Good luck with that, love,' he said, and left. Yes. I remember that.

The air in my room feels greasy, like someone's vaporized cooking oil. My flatmates must be having a fry-up. There's another smell too. Sharp and musty, it tugs on some memory in my mealy brain. I pull the covers over my head and inhale my own concentrated beer-and-smoke odour, which seems the least kind of penance I can do.

'I'm going on a blind friend date,' I'd told grommet man. Tried to drown my recurring nervous cheek-twitch with a preventative pint; pulled the ad from my handbag. She has to be nice, I thought, to answer an ad like this. No 'friendship plus', no 'clubbing, drugs, and alternative sexual experience' or coded invitations to a ritual murder.

Cat pee. That's the smell.

I peel one inch of cover from my face, open one eye. A small black cat stares back with glowing moons. A dark pool sinks into the carpet, the stench like a punch in the nose. 'Bad kitty,' I murmur, and am about to rehibernate when the tugging thought finally budges free: we don't own a cat.

Worry, or ignore it? The cat doesn't blink or move. Maybe it's not real. I pull the blanket tighter around me, pilled yellow polyester with a torn satin edging. I've never seen it.

Olivia had tapped me on the shoulder with a small 'Sorry, are you Meg?' I jumped off the stool and faced her. She was beautiful, all green eyes and shiny blond hair, and dressed in a black suit with short skirt just above her knees. Skinny legs in red heels with silver buckles. I had no idea what to do. I knew what to say – 'Wow, it's so great to meet you!' – and stuck out my right hand in a vague offer to shake. Olivia raised her arm to my shoulder, leaned in and kissed me damply on each cheek. I made last-minute pecking shapes with my mouth. Her sleek silver earrings, elongated cats, shifted light as we both laughed. I assumed it was mutual acknowledgement that this was bloody awkward. 'C'mon,' she had said, hand on my arm. 'Let's snag a sofa.'

Oh God. I bury my head under the pillow. I've never seen its greying rose-print, either. Maybe we could have been like sisters. And I've clearly abandoned her for some poorly hygiened wanker.

I'm fully clothed, though, and appear to be the only person in the room. There's only one pillow. I curl tighter, knees beneath my chin, and stare at the cat, which sniffs its soaked-in handiwork.

A creak, a thump. A woman's voice.

'Oh, Patrick, bad cat.'

I peek out. It's Olivia, wearing red boxer shorts and a white vest, hair in a bun. She plunks a mug on the bedside table. The vibration shoots billiard balls in my head.

'Rough night, babe?' She perches on the edge of the bed. Cellulite puckers the side of her thigh. 'Do you want a Panadol?'

I nod, spurring a billiard-ball avalanche. She pats my blanketed arm.

I paid for two pints of bitter. 'Better for you, and not all girly,' Olivia said, and we both giggled. Followed her hair through the Friday crowd. Everyone's friendlier in this part of town, smiley, sprawled around wooden tables. Where I work the pub crowd consists of twitching coke-fuelled men in pink shirts and ties, and expensively suited women braying over their Chardonnay.

'Cool shirt,' Olivia said when we were settled on a corner couch. I pulled the gauzy sleeves over my hands. Between Olivia's all-black sophistication and everyone else's jeans and retro T-shirts, I looked like a fourteen-year-old on her first night out.

She lit a cigarette, blew a contrail out the side of her mouth and held out the packet to me. I shook my head. We clinked glasses, said 'Cheers', and looked at each other over the tops of our beers.

'Here,' Olivia says now, holding out water and a white pill. I don't dribble, which is nice.

'I'm so embarrassed,' I hear myself whine. Show her you understand, advises some ingrained Voice of Socialisation. Show her you're not a psycho. 'What a nightmare for you, answering an ad and getting this.'

She hands me the steaming mug.

'Seriously. No worries.' The skin under her eyes looks pebbled and purple. She dabs at the cat's puddle with a cloth, biting her lips, making her mouth a thin white line. I squint out of the dusty window at skeletal trees clawing grey.

It was fine. It was fun. Wasn't it? On the back of my eyelids I can see Olivia against the pub's haze, the smiling bright pink lipstick I could never wear and the startling, almost leafy, green in her eyes. She laughed and her cigarette described smoky arcs. Her right foot jiggled, and she dangled the red shoe from her toe. If she wondered why a 'fun female aged 25' sought friends in advertisements, it didn't show.

'It's just, um, my friends moved away, and my boyfriend went all cheating on me, so . . .' I blurted out after our third round. Olivia smiled and nodded, but stubbed her cigarette out in an ashtray and twisted it, hard, into the glass. Her foot jerked an inch too high and the dangling shoe flew beneath a table.

Three men dived for Olivia's shoe in a mini-scrum. The victorious one, shiny and short, waved it over his head and slurred, 'Oi, love, she's no good for you, give us a kiss.' Olivia's wrinkled nose and lowered eyebrows mirrored mine. 'Time to go,' we said, together. I loved how I could tell she was resisting laughter, lest we encourage him, by the skin crinkling around her eyes. Shrugging, he tossed the shoe on to the sofa. We stumbled through the beery fog into the lane, looked up at the narrow pink strip of night sky. 'You can't encourage them,' she said.

'You awake?' Her toothpaste breath shushes against my ear. 'Good for what ails you,' she says, handing me a plate of toast and crawling under the blanket at the opposite end of the bed. Her feet are icy against mine. From outside waft metallic clanks and men's voices yelling in Caribbean accents; a siren; the wooden clunk of a passing train.

My skin feels dry and grey, alcoholic, but gradually glows as I munch toast. Olivia's feet grow warmer. The nightstand holds a framed photo of Olivia and another woman, all teeth and sunglasses in front of a waterfall.

The pavement shone with rain. We giggled past the gauntlet of hooded men muttering 'Skunk? Marijuana? Skunk?' Buildings and the blurred streak of traffic seemed far away, shimmering out of proportion.

Chemical alcopop burned in my throat, and the sweet gritty air of spun-sugar candy. Neon streaks, shouts – a spinning, blinking funfair in the tiny triangle of Brixton's green. Faces whirled past on a rattling mini-rollercoaster. A woman with yellow eyes and a manic afro waved bags of powder; I shook my head and the scene tilted forty-five degrees. 'This is scary,' I yelled at Olivia, and she yelled something back, her face a strained mask, orange in the lights. She grabbed my sleeve and we sprinted towards a bus. I stumbled and my hands sank into the muddy verge. Olivia pulled me away from puddle-spray as the bus moaned off without us.

I should leave. I need to apologize but it feels like we're communicating through Plexiglas, like people in a jail. Patrick jumps on my lap and sticks all twenty-four claws into my thighs with a quiet 'Rrrr'. Yes, he implies, you really should be going.

Olivia hunches over her plate, pushing crumbs with one finger. I peel off the blanket and wobble into the cramped hall. The carpet is beige, patterned with flattened dust balls.

In the tiny bathroom I examine her rows of moisturizers, nail polish, tooth whitener. Under a hot shower I lather myself with creamy coconut soap, wash my hair with minty-sweet shampoo. Steam fogs the room when I finally dry myself with a torn hand towel. I feel underhandedly happier, as though stealing Olivia's toiletries makes me her new best friend.

She's leaning against the wall cradling a mug when I come out. What if she says 'I'll call you?' Is this like dating, which means she won't?

'Look,' she says, pulling a strand from her bun. 'I'm really sorry about last night. I didn't mean to . . . I drank too much, obviously. But I had a really nice time.' Are those water droplets at the corners of her eyes, hovering over her thin smile?

'I should apologize, I was way more drunk,' I say, and pick up my handbag from the hall floor. Before we can launch the apology Olympics – 'I'm sorry.' 'No, I'm sorrier.' – we kiss on each cheek, her fingers pressing into my shoulder. 'Let's meet up. I'll call you,' I say, and 'Thanks so much for everything', which hangs limply in the foyer as I run downstairs.

The street stinks of fish from the chippy below Olivia's flat. I look up at the window where she's standing, holding Patrick. She moves one of his paws in a little wave. The cars, terrace houses, and black trees all glisten with damp. Crows rustle into the air, cawing. I walk towards the swish of traffic, kicking a stone and trying not to think about toast or nausea.

We'd walked through the sodium hush of streetlamps, blowing chewing-gum bubbles and laughing at nothing. Olivia blew a bubble the size of her head, stopped by a rubbish bin, and spat it out; we watched it float down, a sweet ghostly orb against the dark bottom. Olivia linked her arm through mine, squeezed, and guided me towards the fluorescent glare beneath her home.

TRACES

SUE TYLEY

LAURA'S WRINKLE

'Laura's wrinkle' has been in my notebook for several weeks now. It's not a very accurate description, but it's the phrase that was conjured to my mind the instant I noticed the – I'll call it wrinkle again for now – and since then it (the phrase) has reciprocally served to evoke it (the wrinkle) for me with detailed clarity whenever I remember or read it (the phrase). The phrase also evokes the same certainty I felt at the time – an excited, urgent, restless certainty (I think that covers all the nuances) – that the wrinkle will make a short story. So far, I haven't put that certainty to the test, only, periodically, summoned and savoured it – I feel it now – so the wrinkle remains pure potential. Potential for simple description – original, deft, vivid (one hopes) – but even more for significance, to capture and convey the unexpectedness which made the wrinkle poignant, memorable, and resonant with meaning. Because you see Laura is young – twenty-two – and her skin is as smooth, curved and flawless as a fresh, warm egg, or brioche, or as a child's. And her eyes are huge, round, blue, clear, bright with trust, candour, hopefulness – all qualities which, in a scale which I have been made to realize must exist somewhere, like the Mohs scale for comparing hardness, are the antithesis of a wrinkle, at the opposite end of the scale. So when she smiled, and a fan of exquisitely fine lines snapped silently open out from the corner of those eyes, it was both surprising and touching. The frail thinness of the skin apparent, transparent, in the fineness of the lines made me reflect that traces of damage can be found even or already on those whom you would think too innocent and ill-equipped to deserve and bear it. And it's true, Laura *has* been through a lot (things which others judge could also make a story, a very different type of story), things whose traces are perhaps better represented by the San Andreas fault or the wrinkles on an elephant than the filamentary creases I'm talking about here, but that's part of the resonance too: the contrast between the distress and turbidity of the event and the delicacy of its traces. All this is latent in Laura's wrinkle. But to develop it, I'd need a character to give the wrinkle to, and a plot in which she featured, and actually I'm just interested in the exquisiteness and resonance of the image. Which is why Laura's wrinkle is still in my notebook, and not yet in a story.

Where it is written

'Literature would be the poorer without liminal places,' I said, without thinking.

Ewan pounced. 'Ha! Clearly a seven, don't you think?' He appealed to Mel and Barbara.

Barbara smiled with wifely indulgence, but Mel ignored him. I hadn't needed her whispered admission under the duvet last night to know that the novelty value of Ewan's 'Rictus scale' had worn off, and that she was finding it childish and irritating. It measured pretension, on a scale of one to ten. Personally, I was still amused by it – the definitions were an unparalleled piece of cultural iconoclasm (six?) – though less so, I admit, when he applied it to me, which he did with troubling frequency. I hadn't realized. Still, one man's pretension is another man's profundity. Not that I'm claiming profundity; I just say the first thing that comes into my head. And anyway, he was our host.

Mel and I were spending the weekend with our – actually, historically, *my* – friends Ewan and Barbara. The three of us had been at university together; Ewan's sense of humour had failed to graduate. We were meandering through a graveyard, trying to find Philip Larkin. The sun hadn't yet melted the frost, and our footsteps crunched gently on the white grass. It may only have been ten thirty, but I was already looking forward to the promised brandy, brunch and blazing log fire at The Crooked Stile.

Loyally, Mel took up my point and began listing examples of literature indebted to thresholds, to the in-between, the neither – or both – here nor there: '"Dover Beach", "Elegy Written in a Country Churchyard", *Hamlet* . . .'

'*Somewhere Over the Rainbow*,' Ewan interrupted, grinning.

Mel gave up. I took her hand and we ambled away towards a group of yew trees. Before we'd escaped from earshot we heard Ewan explode with laughter.

'"In loving memory of Michael John Trayne",' he managed to read out, wheezily. '"Chewy to his friends". C-H-E-W-Y!' He roared again.

The only other people in the graveyard looked up from where they were kneeling in front of a small patch of earth as dark as freshly ground coffee. The man put his arm around the woman. They were still for a moment, then went back to planting their bulbs.

We heard Barbara's urgent 'Shhhhh!'

The yew trees were blackly green like velvet, and studded with hundreds of improbably plastic-looking berries, tiny red barrels of tar. We turned sideways to follow the faint suggestion of a path which the denseness of the interleaved branches did its best to deny. The branches closed behind us as we emerged into a small clearing, no more than eight feet in diameter, which the yew trees encircled like a formidable funerary screen, tapering up to the infinite depths of a lapis lazuli sky. In the centre of the clearing was a tomb, the finely chiselled corners of its plinth now blunt and crumbling, the taut smooth stone roughly mottled with lichen. All these things caught my eye. But what caught at my heart was the top of the tomb, where moss nestled in the engraved letters like soundly sleeping animals. You couldn't decipher the words through the curled plump softness. You didn't need to.

TRACES

Lia is a Gemini. She doesn't believe in astrology, but her birthsign helps her to naturalize her doubleness. For Lia (baptismal name Olivia) is thoughtful and thoughtless, cautious and rash, conscientious and neglectful, discreet and indiscreet, honest and deceiving, loyal and treacherous, aware and oblivious, innocent and disingenuous. I won't go on. Her friends know only her good qualities and if asked to describe her, would do so unequivocally. Lia and I know better – that is, worse.

She has a habit which I attribute to and find an almost endearing example of her confused contradictoriness: she overwrites (equally, underwrites – both earths up and earths) her affairs with licit marital activity. Thus if she and her lover explore a park, see an exhibition or dine in a new restaurant, she will repeat the visit with her husband, as if to erase the traces by tracing them. On a practical level, this enables her to talk relatively freely to her husband about the park, exhibition or restaurant without betraying herself and her betrayal by forgetting either that she should not mention the park etc. at all, or the lie she first told about the identity of the person with whom she went. For Lia hates to lie, and doesn't do it well. She still has to be careful to match the detail to the right instance, but that's a minor worry and venial necessity once the mortal offence has been absolvingly retraced. Because more profoundly, but with shallow logic, in fact probably subconsciously and without reference to logic at all, Lia believes that the repetition obliterates the betrayal, effects a moral erasure, cleans the slate. So with this alogical sleight, she covers the reminding evidence and recovers her apparent goodness.

That's not how it works of course; like a palimpsest, traces of the earlier writing are always present, always visible to one clear-sightedly immune from the selective blindness of doubled vision. And so I know that even after tomorrow, when our divorce becomes absolute, indelible traces of Lia will remain.

WAYS OF SEEING

You have taught me too well.

Do you remember the first time? I'm surprised to find I don't, though other firsts I do: the first meal you cooked for me (home-made tagliatelle with baby artichokes, wild mushrooms and walnuts in a crème fraîche sauce, ripe mango and ice cream speckled with vanilla – but then, we still cook it together on anniversaries and Valentine's Day); the first flowers I gave you (summer-scented yellow freesias; you dried them; they're downstairs now on the dresser, as light and brittle as rice paper); the first thing we bought together (a tea caddy; we each chose the one we thought the other would like, and got it wrong; when we chose the one we liked ourselves, we chose the same). Perhaps it was our first summer, the pub garden, with blossom floating down into the wine and velvet-bodied bees bumbling through the grass. Or later, in the autumn, as we sat together at right angles at one end of the sofa, two arms of a swivel coat hook, wearing extra sweaters and soft thick socks, to the ethereal tintinnabulation of Arvo Pärt. Or our first Christmas, in Venice, where the canopy of lights over the bridge, its walls buttressed with market barrows, were like netted stars. Or perhaps there was no one specific occasion, perhaps it happened gradually through barely perceptible osmosis.

You would have had to be subtle, cajole; I am too earnest, too competitive, to enjoy games, I lack the ludic temperament. And am ill suited to the role of novice, fret resentfully when my ignorance seems doubly benighted in the shadow cast by someone who knows. You would have had to kindle my interest with artless-seeming artfulness, as a child is made curious by the shielding shoulder and bent head of quiet unassuming industry. You would have explained, gently, almost as if musing aloud and not teaching at all, about locating the definition in the first or last word or phrase (or sometimes in the whole clue, though you probably withheld this possible variant until later); about identifying indicators, the instructions on how to treat the remaining words, the working material of the clue; about spotting codes among the working material itself. You didn't realize until now that I was talking about crosswords? I'm so sorry. No, I see I haven't given any indication – haven't followed the rules of cluemanship. Still, now that you know, are you happy for me to continue? Good, because all this is to your credit – so far. As, for instance, the way you would have volunteered analogies and examples to make it pellucidly clear, even permitting me to become ungratefully impatient with your slow-paced kindness. 'The key,' you might have said, 'is identifying the type of clue, then the rest clicks into place like lock tumblers, like applying the terms in a recognized formula or' – hastily, sensing the bolting panic in my frown (I am a poor mathematician) – 'parsing parts of a sentence. Spotting the type of clue,' you might have continued, or perhaps said on another or over several separate occasions, 'is like adjusting the focus on your binoculars until the blur resolves into a kingfisher on a branch over the water, or like staring at those optical puzzles in the Science Museum until the blobs become a dalmation, or the crone a beautiful girl. Or – one more – like working out just where to stand so that Holbein's skull assumes the right perspective. Because de Bono is only partly there with his lateral thinking: cryptic crosswords require you to think not just laterally but vertically, invertedly, literally, back to front, overarchingly, transparently.'

You would have warned me about misleading contexts which deflect attention from the answer, about clues with mesmerically apparent surface meanings which at the same time tell an utterly different story. You might have cited 'Back number (8)' as a simple example, and quickly released me from the hypnotic meaning 'previous issue' with a snap of your fingers and the alternative interpretation 'something which numbs the back', allowing me to deliver, painlessly, the answer: 'epidural'.

On the surface, our life tells a story of contentment. Our five years together have been years of steady increase – in the value of the precious metal in the name of our credit cards, in collar size, number of bedrooms and bathrooms, garage spaces and litres per mile required, the twice-swollen belly which hasn't quite recovered its original contours, frequency of hair-colour appointments, completed crosswords. We do them together: in the ebb tide of evening after the children are in bed and before the effort of dinner; amid the crumbs, coffee dregs and orange pulp of Sunday brunch; on car journeys where you drive and conjure answers from imaginary letters suspended in mid air and I, who do not get carsick, sit in the passenger seat, reading out the clues and filling in the answers with the benefit of the written words before me. Horizontal and vertical words in a crossword are said to interlock where a letter contributes to two words; our lives are interlocked, with crosswords themselves one of the points of connection.

Anagram clues are simplest, the indicators legion but generally easy to spot: dizzy, ravish, mysterious, excited, restless, suspect, carelessly, sadly, easily more than a thousand. Your favourite anagram clue is

'Dicky came top (4)', for the misleading context, the mesmeric surface meaning of the schoolboy coming first in the exam (*your* context, a cheerful muddied scrum of Hooray Henrys and clever Dickys), the alternative interpretation of 'dicky' as 'unsound' (*your* vocabulary, coyly dismissive, anachronistic, unself-conscious) and therefore acting as an anagram indicator on 'came' which, rearranged, gives 'acme' meaning 'top'. Neat, I agree. Did you know that Melissa is an anagram of 'I am less'? You, Sam, on the other hand, are unyieldingly intractable.

Then there are hidden word clues, where the working material contains a sequence of letters which comprise the answer, indicated by words such as embrace, held by, in. 'Detained in such a noisy capital (5)'. Hanoi. Yesterday's *Guardian*. 'Good morning, Mel. Got earache at four thirty. Couldn't sleep. Didn't want to wake you. Gone for walk – couldn't find my wellies. The dawn is beautiful – haven't been up this early for a while, a very long while. Remember Pitlochrie? Till later, S XXX.' Cheat, lies, leave. The message you left on the kitchen table this morning, propped against the tulips.

I read your mail, the mail you send and the mail you receive. I hope you appreciate the joke. Too bewildered to see it? Checked letters, those letters which contribute to two words? Which result in interlocking? And there's mileage in the term for letters which contribute to only one word, too: unchecked letters or unches. I 'ad an 'unch summat wor wrong. There are accent clue types which rely on peculiarities of speech. Let's see: 'Suspect 'Arry might've 'ad one (5)'. How's that?

The codes, once learned, are reassuring, and make for a world at once flexible, contained, predictable and interlinked, a world where 'way' can be decoded as ai (for A1), mi (for M1), st (for street, but also for saint, denoted by 'good man'); 'force' translates as g (for gravity, which also means gramme or a note or a key or string); tar, salt and AB are all synonymous with sailor; workers are ants and bees; love and ring mean O. We have our own code: '143' means 'I love you'. It will always mean 'I love you'. It's *you* who no longer mean it. And wasn't 143 your room number in Rome, at the hotel where you explained that the switchboard was notoriously unreliable at connecting calls correctly? Another example: 'I'm on my way' can be decoded as you're just going to have one last glass of wine, and a kiss – a probing, bruising, lovers' kiss, a kiss so long you worry about having to swallow, not the puckered dry pecks you and I exchange – and then you'll come home. Or it can, on occasion, mean that you're on the train, alone, on your way home.

Another type of clue relies on being able to break the answer into constituent parts, the more unlikely, resequenced, split and misleading those parts the better. Like the title of the book you gave me: *Pretty Girl in Crimson Rose (8)*. Rebelled. A pretty girl is a belle. Insert belle inside (in) red (a synonym for crimson) and you get rebelled, one meaning of rose. The name of this type of clue is charade. How apt.

It is thanks to you that I have learned to see through the beguiling ostensible contentment, to spot the indicators, the clue types, to translate the code, to detect your – a last clue for you: 'Alter by a devious act of treachery (8)'. Ximenes maintained that the crossword compiler's object is legitimately to deceive. You cannot deceive me. The pupil has outwitted the master.

GOLDFISH

The toilet lid was down. Its edge butted just beneath his ribcage as he stretched across with both arms and clutched at either side. Ice-white porcelain returned his hug with a cool kiss to his cheek. His left leg bent and straightened in an aimless frog kick once, twice, three times. At the fourth attempt, he succeeded in hitching his thigh up on to the lid, then slithered, wriggled and hauled until the other leg had been drawn up too. He shuffled his knees forward to gain crawling purchase; his bottom cranked into the air. Gingerly, he released his grasp and felt his way up the cistern, the trail of handprints evanescing like breath on a window pane. The ill-fitting cover rocked and grated as he pulled himself to standing position; the shelf with its fish tank cargo hove into eye-level view. His face lit up with a beatific smile.

The goldfish flicked to and fro before his eyes. He watched them weave in and out of the wavering, fine-fringed seaweed, loop through the stone arch or hover with faintly fluttering fins above the translucent fragments spilling across the floor of the tank as though just poured from his kaleidoscope. He followed the beads of silver bubbles threading to the surface, and thought he heard the bell in the miniature church ring with a glutinous chime. For several long still moments he stood in wide-eyed enchantment, then suddenly reached up and into the tank, his chubbily unjointed arm only just allowing his fingers to touch the water. Luck delivered a fish against his dabbling fingertips straightaway, and hoisting himself on tiptoe he closed his fist around the gleaming orange body. The flickering tail and slippery wriggling body surprised him, but he kept his hand clenched tight.

With his eyes fixed on the fish protruding from his hand he crumpled down on to the toilet lid, then flattened out on to his stomach and slowly lowered himself over the edge till his feet felt the floor. Then, arm extended in front of him, he walked to the bath mat, knelt and released his prize. He watched and waited, expectantly.

The fish writhed, flopped and gaped.

White-tiled walls loomed above the kneeling child like glittering icebergs. The hard floor pressed coldly through the thin cellular mat and gnawed at his bones. He shivered.

The fish grew still and its metallic brightness dulled.

He heard the front door bell, echoed seconds later by his mother's two-note chimes: 'Ma-tthew! Tom's here! Time to go!' He scrambled up and trotted out of the room.

'He just left it on the bath mat! Of course, the poor thing died! He was such an unholy terror!' Gilda Barrington's voice still rang with a clear timbre. She smiled at her son, ignoring his half-hearted protests. She would have pinched the cheek of the three-year-old boy but was a little in awe of the adult he had become, with his handsomeness an unkissable six foot four inches tall, his vague but highly paid job in the City, and shirts immaculately laundered by his maid. Gilda always enjoyed telling the story to Matthew's girlfriends. Her memory of his boyhood was a garland of such anecdotes, a wreathed celebration of a mother's busy love and a child's mischievous independence. They brought back her little boy.

Fish had been her husband's hobby. He'd had a huge tropical fish tank built into his study wall. After he left, she replaced the goldfish in the bathroom with an arrangement of shells, pebbles, sea glass and teasels. The study was now her studio, and she had filled the alcove left by the fish tank with a *trompe l'oeil* painting of grass-feathered sand dunes seen through a half-open casement window and vanishing into a palely lambent sea and paler sky. She had placed driftwood along the low shelf, which visitors entering the room for the first time invariably mistook for part of the painting. The double deception pleased her.

Gilda showed these things to Lauren, who seemed delighted by the painting and was not deceived by the driftwood. The tour over, they had rejoined Matthew in the conservatory for tea. As her son, seated beside her on the sofa, acceded to persuasion and began to describe another childhood misdemeanour not unredeemed by charm, Gilda studied his latest girlfriend. Lauren sat poised on the rigid edge of a deep-cushioned, linen-cream armchair, the April sunlight undulating through rain-runnelled windows to caress golden gleams into her sleekly pleated hair. Her expression shadowed the story she was being told, eyes rounding in disbelief then dissolving into a smile. Gilda noticed how her almond-tipped fourth and little fingers curled protectively together as she lifted the fragrantly steaming tea cup to lips already framing a delicately expectant 'o'. She admired the girl's legs, glossily sheathed and pump shod, an elegantly elongated parallelogram sloping demurely to the faded silk-threaded opulence of the rug which discreetly adorned the grey sobriety of the slate flag conservatory floor.

She was beautiful, as they all were; Gilda couldn't fault her son's eye for beauty. But she sensed something indefinably different about Lauren. She had warmed to her already, and hoped she would see her again.

'You'll love it,' Lauren was saying. 'It's a different world – a magical, beautiful world – and then the Red Sea has *another* world, too, the world of ancient history and bible stories, which makes it even more special. You'll have no trouble getting your licence, I guarantee – but if you like you could start practising before we go – I could teach you.'

'It's not the course I'm worried about,' said Matthew, still sounding doubtful.

'What is it then? Tell me.' She turned to Gilda. 'Mrs Barrington, perhaps *you* can persuade him to come diving with me.'

Matthew reached for the shampoo then turned and took a small step forward so that the water cascaded down his back. Eyes closed against the foam, he saw again the sunlight gilding Lauren's hair. He sensed his mother's approval and was pleased. Perhaps this time . . .

He stepped back under the shower and surrendered to the drum, clatter and whisper of water on his body.

He turned off the shower, slid back the glass door and stepped onto the mat.

Downstairs the front door closed quietly but firmly. The envelope, propped steeply against the vase on the hall table, toppled gently forward, the letters of his name gliding sinuously through the highly polished surface until stilled and darkly hidden as the envelope fell prone, like the closing of a lid.

JUDE

TAMSIN COTTIS

J UDE SITS AT THE TABLE IN THE LOUNGE. HE IS STUDYING THE *Radio Times* as if it were a bible. The television is his one-way window on to the world outside Sunny Lodge. The real windows have small squares of glass in them and some have swirly bits which make everything on the other side look wobbly. The plain glass is extra strong. Big Debbie threw her shoe at it last week and the large black lace-up just bounced straight back.

Through the lounge window, Jude can see the swing. It was put there for Alicia the autistic girl, who would swing all day and all night if she were allowed to.

Jude looks back at his magazine. He loves the television, even the kids' programmes. He's a man now, thirty-five last birthday. Martha talks to him about when they were children. She's told him that when he was a baby his milk came down a tube attached to his cheek with a piece of sticky tape. The tube went up his nose and down his throat. It sounds disgusting, but he can't remember. He's never seen a photo of it. When Martha was born, he was two and everyone said how lovely she was. He's got a photo of her on his wall. Actually, he's got loads of photos of her. In this one she's up on Dad's shoulders, laughing, all little white teeth and curly hair. The two of them are at the top of a hill, and there's a patchwork of fields spread out behind them. Dad's hair was long in those days and it's sticking out on one side, as though there's a huge hair-dryer just outside the picture.

It can get stuffy in Sunny Lodge and Jude often asks if he can go outside. 'Not just now, Jude, mate,' his keyworker Steve usually says, 'there's no one to be out there with you.' He might open the window for Jude. 'Let's get some fresh air in,' he'll say. But it's not the same.

Today, Jude sits quietly and no one takes any notice of him. In Sunny Lodge you've got to make a noise to get them running. Take Big Debbie. She's on the sofa, roaring and shouting. She's so fat the staff have to get her clothes from a special catalogue. She's got her slippers on now but the tops of her feet are squeezed out, like little pale blue pillows. The residents try and keep out of her way. Jude knows she'll lash out if he gets too close.

'Shut up Debbie shut up Debbie shut up Debbie.' Alicia's getting worked up now. Sometimes Jude thinks he's the calmest one in there. Alicia looks tiny in the corner, her hair all over her face, fiddling with her piece of string. She's rocking backwards and forwards in the armchair.

The staff are in the kitchen. There are three of them on today so it's a bit crowded in there. There are no chairs to sit on, but the staff seem to like it better than the lounge. They're chatting, and their voices go up and down like music. Suddenly they'll all laugh together and make Jude jump. Like when someone lets off a firework.

'What's so funny?' he calls, but they don't seem to hear him. Jude pokes his head around the door. 'What's so funny?' he asks again, and they all go quiet. There's Kathy, the manager. She's leaning up against the cooker with her arms folded. Steve is making some tea. Another one is standing just inside, on the back step, at the top of the ramp to the garden. She's smoking, which is not allowed.

'Naughty!' Jude says to her, but no one smiles.

'Come on, mate,' says Steve. 'Let's go back in the lounge and have a look at your *Radio Times*. See what's on this week.'

The people on the TV get into Jude's head. Tracy Beaker in the children's home who shouts a lot and whose mum never comes to see her; the lady on *EastEnders* who knows her baby will have something wrong and so she kills it before it's born; the man who stole and murdered two little girls (the news, every hour).

Steve sits down beside him and Jude picks up his pen. He's made lots of marks on the pages – squiggles and dots and dashes. It's a special code, telling him which programmes he wants to watch and which ones are boring. He loves soaps and he hates quizzes – except for *The Weakest Link*. 'You are the weakest link. Goodbye,' he'll say to Steve when he's off back to his girlfriend after a shift.

Jude holds his pen like the teachers at school used to when they were marking work. He licks his finger, turns the page, and turns it back again.

'Hey, Steve,' he says, 'there's Britney. She's nice, isn't she?'

'Bit young for you, mate,' says Steve and he turns the page quickly. 'Look, Jude, *Top Gear*'s coming back on Tuesday – we'll have to watch that.'

'Yesssss!' says Jude and he does a high five with Steve.

Jude is about the same height as Steve, though a bit fatter. Steve's great. They have a laugh. Best of all is when he gets to go in Steve's car. It's a shiny black VW Beetle – 1302, with a 1.6 c.c. engine. And he's put alloy wheels on. When they're out in it, Steve lets him choose the radio station and one Sunday, when he was on a double shift, he and Jude cleaned the car together. It used up all the time until the *EastEnders* omnibus.

'You've done a grand job there, mate. Now polish those hubs.'

Jude could see his face shining in the wheel trims but he looked away quickly. He won't have a mirror in his room and he sometimes gets Steve to hang a towel over the one in the bathroom. His face is narrow, and there's not enough room in his mouth for all his teeth. It's as though his face got squashed between big hands when he was born. Mum took him to the dentist lots of times but he was always too scared to open his mouth.

Brad Pitt is special guest star on *Friends* this week. Jude scribbles hard all over his face on the page and the pen rips the paper.

'Hey, go easy, Jude. What did Brad ever do to you?' Steve puts his hand gently on Jude's arm and shows him an ad for the new Peugeot. 'Fancy one of those, Jude?' Then he gets up. 'Got to help Kathy with the rotas now, Jude. You'll be all right here?'

Jude leans forward over the magazine in a huff. He jabs his elbows on the table with a bang and sticks his chin on his hand. He doesn't answer.

'Maybe we can go out and get a video later, Jude. If you're good.'

When he's gone, Jude turns back to the picture of Britney and he strokes her smooth flat tummy. Big Debbie is getting noisier. She needs the toilet. Kathy comes in to deal with her. Kathy's jeans are tight and her face is tired. She's worked there the longest of any of them. 'We're growing old together,' she says to Jude sometimes, but he doesn't feel like a grown-up at all. It's not as if he's got a car, or a job, or a girlfriend. Jude hopes Kathy won't leave yet. Sooner or later all the staff get different jobs. They pretend they're sad, and they say 'Keep in touch' and 'I'll really miss you'. But they won't give him their address and they don't come back and visit.

'Come on, you,' Kathy says to Debbie, 'let's get you upstairs before it's too late. Go on, shift yourself.'

Kathy can be bossy. She even had a row with Martha once, when Jude had been to stay with her. He loves it at Martha's house. She lets him watch whatever he wants on TV and he can choose what he has for tea each day. 'Help yourself if you get hungry,' she says and he can go and get something from the kitchen cupboard whenever he feels like it. He's got his own bedroom there and Martha has decorated the walls with pictures of cars and photos of home. Not Sunny Lodge – their old house in Devon. She's got photos in albums as well and sometimes when he stays, she'll sit on the sofa with him and they'll look at them together. Martha tells him stories about when they were little. His favourite photo is one of him and Martha on the beach. Mum's in it too. 'Tell me again about when you saved me from drowning,' he says.

On the day that Kathy got cross, Martha had let him stand at her garden gate and watch all the cars go by.

'Here's a notebook to write down what you see, Jude. I'll just be in the kitchen.'

He'd stayed out there till tea time. It was fantastic. But then the little girls from the house on the corner walked past, on their way home from school. They'd smiled at him and said hello.

'Hello, girls. Had a good day?' he'd said back, being polite like Martha says he should be; trying to get a conversation going. 'Here, do you want to see my list?' and he pushed his notebook towards them.

'Um, we'd better go,' the bigger one said, stepping back a bit.

'No, don't go. Please look at it. It's all the cars that I've seen.'

He'd walked out of the gate behind them. They began to run and he went after them. The smaller one tripped and he stopped to pick her up. He could see her little white knickers under her grey dress. She screamed and then Martha was right there.

He wasn't allowed any TV that night, not even *Songs of Praise*. Kathy told Martha off for letting him outdoors by himself so now when he goes to her house he has to stand at the big window in her bedroom and watch the cars through the glass.

Jude looks up – Debbie has kicked Kathy and Steve has come back into the lounge to help. Debbie's waving her arms about now, trying to hit them. She pushes herself up from the sofa and runs upstairs. Kathy and Steve go after her.

'Hey up,' Jude thinks, 'that just leaves me and little Alicia.'

He moves the curtain aside, looks out the window. The lady staff who was in the kitchen is standing in the garden, finishing her cigarette. She's blowing on her hands, stamping her feet. She won't be in for a minute or two.

Jude finds Britney again. He squeezes the front of his trousers and glances at Alicia. She's watching her piece of string as she waves it about. Jude knows he's not like Alicia. You can't have a chat with her and she kind of looks through you and out the other side when you try and talk to her. One day Big Debbie's mum was visiting and she sat in Alicia's chair without realizing. Alicia went crazy, screaming so loud Jude had to put his hands over his ears. She grabbed at the woman's hair and Steve had to set her free.

'Bloody hell, Alicia. You've got a big grip for a small person,' he'd said, working her stiff, skinny fingers out of the grey curls.

Looking at Alicia there, all small, Jude thinks about Martha when she was a little girl; gets a picture in his head. Her hair's long, in two plaits. She's wearing her school dress, curled up in the armchair in the sitting room at home, a plate of toast balanced beside her elbow. She's shouting, 'Make him go away, Mummy! Make him go away!'

Suddenly, Jude is up and across the room and grabbing at Alicia's boobs. She screams and scratches his face. He puts his hand between her legs and she goes still and stiff. Kathy and Steve come running downstairs. Jude's not quick enough back to his seat. That's always been his problem. He's too slow. They see him leaning over Alicia, and Steve pulls him off.

'They're in trouble now,' Jude thinks. 'They shouldn't have left me here with Alicia. I'm not supposed to be on my own with the other residents. Kathy put it in my notes.'

Jude gets sent upstairs and for a while he lies on his bed, thinking about Alicia's soft body. Downstairs in the office Kathy is on the phone to the social worker. The door's slightly open and Jude goes to stand on the landing, so he can hear better. He rubs his hands together very fast and screws up his face. He loves it that they're talking about him. There'll have to be a meeting now. Maybe Martha will be invited and she'll come and see him at Sunny Lodge. He imagines her coming up the drive – her bright blue Renault Clio crunching like crisps on the gravel.

'Jude' is an extract from the novel *Barefoot on Sharp Stones*

HELLFIRE CORNER

HELEN PIKE

I AM LYING ON THE BED IN THE SPARE ROOM; THIS WAS THE ONLY place to be, once I had decided not to go to work today. In our bedroom I can hear my husband making love to Marieke, his dead son's Belgian girlfriend. When I heard David's key in the lock, I assumed that Marieke had left something behind. I imagined David on his way to the ferry, trying to hide his annoyance at having to double back. But then he opened the door furtively, as if he knew that I was here; and I hesitated. They headed straight upstairs.

Marieke does not come quietly. She also does not like to be referred to as Belgian. She is Flemish, and I have never been sure how to pronounce her name; I have always assumed that Marieke rhymes with shrieker, which turns out to be appropriate. Luke called her Ma, and she called him her 'boy toy': she is eight years older than Luke, and eight years younger than me.

Luke was killed when a lorry veered into them on the N313 in Belgium, just north of their village of St Juliaan. He was killed in front of a memorial to the first victims of poison gas on the Ypres Salient in April 1915. That the site is known to the world as Gas Corner and not Luke Craven Corner might well be the death of my marriage.

Luke and Marieke had settled into a prosperous Euro-lifestyle being subsidized by the EU for not growing rape seed. Luke looked like one of Marieke's four brothers. When they sat around the table last Christmas Eve, the family's faces glinted in the candlelight like golden coins.

In the six months since Luke was killed at Gas Corner, we have been to Belgium more than in the four years he lived there: nine trips. Marieke was there every time we visited, of course, but only as a blond haze, keen to join us, then making excuses at the last moment. She has a sweetness that is coming at me from under the door like the sweetness of mustard gas.

'I lost my son on the Salient,' David says to anyone who will listen. Symmetries of bloodshed shimmy like poppies in the disturbed ground of his grief. During our second trip, he added 'My son died at Hellfire Corner', but instead of clarifying what had happened to his son and where, he only confused his listeners.

'Why did you say "Hellfire Corner?"' I asked David. Hellfire Corner was the spot where soldiers on the Salient were most likely to be shot, but it is on the N8, just east of the Menin Gate, a good five kilometres south of where Luke was killed. David is a cartographer, so these things matter to him.

'And when,' he said, 'did *you* become so exact?'

David likes to take in the terrain, appreciates Belgium because the landscape looks like a map, its low ridges only just sketched in, cemeteries marked with a cross, jagged trench lines yielding to Roman roads. He sees the world in Ordnance Survey glyphs. It was one of the things I loved about David, how he treated our life like one of his Landranger maps. Above our bed is a map of our house and garden, with the telephone marked in the hall, and a trail of black Ordnance Survey bootprints leading to our bed. Scale: one to twenty-five.

Two doors down, the ecstatic sobs of Marieke's orgasm confirm what I have always suspected: that the wonderful sex that David and I enjoyed before Luke's death had very little to do with me. I assume that David has never betrayed me before, that I would have known if he had. It has always been important to him that I know where he is. Before I heard what he and Marieke intended, I imagined that David would come to the surgery with me. Perhaps, after all, the problem would turn out to lie with him.

Luke's village, St Juliaan, is famous for its Crucified Canadian. Nailed to a barn door in 1917, he became a byword for German perfidy – then historians began to question whether the crucifixion ever happened at all. It happened; of this David is sure. Think how the parents of their son would have felt, he said, being told by some academic that their son's execution was a legend, adding his face to the thousands of others lost in the mud.

David chose a marble headstone for Luke, a defiant white flag among all the grey Flemish crosses. For all our trips across the Channel, we stopped only briefly at Luke's grave. David spent the little time he was there, including during the funeral, staring at the cross of sacrifice in the military cemetery on the ridge. Over Luke's coffin, he pledged to visit every cemetery of the Great War. Only then, he said, would he be able to understand loss, and his place in it. (Scale: one dead son to six million.)

There are over two thousand of these cemeteries.

What David had in mind, I consoled myself, were tours of the Salient, and of course the Somme, to be taken in a few brief bursts. I bought him a *Militair Toerisme* map – the entire Western Front cunningly spread over two manageable sides.

I had bought the wrong map.

'We are not tourists,' said David. 'We are –'

'Pilgrims?' I might have said, but this was the week after Luke's funeral, when I did not understand that my way of remembering Luke did not count because I had not known him before he was seven.

'Look at the scale on this,' he said. 'One to two hundred and fifty thousand.' The site of Luke's accident was a mere speck on it.

He went out and bought *Geografisches Landkaarte* with a scale of one to twenty-five thousand. One map for Ieper (Marieke's Flemings have prevailed in their spelling of Ypres, just as St Juliaan was St Julien in 1919), another for Langemarck only ten kilometres away, and so on. Navigation was hazardous: roads crept up on me so quickly that the map felt larger than the country; my directions were all overlaps and black holes.

On her back on my bed, on my side of the bed no doubt, Marieke must remind David of the undulating, easily invaded land where he lost his son.

The cemetery tours were worse than I imagined. While David took photographs of any graves of men of Luke's age, I read the visitors' books. *Moving / fascinating*, wrote most. In the gloomy German cemetery at Langemarck, the bones of thirty thousand German raw recruits were jumbled in a patch of ground begrudgingly handed over by the French. David lapped it up, the injustice of the place. He preferred the spookily realistic statues of German soldiers to the soaring Canadian monolith at Gas Corner.

In the Langemarck visitors' book, the usual bland remarks were broken by a red-inked comment which bore the mark of a teacher who had been away with too many pupils for too long. *The Germans deserved this. I have no sympathy for them. If they had the chance, they would do it again.* Sure enough, it was surrounded by bubble handwriting from a school in Leeds.

I did not show David the teacher's comment. He was not ready to engage with a world in which some people thought that justice prevailed.

David is on the landing. I hold my breath. My stomach rumbles mutinously, and I wave a shushing finger over it. Does David stop for a moment, sensing something, a third soul in the house?

If I wanted to confront David, this would be my moment. But I am afraid that David would try to hide his nakedness from me, and I know what he would say. He would want to know why the bloody hell I had not made my presence known earlier. He would ask me to understand that this is his way of getting closer to the body of the son he has lost. Marieke, I realize, must have the look of Luke's mother. Elise, David's second wife, died of breast cancer when Luke was five.

I imagine that David will have checked Marieke's breasts for lumps; oblivious, she will have swooned at his attentiveness as a lover.

I am relieved when he is back in the bedroom.

Often he tells the ceiling above our bed that women of my age can take a year or more to conceive. Since Luke died, we have been making love every night, a slow swansong of sex. I threw away my diaphragm after the funeral. There was no need to discuss what we were doing.

By the time our cemetery tour reached the Somme, we were no longer stopping to have elegiac sex in sunken lanes. David was disappointed at the Somme's milky terrain, at how its chalk had erased the marks of war. This was not Luke country, so we would find our own way, that day. Go wherever the mood took us, for once.

The mood took us back over the Belgian border. The only music permitted was mawkish Britpop anthems from Luke's teenage years. *Bittersweet Symphony* would send us on to the verge, bawling. This is what I needed to be doing, but I wanted to be doing it at home, on the lumpy single bed that Luke used to complain about. I am lying on it now, and I see his point. David joked that if we replaced it, Luke would never leave home.

By our seventh trip it was July and we were near Ypres again. When we reached Essex Farm cemetery and the poet Robert McCrae's bunker, we were quarrelling. A coachload of children were gathered around an angelic boy who was reading 'In Flanders Fields'. 'We are the Dead. Short days ago / We lived . . .' Three boys had separated themselves from the group and were having what sounded and smelt like a farting competition. A girl in a wheelchair was trying to move away from the boys and the farts, attracting the confused disapproval of one of her teachers: surely cripples can't be badly behaved?

'They shouldn't be here,' David insisted, even though school parties had been crawling all over the Salient. David wishes I was still a teacher, even though I told him that my job was the reason why I had not wanted another child, a child 'of my own', as David put it. Two years ago, during a grisly Year Eleven class trip to the Imperial War Museum, I had shouted at a member of the public for walking in front of me during a slide show. The woman's outrage turned to sympathy as she looked at me and the group I was with. I handed in my notice the next morning, afraid of the person I was becoming.

While I was working with nine hundred children, my sanity would not permit me to entertain another one at home. Luke had slipped into my life at seven years old, and I loved my leonine motherless boy ferociously.

'It's outrageous,' David said. The children were alive, they were here, in the fashions of 2003, they were enjoying themselves. In their trainers they trampled over David's grief.

The wheelchair got caught in a bank of flowers in front of a row of graves. The farting boys helped the girl; she kept her hand over her nose and mouth.

'Being your next of kin is a risky business, isn't it?' I said. I felt as though I had stepped over the coupling of two high-speed train carriages.

'What on earth do you mean?'

'I mean,' I said, aware that I was being mean, but giving in to the dark currents sluicing beneath me, 'that loving you means being either dead or barren.'

I feared, I told him, for our unborn child.

Hope bloomed in his face.

'No, I'm not,' I said.

Wouldn't it be easier, I wanted to ask, if his next child were deformed in some way? Caught in a wheelchair on a bank of flowers in front of a row of graves? Then we could get the tragedy over with, know what we were dealing with, have less to be taken away from us.

I look at my watch: eleven thirty-seven, so too late now to book a doctor's appointment – and tomorrow is Saturday, so the surgery will be closed. And David, no doubt, will have a cemetery or two lined up for us to visit. The only weekend I have spent in London since Luke died was the wake for Luke's university friends, all of whom had got drunk and stoned, and sombrely, respectfully trashed the house.

Perhaps I will lie here on Monday as well. Perhaps tomorrow I should plaster over the cracks where the cornicing meets the ceiling – it looks as though someone took the lid off the room like a boiled egg and tried to stick it back again. I am hungry; I place a hand on my hollow, noisy stomach. Did David tell me that he had any meetings this afternoon? But then, he told me he had a big meeting this morning. David and Marieke are at that stage again where they would not hear me if I were to get up and phone the doctor.

What will we do this evening? He and Marieke will have to leave at some point. Only an extraordinary event will save me from having to listen to the expurgated version of this morning. I wonder if they are using contraception; I used to be able to separate sex from procreation.

The Martyr of St Julien. David is writing a book on him. I have yet to read any of it; David became interested in history soon after I had finished with it. Tonight I will ask David about him. I, no longer an historian, will ask him for how long we owe ourselves to the past.

Nailed to a barn door – who knows how long he hung there before he died?

'Hellfire Corner' is an extract from a novel in progress

ALL THE HARD WAYS
WILLIAM WEINSTEIN

W HEN HE WAS DOING HIS NATIONAL SERVICE, THEY PLAYED DICE on the floor in the latrine, lines and numbers scrawled in chalk on the rough cement. That was where he first learnt about gambling. The smell of urine made him gag and the hard floor punished his knees. But the other players made room for him and someone handed him a pair of dice. For once, nobody called him Jew Boy.

Driving down the Cromwell Road, Harry can remember the rush of excitement as the dice skittered across the chalk lines and the young men bayed for a winner, their voices crashing off the grimy tile walls. They bet whatever they had – pennies, chocolate, cigarettes. They wrote IOUs and made extravagant promises: 'I'll black your boots for a month.' 'You can take my sister out on your next leave.' He remembers the shouting, the jostling bodies, the camaraderie – he couldn't call it friendship. Away from the dice game he was treated as coldly as ever.

The dice table where Harry plays now is in a basement casino in West London. He stops the Audi outside the entrance and opens the car door to the cold and the smell of yesterday's garbage. The canopy over the front door is faded and a torn piece flaps in the wind.

At the front desk the receptionist greets him by name, with an easy familiarity. It is a similar story in the casino. The dealers call him Harry much more than he cares for. When you are sixty years old, when you are one of the club's founding members, you should be 'Mr Ruben' or perhaps, like in the old days, 'Mr R'. But they know him too well and so they call him plain Harry. Except for the new dealer, Max, who doesn't call him anything but stands at the table with an infuriating half smile on his lips.

Harry hates new dealers. He likes to talk quietly and fast. He doesn't like to repeat himself. New dealers don't understand his bets, don't see the thought and the beauty behind them. New dealers cannot work out what bets pay. They flounder, reddening, dropping chips, sweating in their panic. New dealers want seven to come because when it does, you grab all the money on the table. They all know how to do that. There are more ways to make a seven on two dice than any other number. And when you do, you don't just lose your original bet, you lose everything that is still in play. All the bets you made that you hoped would pay while you were waiting for your main bet to win. Wiped out.

Harry thinks sometimes that new dealers can *make* the seven come. And Max is a new dealer. But he's different. He knows the game – forwards and backwards. He handles even the most complex bets with lazy, insolent grace. Harry can't help catching his eye whenever he's losing and Max always seems to be laughing about it. Harry even complained to the manager once, but nothing happened. Max was still there the next day, calm and polite, still smiling. Harry wonders whether there isn't a shred of pity in that smile as well. And that is even worse. Harry pays more in taxes every year than a dealer like Max makes in salary. Harry doesn't have to spend every night hunched over a dice game, eating cigarette smoke, wasting his life away on shift work, hoping for the last break and an early out. Harry hates him. All the players hate him.

The moment they spot Harry, a cry goes up around the table.

'Here he is,' someone calls.

'Now *here's* someone who can throw dice,' announces Signor Gitti. 'A real shooter. You can't go wrong betting on his roll. Harry is a professional.'

The other players ignore him, but Harry thinks he detects a note of mockery in Gitti's voice and stares at him irritably.

Gitti is a louche Italian running to seed, his once-expensive suits fraying at the cuffs and collars, his chiselled features relaxing into bags and lines. The ends of his trousers are an inch or so above his shoes now that the spreading of his stomach has hitched them up. There are still hints of his old beauty, his former elegance. The hair is still thick and dark, untouched by dyes. He holds his cigarette between finger and thumb, smokes it with his palm to his face, fingers splayed. He does not bite his nails so much as consume them, gnawing with his molars like an animal trying to escape a trap.

He is at the dice table promptly at half past seven every evening and never leaves before the table closes at four in the morning. Often he has lost all his money by midnight but he stays on anyway, chewing his nails and commenting on the performance of every shooter. Occasionally his wife accompanies him and watches the game, her sad head bowed uncomprehendingly as the red dice skitter and fall. Her anguish is plain to see as her husband insults yet another failing shooter.

'Hush,' she says to him. 'You didn't do any better.'

But Signor Gitti – everyone calls him 'Signor' – is oblivious. He glares at the shooter who has just sevened out. Max grins at nobody in particular.

'What are you smiling at?' Gitti snarls. 'Deal your game.' He throws some chips down roughly on the table so they bounce in different directions. 'Give me eighty-eight the insides, twelve the hard eight.'

'Working on this roll?' says Max, retrieving the scattered chips.

'Working, working, of course working,' he says. The stickman passes the dice to the next shooter who picks two and throws them.

'Winner seven,' intones the stickman, retrieving the dice from the end of the table with his crooked stick. 'Working bets are gone.'

Max sweeps up Signor Gitti's bets and looks at him benignly. 'Same bet again?' he asks.

Gitti says something foul in Italian and turns his back on the table, teeth tearing at his fingers.

Beryl, crowded into the corner, is as desiccated and humourless as a dead tree. She too has expensive clothes that have been worn too long. Her fawn trouser suit hangs off her scrawny limbs and the elbows of the jacket are shiny and discoloured. Her voice is rough, the glottal scratch of a heavy smoker and, combined with her ill-fitting teeth, she is almost impossible to understand. Within the maelstrom of the dice game, the dealers struggle to hear her mumbling.

'Fifteen ac . . . four hard . . .'

'Fifteen across,' repeats the dealer loudly. 'Four the hard what?'

The dice are in the air.

'Ten,' says Beryl, lips curling around her dentures.

'Four the hard ten,' says the dealer to the stickman, who puts up the bet and then takes it back down when it loses on the next roll.

'Back up the hard . . . three . . . any,' Beryl mutters.

The dice are in the air again and they land, scattering chips as they roll on to a two and a one.

'Where's my bet?' says Beryl, unusually clearly.

'You didn't have one,' says the dealer.

The supervisor groans.

'Put up the bet,' he says to the stickman.

The dealer makes the payout but Beryl doesn't pick up the chips.

'Goes to twelve centre . . . deuce,' she mutters, a tiny smile stretching her mummified face. The dealer has to go out and retrieve the chips and the dice are already in the air.

'Hands!' everyone shouts, but it is too late. The dice bounce off the dealer's hand and hit the end of the table.

'Seven out,' says the stickman, bringing them back to the middle and a storm of abuse envelops the table.

'Coming out,' says the stickman, ignoring the angry voices and dumping five dice into the crook of his stick. 'New shooter.'

He moves the dice to the next player, Mr Campbell. Prematurely wizened, the marks of forceps still clear on his hairless skull, Campbell stares back incredulously, as if he has been presented with a plate of dog shit.

'Pass,' he says finally, waving the dice away and fingering the twelve one-pound chips he has been hoarding for over an hour.

Then Signor Gitti. He turns his back to the table again. His wife shakes her head as the stickman catches her eye. She hates to shoot: the false bonhomie, the creaking compliments about lucky ladies when you win. And the abusive mutterings on all sides when you seven out. Only the fact that she is here with Gitti stops people like Campbell from openly insulting her.

Mr Danvers is next. He is a solicitor, in his customary crumpled suit and brown Hush Puppies. A high domed head with a few wisps of hair carefully combed over. He has a long, pointed nose and weak eyes. And most of all, a sour temper and a sarcastic tongue. Harry can imagine him presiding over some Dickensian office: clerks on stools, dusty floorboards, mildewed ledgers. And going home to a brown-toned house. Lamplight and boiled food. A tight-mouthed matronly wife. The reality is that he lives alone in a one-bedroom flat on the Edgware Road and takes a bus to his office in Little Venice. He has had to sell his Mercedes. His secretary resigned, unable to cope with the stream of angry clients. Danvers misses at least two meetings a week when his body, exhausted from sleepless night after sleepless night, simply collapses and passes into what is not unlike a coma.

He looks down at the dice lying in front of him as if he has never seen such a thing before.

'You want to shoot?' asks the stickman.

'Only if it's you,' says Danvers, looking up with no trace of a smile.

The stickman goes all the way round the table; ten players. No one will shoot. He pours the dice back into the bowl and pushes it in front of the supervisor.

'No shooters, no war,' he says laconically. The other dealers begin putting their stacks of chips away. Harry waits until they have finished – a small victory, inconveniencing them – before pulling out a fifty pound note. He throws it in.

'Twenty the line, five each crap eleven,' he says. The game limps back to life.

Harry picks up two dice, rubs them in a circle around his bet and, with a curious double-pumping motion of his elbow, throws them strongly down the table.

'Eleven, eleven, front line winner,' calls the stickman. They pay Harry's line bet and the stickman taps his stick.

'Seventy-five pounds.'

Something is different. Harry feels it through his fingertips, through the metal taste on his tongue. It is as if the world has tipped minutely, and everything has slipped sideways. Nothing is the same. Harry staggers, feels a power surging through him. Gravity, probability; everything is in flux. Suddenly he knows he cannot lose.

He looks up. 'My bet goes to eighty centre, high twelve.'

'No change,' says the stickman and adjusts the bet. Harry throws, the same exaggerated motion.

'Twelve crap, twelve,' says the stickman, with a flicker of interest in his voice. He taps in front of Harry again. 'Seven hundred and sixty-five.'

Harry presses the bet again and watches the other players scrabble for their money. They feel his power too, they sense that this will be a roll. The stickman puts down the stick and grabs two handfuls of chips. He lays a blizzard of bets across the layout as the players on either side shout them at him. Finally the storm dies down.

'Any more?' he says, moving the dice. Harry picks them up as Beryl, always late with her bets, pokes the dealer with a bony finger and coughs, 'Two any.'

Harry blocks them all out, rolls his shoulders and pushes back his cuffs. He can feel the smooth silicone of the dice between his fingers, the sharp corners, the microscopically raised edges of the spots.

Around the bet, lean, lift, hand back, elbow out, pump, arm out, release –

'Twelve crap twelve,' shouts the stickman above the roar that envelops the table. The other players are calling Harry's name, pounding him on the back. He struggles to contain his glee, to keep his emotions under control. 'Mr Cool', Signor Gitti likes to call him and he smiles fractionally as he accepts the compliments.

'One more, I think,' he says, stacking his chips. The stickman is struggling through the payouts and Beryl's voice is saying over and over again, 'Have you got my bet?'

It takes almost five minutes before all the players are paid, the arguments settled, the crap bets pressed. He has promised them one more winner and when he rolls a three, ace and a deuce, the table descends into chaos. Everyone in the casino is looking at them as they dance and scream. Harry stands silent, a pillar of sanity, he thinks, among the madmen. When it is his turn to be paid out he calls, 'Give me my bets down.'

The dealer collects all his bets and gives them back to him. He drops them carelessly on to the winnings in front of him, ignoring the shocked faces of the other players. He is rubbing their faces in it. Nobody ever takes a winning crap bet down. There are complaints around the table but they are muted. Harry is now the top player present. The power of his arm has granted him immunity from insult. He can no longer be directly challenged. He rolls a nine and watches in satisfaction as the stickman wipes up the losing crap bets.

'You're just so smart, aren't you,' Danvers mutters sourly but when Harry meets his eye, he looks away and pretends to be talking to someone else. Harry dismisses him, dismisses them all and focuses on the dice. He blocks out the smoke and the smell of the tightly packed bodies around the table. Only the dice matter, only avoiding the seven matters. He throws and his shoulder feels as big as a gorilla's. He can throw all night. A delirium, not unlike joy, rushes through him and he remembers what it feels to be young. The smooth efficiency of his limbs. The loping power of young muscles, taut and sinuous under tight, smooth skin. Below the shelf of the table his cock is jutting hard against the front of his trousers. And for several moments he is so happy that even Max's sly grin cannot disturb him. The chips pile up in front of him and the other players are holding their breaths, willing him to continue. But even though the numbers still come, and the money, the joy begins to fade and the excitement, so intense just a moment before, begins to curdle like milk left out in the sun. He can taste the sourness, smell it. A terrible sadness rushes in to replace the last threads of joy, even as the numbers continue to pour out of his arm.

The dealers lunge across the table paying bets, sweat glistening on their faces. Gitti calls his bets off, as he always does, and stands fuming as Harry still keeps rolling, number after number, winner after winner. The hundred-pound chips fill the rack in front of him and the dealer switches to five hundreds. All around him the other players are shouting and laughing. But Harry is not laughing. He can feel his jaw clenched, his eyes staring and inside he is shrieking, torn this way and that as the dice tumble towards a loser then skid the other way and he wins again. And suddenly, his breath catching in his chest, he is remembering a time when playing dice was no more than an occasional pleasure. When every night was not spent in a basement, beating his head against an uncaring wall. He remembers walks by the river and evenings on the sofa, reading. And Lucy, long gone now. The memories fill his head like water rushing up the neck of a bottle. Lucy. Somewhere she must be living her life without him. How would she look now? Would they recognize each other in the street? Would she speak to him now? Forgive him?

He looks away from the table, up towards the smoke-stained ceiling and, as his concentration wavers, he finally sevens out.

Eyes around the table run jealously over his winnings, assessing, counting, trying to remember what he started with. Campbell slides closer. He has increased his twelve pounds to twenty-eight.

'Good roll, Harry,' he says, his eyes on his hands as he carefully lines up the coloured flecks on the sides of the chips to make one solid line along the whole length of the stack.

Harry ignores him and piles his chips on the table, pushing the memory of Lucy firmly back into its dusty drawer.

'Colour change,' he says and watches while the supervisor counts the chips into neat piles of twenty.

'Twenty-seven thousand six hundred,' the supervisor announces finally and the dealer passes the larger chips across the table. The dice are moving again but Harry doesn't bet. For a few minutes he stands and tries to savour the taste of victory. It is not the money. It is the status. If you can shoot a winning roll, you are a hero. Everyone is your friend. Everyone loves you. It takes concentration to make a good roll. You have to keep the seven at bay, fight it off with the power of your will. And you have to throw the dice exactly the same way every time. The right way. Not Danvers' malicious shove that lands the dice among the dealer's neatly placed chips. Not that limp Eyetie flick that Gitti does, where half the time the dice don't even make it to the end of the table and flop backwards on to a seven. No. You have to show them that you are in charge – the master. Then they will do your bidding.

Feeling better, he watches with quiet amusement as the dice seven out almost immediately.

'Normal service has been resumed,' comments the stickman and earns a foul look from Danvers, who chunters away to himself under his breath for a good two or three minutes. Two other shooters try their luck with similar results and then everyone is passing the dice and calling his name.

'Harry, Harry,' they shout.

'Star shooter.'

He waves a self-deprecating hand, allows the men on either side of him to give him more room.

'Four hundred the line, fifty each crap eleven,' he says recklessly, throwing in five hundred. The dice slide across to him in a red line, one behind the other. He picks two and, without hesitation, sends them on their way.

'Eleven, eleven. Front line winner,' the stickman calls and the whole table cheers.

Harry rolls a nine on the next roll and every single player at the table bets whatever he can afford on the numbers. Harry watches his own hand reach down into his chips and as he does, an idea, as quick and slippery as mercury, runs through his head. He slides it around, awed and excited by its audaciousness. He will win, again. He knows this already. But now, he will win big. Massively. He will let these losers watch while he rolls numbers until the table closes at four in the morning. And then he will walk out. Walk out and never come back. As his fingers touch the pure edges of the dice he realizes how he has come to hate this place. He takes a deep breath, feeling the bite of the smoke-laden air in his lungs and lets the words dance across his mind. *He will never come back.*

'Twenty-seven thousand across,' he says and revels in the hush that falls around the table. He watches the dealer slot his bets in amongst the others, the fives and tens of the little people. *Twenty-seven thousand.* Who else dares to bet that sort of money? Who else has the power that he wields? He watches the stickman shortening his grip on the stick, turning the dice and sending them sliding towards him. Everything is slow. Smooth. He looks up and sees the faces looking awestruck at him. He sees the hollow eyes and badly shaved chins. The nicotine-stained fingers and greedy mouths full of bad teeth. How many years has he wasted with these degenerates, huddled over this battered table, choking on their smoke, stomach knotted with fear and rage? This last roll and he will step out into the night air and he will be free. Anything might happen. A picture flashes into his mind, of a page in his address book, lying open on the telephone table. A name – Lucy Partridge – scored out in heavy strokes. The paper torn in one place by the point of the pen. But the phone number, still legible . . .

He receives the dice, sets them, elbow out, pump, arm stretched out, release – and with them turning in the air, turning, tumbling, he takes his eyes off them for a fraction of a second and meets the lazy, cynical smile of Max, the new dealer, who is staring at him from the other end of the table.

'My bet's off,' he tries to shout, but the words are strangled in his throat.

'Seven out, straight out,' calls the stickman and a huge groan followed by a storm of cursing stabs at him from all sides.

'Marvellous, marvellous, shoot again.' Danvers' sarcastic voice rises above the others like a whip, his pasty face flushed with anger. Fury seethes around the table like a poisonous tide and Harry's protection from insult is gone. Even Beryl has a sour word for him as she leaves the table. Harry stands, arm still extended, his empty hand frozen in mid air. One by one the players drift away, bodies twisted with disappointment and shock until only Harry and Gitti are left. The dealers ignore them now, tidying the chips and laughing among themselves. Gitti looks at them venomously.

'They don't fucking care, do they?' he says. He touches Harry's arm with real tenderness, all his anger gone. 'You were so close to it, Harry. I could feel it.'

Harry stares down at the green surface of the table, not yet able to talk. The world has faded and resumed its dull colours. His arm, which had felt so smooth and powerful, has withered and shrunk again. Slowly he raises his head and looks around. The roulette tables are closing, and players, desperate for one more chance to win, are running from one to the other, swept towards the last bet of the night like pheasants towards the guns. The lights come up and the casino is exposed in stark detail. There are cigarette butts ground into the carpet. The abandoned drinks that litter the side tables are tainted with ash and lipstick. Half-eaten sandwiches lie everywhere, the bread marked with fingerprints by hands grubby from handling money.

Gitti drinks the last of his cold coffee and lights another cigarette. 'Come on,' he says. 'Let's get out of here.'

Outside, they stand waiting for the doorman to fetch Harry's car. The rain is falling and the gutters are choking with dead leaves.

'It was a great night, Harry,' says Gitti, coat thrown over his shoulders, maestro-style. He gives a harsh laugh. 'You scared everybody tonight.'

Harry nods.

Gitti is counting the change from his trouser pocket. 'See you tomorrow then,' he says.

'Yes, see you tomorrow,' says Harry, buttoning his coat against the wind, and the rain.

'All the Hard Ways' is an extract from the novel of the same title

ANAMORPHIC BREAKUP
AMANDA SCHIFF

I THINK I MUST BE DREAMING THAT I'M AWAKE, BUT AS I LIFT MY head from the pillow it feels too heavy for my neck, full of scrabble and scratch. The darkened room is unfamiliar, and I don't recognize the shapes of the furniture. This isn't *our* bed; the sheets are rougher and there's the unaccustomed weight of a quilt. I'm alone. But when I finally get up and open the shutters, I'm startled to see that the room overlooks a small canal; I don't recognize the decayed houses across the water.

Opposite the bedroom is an old-fashioned bathroom with a square white sink and deep bath. The towels have been used and are still damp. Toiletries and cosmetics from an Italian supermarket litter the surfaces. As I sniff the unfamiliar lotions and squeeze tubes of cream, I catch sight of myself in the mirror and recognize the face. It isn't that I don't know who I am, but that there is no memory of who I was yesterday, or the day before that. Perhaps I'm still asleep, dream-walking through these unknown rooms; but it feels concrete, and as I stub my toe on a small table in the hallway, the pain is real enough.

In the bedroom is an elaborate antique mahogany wardrobe, and this must be where I will find my clothes. They're all monochrome, stylish but not fashionable; black, white or charcoal grey. All the labels are Italian, but I can't remember buying any of them.

In the bottom drawer there's an envelope with three thousand euros and a passport; it has my photo, and the name, Fran Blake. *Yes, I know that's right*. I must have a handbag, and look for it in the living room. It's underneath the sofa, in the large light room with arched Gothic windows. There are ashes from a recent fire in the grate. The kitchen at one end has the remains of a meal that I don't remember eating and dirty pans in the sink.

Slow-witted and hungry, I should find somewhere to have a strong coffee and something to eat, and then perhaps I will see things more clearly.

Taking the key from a hook by the front door, I double-lock it behind me, noting how reflexive this action is. A young man with dark curly hair comes up the stairs and he smiles at me and says '*Buon giorno, Nina, come sta?*' I'm confused, not sure exactly what he said, and by the time I call after him 'Excuse me . . .' the door a few floors above slams in reply.

The front door opens onto a tiny courtyard, which leads into a narrow alley. Instinctively, I turn left and then right on to ever-widening streets. I realize now – *this is Venice* – how could I not recognize it, even if I feel sure I've never been before? I have no memory of booking tickets or getting on a plane. How had I found the apartment and how long had I been here? I reach a large square dominated by a vast red brick Gothic church. There are *caffès* around the edges of the square with tables and chairs in the middle along the flank of the church. I head for one called Rosa Salva, and a waiter waves and shouts 'Ciao, *Nina*' to me before he ducks inside. I hope that I have misheard him. By the time I sit down, he has returned with a ristretto and a small pastry. I want to ask him how often I come here, and why he calls me Nina too, but I don't know how so I just thank him.

I empty out the handbag. There's a wallet with cash but no credit cards and receipts and business cards for restaurants and shops. Sunglasses, a pen, some tissues and a lipstick (red). No mobile phone, diary, address book or camera. In a zip pocket, though, there's a small notebook bound with swirling marbled paper, with two pages of notes in a dense, peculiar handwriting, which I can't decipher. Is this still part of the dream? Woolly-headed, I can't keep track of what is real. It seems likely that the answer is in the book, but it's frustratingly obscured. I look up, distracted by the excited twittering of a group of nuns, like a flock of magpies in their black and white habits. Tour guides rally their parties, who stick close together, terrified of getting lost in the maze of streets. I leave some coins on the tray and wander across to a canal that runs past the open fourth side of the square, and cross a small bridge.

It must be late October, because there's a chill to the day in spite of the bright sun. Am I the sort of person that panics? If I am, now would be a good time to do so. But I'm confused, light-headed rather than scared. The vistas like stage sets, and the misleading acoustics of the canals, suggest that reality isn't a useful concept in this place. Walking past souvenir shops, an undertaker and a haberdasher, it seems familiar as if I've walked here before. There wasn't a map or guidebook in the bag, but I don't feel lost. I cross the next bridge. The Ponte dei Miracoli: the Bridge of Miracles, which seems significant.

Walking through the streets and alleyways, emerging into unexpected squares or abrupt dead ends, I'm trying to formulate a plan. I could go to the English consul, and explain . . . what? That I can't remember how I got here and people seem to know me – but call me Nina? I *know* I am Fran Blake, and the passport obviously confirms that, but I can't think of a single person in England that I could call for help. I can't remember what it was like to be Fran in England, what her life was like or what job she did or even if she had children. I'm now-Fran but not then-Fran. If I keep moving, maybe I will eventually arrive somewhere.

On a rack of newspapers outside a shop I see the date, 30 October. This small piece of information is a fact, something real, like my bruised toe. I have to hold on to these reassuring shards and hoard them against the weightlessness that is claiming me in waves. Perhaps it's all the tidal water washing in and out of the arteries of the city, but I'm starting to feel seasick and out of kilter. By the Canareggio canal, at the entrance to the Ghetto, a Jewish restaurant has tables by the water's edge. Shopkeepers are starting to wind down their metal shutters and close for lunch. Pigeons hop over the cobbles, searching for crumbs. A water bus approaches the mooring, grinding its gears and belching diesel fumes. It crashes against the pontoon, creating a backwash that agitates the smaller craft.

I enter the Ghetto through one of the old gateways, and get mixed up with a group of American tourists. The Venetian guide is explaining in fractured English about the history of the Jews in Venice, and when her party follows her through a doorway into a hidden synagogue, I try to tag along. She closes the door behind the last of them, as if she hasn't noticed me, before I too can enter.

The sun has gone and the cold and damp are working their way up my body through the thin soles of my boots. I have been noting the designations in the topography of the city: *corte, fondamenta, salizzada, rio*. The squares are called *campo* and the smaller streets, *calle*. In a working-class neighbourhood I come upon a small oily canal, where men in grubby vests with cigarettes dangling from the corners of their mouths are repairing motor boat engines. Around the corner, there's a church undergoing restoration. It has a marble facade with niches for a badly weathered statue of the Virgin Mary and two female saints. The board tells me the church is San Nicoló dei Mendicoli. I know I've seen the interior, but the doorway is barricaded with metal gates. I sit for a while on a nearby bench, trying to pin down an elusive sense of familiarity.

It's after midnight, and in the fog and silence I feel the fracturing of time and displacement more keenly. Is this an experience I have already had, a memory; or a premonition of something yet to happen? Maybe it's just an endless now, unfolding in front of me as I walk, like a roll of carpet.

Finally, giving in to fatigue, I make my way back to the apartment. I've been walking for hours, but even without a map I manage to navigate through the labyrinth – as if I have an internal gyroscope, which constantly finds its level and maintains my equilibrium.

After a night of deep and dreamless sleep I awake tired and unrefreshed. When I try to study the notebook I still can't make out any of the words. And yet when I'm walking I feel fully conscious, perhaps for the first time in my life, because I have no point of reference. It's possible to look at something – a building, a view of rooftops, reflections in the water – and see it as a random collection of shapes and colours, a configuration of planes and space. In this abstraction, I can take my place in the world. The uneven colours and textures of buildings, where layers of protection and decoration have been broken down by time, give me a simple visual pleasure that is entirely stripped of meaning. No symbolic resonance, everything is as it appears, because I don't care to know its history.

It's getting dark early, and when I return to the apartment, I run a hot bath to soothe my aching muscles and sore feet. Sitting in the deep marble tub, I'm aware of little animal noises, whimpers of fear and distress, and realize that they are escaping from me. They betray something that I haven't allowed myself to feel, but can't leave unexamined any longer.

Now that I know what it is to feel truly alone, with no sense of purpose or continuity, everything I do has the same weight and value. I have lost all context and meaning, so that if I drink a cup of coffee, or draw a razor blade across my wrists, neither act has more importance than the other. I'm floating, carried on tides I can't control. The only possibility is to try to live in a continuous present, moment by moment. There is nothing to go back to. I have been cut loose from all connection to the world.

If I stretch my arm out of the window, I can shake hands with the person who lives opposite. I peer through the shutters, and in the other apartment I see a man, woman and small child sitting around the kitchen table eating their supper. A TV is playing in another room, and they are chattering away to each other. The room is cosy, and this is a fantasy of perfect family life, but it doesn't spark any memories in me.

1 November is *Festa dei Mort*. As I approach the church of San Francesco della Vigna, a funeral procession emerges from the portico, the mourners wearing ceremonial robes. I get caught up in the cortège, but no one pays me any attention. The procession comes to a halt by a wide canal, and the pallbearers place the coffin in a motor boat. The launch heads off for the open waters of the lagoon, towards a small island where I presume the burial will take place. The undertaker wears dark glasses and his jacket draped over his shoulders. He talks loudly into a mobile phone.

And suddenly the revelation stabs me like a migraine.

I am a ghost. *I was the one that died.* That would explain everything. I have no memory of my life before I died, and I'm retracing my footsteps endlessly. *An unquiet soul.* The people I knew before I died still recognize me, but no one else can see me. So . . . How did I die?

I don't know whether or not to be relieved. It's as good an explanation as any other, but it contains the depressing prospect of an endless loop of existence.

The light is fading and as I emerge into another empty *campo*, I startle a young woman entering from the other side. She looks at me with fear and suspicion, and this confirms my conclusion. I feel chilled, as if I will never be warm again.

Maybe this is how it is for ghosts. I feel insubstantial, as if I'm made of smoke.

As we pass each other by the marble well-head in the middle of the *campo*, I stare at the woman, who lowers her head and avoids my eyes.

Noticing a light burning in the ground-floor window of an ancient house, I take a closer look. A brass plate by the door reads '*Gabinetto di Curiosita. Museo del Mundo*'. There are no opening times, but I push the brass bell and a buzzer admits me. The wood-panelled hallway is dark and smells of candle wax and polish. On a desk a sign reads '*Entrata 4 Euros*' and I rummage in my purse for change, taking a photocopied museum guide in English. The floor plan of the museum is laid out over three rooms: The Chamber of Wonders leads to the Chamber of Artifice, and then into the Chamber of Miracles.

Opening the heavy wooden door beyond the staircase, I enter a room filled with glass-fronted wall cabinets and vitrines. These are crammed with specimen jars of preserved reptiles, works of art and scientific instruments, exotic shells and corals. Drawers are haphazardly open, containing antiquities, coins, archaeological and ethnographic treasures. Cases of stuffed birds and animals and boxes of bees, beetles, moths and butterflies are stacked on shelves. On a pedestal stands a mermaid skeleton made from the top half of a monkey sewn to the bottom half of a fish. A narwhal tusk, like a unicorn's horn, lies gathering dust on a window ledge. The lighting is subdued and the effect overwhelming and disorientating. Here is a universe in microcosm, the world captured and reduced to taxonomy and meticulous annotations. It exposes the secret foibles of the collector, something slightly shameful or pathological. There's nowhere to rest the eye, except on a jar containing a two-headed calf or a case of *ex voto* tokens. And yet it's inexplicably marvellous in spite of all this.

Something inside my head begins to slide and expand to fill the room. I feel as if I might faint and put out my hand to steady myself, but find nothing to support me. I turn and come face to face with a wall of photographs and engravings of deformities and medical freaks. There's a shifting movement inside my brain, as if my internal furniture is being rearranged.

I notice another doorway – is it my imagination or is it slightly smaller? I push at the half-open door and step through into the next room. This is almost in darkness, except for two objects, dramatically spotlit. In the middle of the room, on a table, is a glass-fronted box. I peer at it, and see inside a painting composed of large swirls and pools of colour, which makes me think again about the notebook. An arrow on the side of the box points to an aperture, and I bend down to look through it. An image is revealed just by moving my position slightly – the random shapes take on recognizable meaning, a man and woman intertwined. The guide reads: 'Anamorphic image of the Greek goddess Mnemosyne, mother of the Muses, and Zeus. From the Greek *anamorphosis*, to transform'.

At the other end of the room stands a life-sized figure, also spotlit, and dressed in the costume of a medieval doctor. As I approach, the doctor beckons with his long fingers, and gestures for me to hold out my hand. When I'm within reach, the mechanical man takes my wrist in his hand. He appears to be taking my pulse, his head tilted to one side, nodding and inspecting my face. His eyes search mine, questioning me, challenging. The illusion is breathtaking. In this moment, I know that I'm alive, human, certainly not a ghost. I'm bewitched by this creature constructed from cogs, wheels, levers and gears, marvelling at how something that appears so animate is not a living being.

The automaton completes his circuit and releases me. I go to the next door, and open that too. Do I have to stoop slightly to walk through?

The third room takes me by surprise. Its dazzling light is reflected and refracted in countless mirrors, but I'm drawn to the far wall by a cabinet containing three mirrors. The first is a burnished bronze convex hand mirror. The guide says it is 'Fifth century BC. Catoptrics, the Greek science of reflection in mirrors, encomposed Esoptrimos, Katoptron and Epiphanein'. As I look at my reflection, it's like gazing into a deep clear pool on a hot day. The fractured jangling sensation in my brain that has been with me since I woke up in confusion a few days ago is unscrambled and stilled.

Reluctantly, I move on to what the guide describes as a 'Witch's Mirror'. This is flat and rectangular; seven smaller convex mirrors have been attached, so that they multiply the image. As I look into it, I see someone else reflected over and over, in my place. My breath catches in my throat. All I can hear is the drumming of blood racing through my veins. It fills the room and beats against the glass cases. The mirrors hum and rattle and I'm afraid they will shatter. *Isobel*. I can't say how I know this, but from one moment to the next the thought appears, and once acknowledged can't be unthought. When I look at her I see myself, and when I look at my own reflection, I see her. That *Isobel* is in the past tense and I don't know why. I look away; I try to leave the room to avoid thinking about her, but I'm drawn to the third mirror. This is circular, bright, and shows no distortion. I look at the guide, which says this is 'The first modern mirror, invented by Domenico D'Anzolodel Gallo on Murano, 1507'. It shows me my own reflection with a simple guileless truth that makes me remember something important, about then-Fran. When we were small, Isobel and I would use mirror writing so that our parents couldn't read our diaries. *I had a twin.* Shaking, I search in my bag for the notebook, and hold it up to Domenico's mirror. For a few seconds I can't quite understand what I am reading. I have the sense of the words, but not the emotions behind them. In the book I had written this:

> *Without Isobel, how can I live as Fran? I don't know how to be Fran without Isobel. I want to leave this trace, so that if I need to find my way back, it will be a ball of string to lead me out of the labyrinth, like Ariadne gave to Theseus. There's a picture of our parents on honeymoon, in a gondola, and they're so full of hope for the future, so beautiful and in love with life. I want to see what that feels like. I've never understood it before, but I need to see if I'm capable of it, otherwise there's no point in living a day longer like this.*
>
> *I was driving Isobel to Mum and Dad's for dinner. It was raining, and we were late. Isobel was very angry with me. I told her I was thinking of leaving Jack. She said I was selfish and that I gave up at the first sign of trouble. I told her that she had no idea what I had been going through. I had kept it from her, because I knew how much she liked him, and didn't want her to have to take sides. I said she was being judgemental and unfair to me, and that she had never been married so she didn't understand. I must have turned to look at her only for moment, but it was wet and dark in the country lane, and I didn't see a milk tanker coming towards us.*
>
> *I held Isobel for two hours as she was dying while the*

firefighters cut us out of the wreckage, and then she died there by the side of the road. I had almost no injuries, just a few scratches and bruises. Everyone said it was a miracle, but I can't see how that can be. I killed Isobel, I was responsible.

It is as if the person who has written this is waving to me from behind the mirror where she's being held captive, but I can't help her. I don't understand how I could have written this and then forgotten everything – it seems too wilful and self-aware. The woman inside the mirror is then-Fran and she is trying to send me the end of the ball of string so that I can follow it back to her. But I can't find the way to climb through the looking-glass into my old life, even if I want to.

I walk back through the deserted entrance hall with its rosy lighting and beeswax scent. I open the front door, but still no one comes.

Returning home, I climb the stairs to the apartment at the top of the house and ring the bell. The young man I met earlier opens the door. He smiles at me and waves me inside.

I ask, 'Do you speak English?' and he looks puzzled.

'Are you making a game with me, Nina?' he replies.

'My name isn't Nina. It's Fran Blake. I'm sorry, but I don't know yours.'

'Marco,' he says, looking confused. He takes my hand and leads me to the sofa, and I sit beside him. When his hand touches mine, I think, 'Have I slept with you?'

'I don't know why I came to Venice, or how long I've been here.'

Marco answers my questions, when he realizes I'm tired and anxious rather than crazy. The apartment belongs to someone from Milan, who rents it out through an agency. I have been here about a month.

'Have we had many conversations?' I ask him.

'We had coffee near the Rialto market when I met you shopping. And I made you *risi e bisi* one evening.'

I raise my eyebrows for him to continue, but there isn't anything else, and he just shrugs. I have no idea if he will understand, but I tell him the story I have read in the notebook.

Marco asks, 'Do you remember any of this yourself now?'

'I remember Isobel, but not the accident. It's a blank until I woke up in Venice,' I reply.

Marco teaches architecture at the university, and he calls a professor in the Faculty of Medicine for some information about my condition. The doctor thinks I'm suffering from a fugue state, an extreme form of amnesia, caused by the emotional trauma of the accident. I suppose it makes me feel better, giving a name to this confusion, knowing that I'm not mad.

'Did you know that twins see their mirror image in a different way from other people?' Marco asks me. 'Because they have the mirror in each other?'

We are sitting on a bench in the sculpture garden of the Guggenheim museum, underneath the naked trees. We have been to the British consular office, where they have told me more information about myself. They contacted Jack, who offered to come and get me. I'm touched by that, but said I was well enough to return by myself. Marco offers me his phone, and I call Jack myself.

'I was worried when I didn't hear from you after a few weeks,' Jack says.

'Had I already moved out, then?'

'You didn't want to come home from the hospital. You moved into Isobel's flat. We didn't think that was a good idea but you insisted.'

'I don't know what I want to do now. I'll come back and sort things out, but I can't make any plans.'

'You don't sound like you're OK, love. Are you sure you can do it on your own?'

I'm annoyed with him for this. 'I think I have to.'

'If you're sure . . . Take care of yourself.'

I can't remember what he looks like. His voice doesn't sound familiar. It's like discussing the weather with someone you've met at the bus stop.

Marco takes me to the airport and I buy a ticket. He sits with me until my flight is called, and says that if I come back to Venice I can always stay with him.

'Have you ever been to the *Gabinetto di Curiosita*? I can't remember where it is. Somewhere near the Arsenale, I think.'

'Maybe, when I was a child. It sounds familiar.'

But if he had been there, he would never have forgotten it.

'May I call you Nina? It suits you, and I don't really think of you as Fran.'

I don't know if I'm Fran or if I want to be Nina. I don't even know where that name came from. I can't say if I want to go back, or put my old life behind me for good. Maybe it is possible to start again with a clean slate, but I'm starting to get flashes of it at the periphery of my vision: sidelong glimpses of Isobel, tugging on the ball of string.

JUSTICE

ANNE KOCH

T HE TIN CAN HURTLED DOWN THE AISLE OF THE UPPER DECK, shooting sticky brown drops of Coke. George kicked it away and grabbed the handrail as the 134 bus abruptly accelerated. The woman sitting in front of him turned around sharply. She frowned, holding one hand up to her head in irritation. George realized that he had pulled her hair. It was long and light brown and spilled over the back of her seat. 'Oh, I'm sorry,' he mumbled, sitting back to regain his balance – and his distance from the sheaf of thick hair. The woman turned away. Her shoulders looked resigned. What else did she expect? he wondered. I didn't do it on purpose.

A drop of sweat rolled slowly down George's side from under his left arm. He noticed a few strands still caught in his fingers and he shook them off into the aisle of the bus. The hair floated slowly down to the filthy floor. He felt nauseated and looked up to see if the small window could be opened further, clutching for the rail again as the bus jerked forward.

It was a late afternoon in early December and George Bowen was returning home. He had been to see Peter Dalgleish, his lawyer of more than thirty years. George found it hard to believe they were still talking about a trial that had taken place more than two years ago. After all, I won the case.

> *We can now conclude proceedings on this fourth and final day of Bowen v. Parkinson. Thank you to all our jury members and, indeed, to all involved. The jury has decided in favour of the plaintiff, George Stephen Bowen and, guided by the court, has awarded him £350,000 in damages which will have to be found by the defence. All rise.*

It had been an extraordinary day. George woke up early and managed to drink his usual two cups of tea, but the slice of toast remained, untouched, hard on the white porcelain plate. He mindlessly put on some old rubber boots and went out into the damp garden; the bracing air had no effect on his bilious stomach. Vacantly, he dead-headed a yellow climbing rose which somehow managed to produce flowers year round.

A few hours later, on his way to the Old Bailey, he needed his sunglasses, although he suspected this had as much to do with his sleepless nights as the sudden appearance of the sun. When George ducked into Court 4, the room was half empty and all he could see was a blur of dark heads, oak benches and green leather upholstery. He had a strong urge to run away. But it had been his decision to bring the case against Helen.

The judge, the Honourable Andrew Caldicott QC, had the flaccid roseate complexion of a man who lost count of his weekly intake of alcohol units. His excess facial skin had collapsed just above the starched gull-wing collar of his white shirt. Like all the barristers, he wore the uniform wig. Its white regimented pin curls and his pink face made George think of a corpulent rabbit.

George's own barrister, Nicholas Smythe, appeared much like the judge – with robes, white shirt and wig. But he had a hungry look and blue eyes that watched everything.

> *My esteemed client, Dr George Bowen, has been a doctor for twenty-one years. During this period he has practised medicine, he has worked closely with dozens of other medical practitioners and attended to thousands of grateful patients. Throughout this entire time Dr Bowen has not had even a single complaint made against him. Indeed, we shall be hearing from colleagues and patients who are keen to appear before you to defend his estimable reputation. As you will appreciate it was a huge shock to my client to be accused of this very grave offence, an odious allegation that would have impugned his reputation as a doctor and a human being and ruined both his professional and personal life. With a heavy heart my client took the difficult decision to sue the defence for slander. The allegation that my client molested women is baseless and has been made by the defence for what can only be malicious reasons, as we shall see.*

The bus braked in front of a greasy kebab shop, all yellow and red fluorescent lights, the huge side of shiny grey lamb turning slowly in the window. George had to take the rail again but carefully avoided the shiny, cascading hair. One of his knees smashed into the back of the plastic seat in front of him and he wondered why the bus driver was in such a fury. But then, London bus drivers were permanently enraged. Doctors, too, were a troubled bunch, but they took it out against themselves; their suicide rate was one of the highest in the country. Bus drivers just wanted to kill everyone else.

George Bowen's medical practice, shared with his partner Anthony MacKenzie, had survived for fifteen years. It was a small, busy practice and they regularly turned away potential new patients because although George and Anthony loved medicine, they didn't want to work away their lives. Some colleagues accused them of a lack of ambition but George and Anthony took this almost as a compliment. Then Anthony had a massive heart attack on his way to work and George went to St Pancras morgue to identify him. The metal door shut on the still, perfect body of his friend and Anthony was gone forever.

George still missed him. At the end of the day, the two had sat in Anthony's office. Often Anthony brought out a bottle of Islay single malt whisky, but they had to hunt for decent glasses and usually drank it neat from coffee mugs. They discussed patients and colleagues, politics and books and, sometimes, very personal things which men didn't usually choose to share. Both had been the first in their family to go to university. Both were uncertain about how far they had been able to escape their background. Anthony generally left before George to go home to his family. George didn't have to hurry back: his children were older and his wife, Jean, would be preoccupied.

After Anthony's death, George had staggered on for just over a year. He knew he would either need to find a new partner or close his practice and work in a bigger surgery. Joining up with Dr Helen Parkinson was almost an accident. A tall, large-boned woman with ash-blond hair, she was introduced to him by a friend at the Royal Free Hospital. She seemed nice enough when he met her, if a bit posh in that unexamined way he hated. And she was cold. But she had plenty of experience as a GP and discreet enquiries didn't unearth anything to worry about. He had thought that a woman partner would be good for the practice. But I didn't check her out enough, he thought. I was too lethargic and depressed. And then, what could I have turned up anyway?

For the first two years she seemed all right – the work was done and she got along with the patients and the secretary.

Actually, he thought, there was always something unpleasant about her. George remembered how she would make petty, disparaging comments about patients when she thought they couldn't hear. He was convinced that Mrs Butler, who was nearly eighty, had heard Dr Parkinson call her a stupid bat after the old lady had complained about an illegible prescription. And a few months after she joined him, he was walking by her office and overheard her on the phone. 'How can anyone who looks like he does give advice to other people about their health?' she was saying. He could see the expensive stilettos propped up on the desk as he passed her open doorway. 'But look where he comes from. What can you expect? It's his background, you know.' George had audibly cleared his throat and, moments later, he heard her closing her door.

He wondered if he made enough of an effort to be sociable so he invited her for lunch on the last working day before Christmas. He booked a table at a pleasant Italian trattoria around the corner. In the middle of the meal, the restaurant took delivery of a huge fridge and Helen seemed to take the disruption very personally.

'I really do wish they would shut the door. It's so damn cold in here. And noisy.' Helen, in a thin beige silk shirt, hugged herself and frowned. 'What do they think they're doing, delivering a fridge in the middle of the lunch hour?'

George could feel the cold blast from the open door. 'Why don't I get your coat and you can drape it over your shoulders?' he suggested, standing. A couple of bemused fellow diners had left their tables to help ease the fridge through the door.

Helen ignored him. She poked her rapidly congealing risotto with her fork. 'Why don't we just leave. This is totally unacceptable. I'm probably going to come down with the flu now.' She looked up. 'Oh, I guess we can't leave, can we, given the stupid thing is blocking the way.'

George noticed that Maria, the owner, had overheard Helen's remarks. She came up to their table, barely looking at Helen.

'I'm terribly sorry,' she said. 'The delivery people promised me they'd come at eight this morning.' She plucked at her apron nervously.

'It's all right. They'll get it in here soon. Don't worry,' he said, avoiding Helen's pinched face. 'If you could get my guest's coat, please – I'm sure that'll help. Thank you.'

But Helen refused to take the coat despite George's urging. Moments later, the fridge was forced through the door and carried to the kitchen. The other diners cheered but Helen sat, examining her long polished nails. Maria offered to replace the food but Helen wanted to leave immediately.

There was something so humourless, so narrow, so mean and selfish about her, George thought. She hates people like me; she despises me. He should have known then. He should have done something then.

In the year or so that followed, Helen worked hard in the mechanistic sort of way he and Anthony had observed in many of their colleagues. He wondered why she hadn't hooked up with someone on Harley Street. Why me? he wondered. They had short routine meetings about practice business and the occasional polite drink in the office. But after the Christmas lunch débâcle, George kept his distance. He was depressed and preoccupied, too, with things at home: Jean seemed weighed down by an unspoken and unaccountable sadness. Increasingly George found that he had nothing to say to Helen and when they did speak, he felt defeated. He told himself that after Anthony, he had unrealistic expectations about the partnership, but once, after George had a week out with a bad cold, the office was redecorated entirely in shades of beige. It didn't feel like his any longer.

Then Helen bought a thoroughbred horse and talked of little else. How could he relate to a person who went riding all weekend and had pictures of her horse in her office – large pictures? And her plummy voice seemed to get louder as the months passed until he could hear virtually every word reverberating through the sturdy walls between their offices as she whinnied her way through conversations. She was always in the office when he arrived and still there when he went home.

George looked out of the bus window. A television flickered on a formica shelf in the corner of the kebab shop. The six or seven dark-haired men standing around inside looked out into the darkness. One hiked up an old pair of shiny brown trousers with one hand. Another went to the doorway and gobbed into the street. As the bus pulled away noisily, the greasy slab of meat continued its slow turn and the tin of Coke bounced towards the front of the bus.

The hell had begun one cold morning in October. Jean had wanted to talk but he hadn't been able to get out of bed and was so late he hadn't even had time for tea, let alone conversation. In the office the water cooler gurgled away in the corner as waiting patients turned the tired pages of aged magazines. He hung his coat up and, barely glancing at the case list, returned to the waiting room to greet his first patient, an elderly lady called Mrs Timpson. Helen, in one of her pale suits as always, was in conversation with two middle-aged women sitting along the far wall. She turned, her eyes blinking behind expensive reading glasses, as she said, 'And he – yes, our dear old Dr Bowen. Well, now, he's often late. He has a lot on his plate, you know.'

George ignored the last comment and asked Mrs Timpson to follow him into his office. He saw patients all morning and when the surgery closed for lunch he decided to walk up the road and buy a bunch of irises for Jean. He knew they would have to sit down and talk things over that evening. As he was putting on his raincoat he realized he hadn't had a chance to go through his mail. He sifted through the pile and opened one letter. It stated that he was going to be investigated by the General Medical Council – investigated because of allegations made by one Dr Helen Parkinson – that he molested women. Groping was the word in inverted commas, Helen's word. The letter asked for his co-operation. He sat down at his desk, the letter shaking in his hands. Was it a joke? Should he confront her? Would she apologize? He was frightened and got up to lock the door of his office.

By mid-afternoon, however, his anger made him more energetic than he had felt since Anthony died. He was going to get rid of her honey-beige presence. He wouldn't work with her for even one more minute. George told his lawyer that he didn't care if his chances of winning a slander case were practically nil. He was going to sue the bitch. He was going to get her.

Dr Helen Parkinson hired the best defence barrister money could buy. James Morrison QC wore pince-nez that were probably made of real gold and throughout the trial appealed directly to the twelve members of the jury.

> *We shall be hearing from our witnesses shortly but my friends I would like to ask you to bear the following firmly in your minds when you consider this case. The defendant is an upright member of the community, a happily married woman, a highly respected medical doctor. Why would she accuse the plaintiff, a fellow doctor, her partner of some two years, of molesting women if it wasn't true? We have to take these charges seriously not only because they are true but also – and surely this cannot have escaped your notice – because this case is a matter of grave public interest.*

But I didn't do it. I didn't. He closed his eyes as the bus jerked forward. The jury knew that and decided I was innocent. I am innocent. And I won.

The bus stopped in front of a clean green and white store front: 'Green Endings – Funerals of Your Choice'. The first time George had seen a cadaver as a young medical student he'd had to leave the room to throw up. Then it got better and dead people became mere bodies. He shifted uncomfortably on the ratty bus upholstery. I didn't do it. I won my case.

The young woman in front of him stood up to get off the bus. She tried to walk but the lurching bus made her stumble. He wanted to get up and help her. She turned to go down the stairs and her long hair flew up behind her. She didn't look back. Squinting out of the streaked window for a last glance, all he could see was the beam of car headlights and intermittently his own face. He looked away. I must take better care of myself, he thought, looking down at his trousers. The bulky waistband was bunched up inelegantly and the only thing keeping them up was a leather belt with new holes he had drilled using an old corkscrew.

Jean left because I worked too hard and, well, no, I didn't give her enough. But I didn't really work hard at all. Only one month after the last of their three children moved out, Jean announced that she, too, was leaving and a week later she was gone. I didn't do enough to stop her, George thought, but then, she seemed so determined – like she'd been planning the escape for years. They'd had their ups and downs over the years but had always been able to talk. This time there were no words.

When it came right down to it, he didn't know why Jean left him. Everything felt concealed from him.

He remembered when he and Jean had taken the same 134 bus to go to an exhibition of Venetian paintings at the National Gallery. She had taken him straight to the Titians. On the way back to the bus stop, she stopped in a delicatessen and bought a large container of fruit salad. In the bus Jean took out the salad. 'Here,' she said, passing him a napkin. And then, 'Open your mouth, darling.' He remembered the pieces of pineapple, mandarin orange, kiwi and the one soft lychee swimming in syrup. She had shared the fruit salad between them, feeding first George and then herself with the single white plastic spoon. When she kissed him afterwards, he could taste the pineapple on her lips. It was only a few years ago, well, maybe ten years ago, George thought, yearning for Jean's round, dark-eyed, creamy, adorable face – a face he had seen in the Titian paintings that day. He squeezed his eyes shut. I still love you, Jean, he thought. You're so beautiful. You're more beautiful than any painting anywhere.

Peter Dalgleish had dealt with the divorce too. My lawyer, he thought scathingly, merely one of my numerous lawyers. Since he had decided to sue the bitch – he couldn't think of Helen Parkinson in any other way – he engaged a whole raft of expensive solicitors and barristers. But Peter was his regular guy, the solicitor who'd handled all of his legal affairs for years. He trusted him. Peter had called him twenty-four hours before to warn him that Dr Parkinson was trying to declare bankruptcy. The meeting hadn't taken long, barely half an hour, and now, just before six p.m., George was on the bus returning home. He could still feel the arm around his shoulder as Peter comforted him after delivering the bad news.

'George, look, there's no getting around it – the news I have today isn't good. Not good at all.'

George looked at his lawyer across the big mahogany desk. He felt like a small speck of dust and wanted Peter to blow him away.

'What is it? What's happening, Peter?' George tried to push his shoulders back and lift his head.

Although Peter was pushing sixty, he had an open boyish face. He was a man who went into the law for a quiet life and preferred to deal with property and money rather than with conflict and collapsing marriages.

'Well, you know that Dr Parkinson was in court today declaring bankruptcy. Well, she was . . .'

George staggered to the top of the steps of the bus, kicking the dented Coke can out of the way. The door was already folded open when he reached the bottom of the stairs and, worried that it would close before he could get clear, he almost threw himself on to the pavement. He stumbled and when he regained his balance, he noticed a man approaching him. 'Eighty pence to get something to eat. Please, Governor.' He reached into his raincoat pocket and gave the man two pound coins. Looks a bit like me, he thought. Soon I'll be broke too.

Huge lorries roared by en route to the M1 and George hurried the half block up the hill and turned the corner to face a quieter road. He was sweating central London dirt as he walked slowly towards his house and felt in need of a hot bath and a big glass of whisky.

Poor old Peter had trouble delivering the bad news. 'Well, she was successful in her court application.' He said this very quickly, looked past George and swallowed.

'What do you mean?'

'Well, it doesn't affect the outcome of the trial in one sense. You, of course, won the case. But, in short, if she's bankrupt, she has no money and therefore can't pay the damages she owes you – or your legal bills for that matter. The latter, as you know, George, are substantial.'

'What?'

Peter didn't reply. The two men sat there without speaking. George could hear cars in the street and a roaring in his ears.

George spoke first. 'Is there anything at all we can do to get the money back? Can we appeal? I mean, I won the case, didn't I?'

'Yes, you won. But no, I'm afraid there's nothing we can do about the money.' He looked down at his hands, carefully placed on his desk. 'What we need to do is to talk to your bank about how to manage your debts. When all of the investigations clear you, as I'm sure they will – I mean, that's certain now that you've won your court case – then on the money issue, perhaps you could go back to the General Medical Council or one of the other professional bodies or . . .' He was about to go on, but decided against it. George could see his massive legal debt floating above them like a barrage balloon; it seemed to spread and take up most of his lawyer's office.

How did she pull it off? Bankruptcy. He pictured her sitting on her pristine white sofa in her immaculate, vast and very expensively furnished pale living room. He'd only been there once and felt like he might dirty the room. She certainly thought he might. 'Oh, George, would you mind awfully taking off your shoes and sitting on this chair over here? The sofa's just been steam cleaned.'

George's red brick house was half a block away. The upstairs windows were silent. He tried to catch his breath. Even though he hadn't received it yet, he'd already spent more than half the £350,000 award. George felt sick. He still had to deal with all the investigations and he couldn't do that without lawyers. How much did he still owe Price, Gerrard and what's their names? And he had to shore up the practice. He laughed aloud at the thought that the damages – all that money – once seemed unimportant, inconsequential compared to his honour and his integrity.

He unlocked the big black door and entered the dim hallway, quickly closing the door behind him. The darkness felt safe but gradually light from the street picked out the silhouette of the hall table and the banisters going up to uninhabited bedrooms. George reached for the mail on the floor, wincing when he noticed one very white, expensive-looking envelope. He went into the living room and sat down in the burgundy winged armchair with his coat still on.

The picture frames on the black marble fireplace jutted into the gloom; his children's shadowy faces smiled down on the room. George looked at the large photograph of Michael, his youngest. He looked like Jean – the same brown eyes and pointed chin. George thought of phoning him to find out what Jean was doing but decided to wait until later.

He pulled himself up and closed the red velvet curtains Jean had made. Red was her favourite colour and she nearly always wore the garnet and gold necklace he had given her for their tenth wedding anniversary. Was she wearing the necklace when she made the curtains? he wondered. She was wearing it when she left that day, the day she left and didn't come back.

She had been standing by the front door. He could see the garnet resting just below her collar bone. She hadn't taken it off. It was as if she wanted to say that he shouldn't take her departure personally. And then she pulled up the collar of her coat. The garnet was concealed and she was gone.

He locked the door and then went to the kitchen to pour himself a large glass of whisky. Any old thing would do now, he thought. He leaned on the counter and looked out of the big window at the invisible garden.

George could see the blinking red light of the answering machine in the corner reflected in the window. He poured himself another glass of whisky before approaching it. Maybe one of the children had called. Maybe it was Michael, or maybe, maybe there was a message from Jean. Maybe Jean's clear voice would be there on the machine asking him to join her for a walk on Hampstead Heath. She wouldn't like the mud but they would walk anyway and then warm up over a cup of tea in the café at Kenwood. He pushed the start button on the machine.

Hello Dr Bowen. This is Susan Purcell from Price, Gerrard, Peterson and Taylor. Mr Gerrard has asked me to remind you that he sent you an invoice more than eight weeks ago and a reminder last week. Could you please call me as soon as possible. My number is . . .

George flicked off the machine. They would all have to wait for their money now. What was he supposed to do? His medical practice had deteriorated because so much of his time was spent on legal matters.

The whole court case was probably a big bloody mistake.

George sipped at his whisky but the glass was empty. He filled it again. He started taking off his shoes but stopped to pick up the pile of mail on the table. It was pointless opening the barrister's bill. The envelope glowed in semi-darkness. It hurt his eyes. He closed them and, leaning back in the armchair, stretched his one shoeless foot.

Dr Helen Parkinson appeared on a big white horse in front of him. Her hair was long and white blond. Her skin was pale, her lips silver. She was wearing pale beige riding gear and her long fingernails were painted white. She was silent and motionless as she looked at him, high on her big white horse. She waited and said nothing. Then, with a slight nudge of her white, knee-high riding boot on the horse's flank, she turned and rode away. Her long, white-blond hair flew up behind her. She didn't look back.

George knew he wasn't going to get anything; he had been defeated. George Bowen had lost his case.

PRECIOUS

ALISON HUNTINGTON

S HE'S WEARING THE BIGGEST DIAMOND RING A GIRL COULD DREAM
of. Fat, sharp and sparkling. Blue and yellow. Wide, smooth facets.
A real mouthful of a gemstone.

*

Scooping sapphires, celestial gravel, into my wet mouth. Saliva slips
over each, trying to create a whole from the shoal. A ruby, the size of
a child's furious fist, pounds its way into my navel. It fills a gap and
creates a chasm.

You never wanted children.

*

And you never bought me a ring. You didn't believe in marriage. So
when I watched you walk down the aisle with Sophie, I wondered
where you were when you changed your mind. And if it was the time
I woke at three in the morning next to a rigid shadow.

I wasn't going to go to your wedding. Churches in May make me
sneeze. But then I thought what the hell, if you're stupid enough to
invite me. What better time to start drinking again than on your free
champagne? I dressed carefully, low front, hair up. Remember how
you fell in love with the back of my neck? Several pairs of eyes told me
I'd upstaged the bride. It was a cheaply satisfying feeling. And hardly
my fault traditional doesn't work for everyone. White satin made her
pale skin look green. She wore her veil as though she'd run into it in
the dark. Does she call you Rob or Robbie?

In the front row your mother-in-law, funny words, panted like an
overweight jockey in emerald riding silks, low-slung jowls basting
turkey roll breasts. Does she call you son?

I found a drinking partner, a miserable-looking boy whose
girlfriend wouldn't speak to him. He said he'd proposed and she'd
turned him down. We kept each other topped up and laughed a lot.
Loudly.

Don't they make a lovely pair? You sank a bread knife into baby
pink sponge as Great Aunt June laid a spaghetti-veined hand on my
arm. She'd forgotten she met me at your parents' thirtieth anniversary.
I looked down. Her third finger was pale blue, lightly throttled by a

ring that had shackled her to a memory since 1944. The daisy of tiny diamonds was dull, filmed with grime and time. For a moment the champagne made it look pretty.

Though not, of course, in the same league as your charming wife's. I'm amazed she could lift her wrist to pull those baby doll curls out of her eyes.

And all the time I can hear you.

Diamonds are just bits of carbon.

Prices inflated by bastard big business with a nifty line in advertising.

A month's salary to last a lifetime. What fat fuck invented that?

Great bread queues of sad blokes in bad suits shuffling miserably into the house of a god they don't believe in, because they've all bought the same idea.

Makes me want to puke.

I loved the violence of your beliefs.

You used to see through all this. You knew it didn't matter. That it's arbitrary. That someone made it up.

Maybe you're tired of thinking.

I hate you for that more than anything.

*

The Monday after the wedding I went to the bank. Withdrew all my savings. I'd heard about this place in Hatton Garden. An antidote for the rockless. I'd been told it said 'engagement rings' in the window. Most of them say 'engagement rings' in the window. But this sign was red neon, like bloodstains on cake icing. I was to ask to see the diamonds. The big ones.

The guy behind the desk was dark and handsome. His teeth sparkled. He stared at me hard. I think we can help you madam. Won't you wait just a moment? I crossed my legs so that my skirt rode up a little. I could feel the hem hitching itself on my stocking tops. The sidekick standing at the back of the shop winked at the dark guy and came over. You know how much it costs? Yes, I said. A lifetime's salary to last forever. He smiled and took the envelope from my hands.

The dark guy slipped a keycard across the door at the back between two display cases of rings. The glass still carried the fingerprints of Saturday's eager fiancées. He beckoned to me. I stood up. I walked between the display cases and left the outside world behind.

The door led into a red-carpeted room. In the centre was a chair upholstered in jade green. To either side, shelf after shelf carried jars of gemstones like a storybook sweet shop. All un-set. Most cut, some simply polished. All different sizes. The dark guy smiled at me. I can leave you alone now. I promise not to come back and disturb you. Is that what you want?

I nodded.

He pushed me gently back into the velvet chair with one hand. With the other, he reached for a jar on the top right-hand shelf. He pulled it down. It shimmered with the dull ache of rubies. He unscrewed the jar, pressing it against his body. He took out a handful of blood red and rained it down on my throat. Some slid inside my shirt. He pulled my collar aside to let them fall further. Then turned and left. I heard the lock click, and smiled.

*

For the past – I don't know, it's dark in here, three days? – I have gorged myself. There are sapphires in my mouth and pearls between my toes. Diamonds sit in my eye sockets and in my armpits rest two fabulous rocks of amber. So many gems are pressed against the back of my throat that I can't swallow. The saliva has long since stopped trickling down my face.

I hope you're happy with your lot. Your terminal bit of flesh and bone, with a diamond attached. You'll have to chip it off, when she dies. Or bury her with it, circling a finger that grows greener by the day.

And me? Don't worry about me. I'm planning on glittering forever.

IN LIMBO

NADINE GRIEVE

THE CAB STANK OF CIGARETTE SMOKE AND KEBABS. FOAM AND kapok oozed from splits in the plastic seats. Andy sat upright while Dora snuggled into his shoulder.

What a party, he thought. Andy had been pouring himself yet another drink when Dora came up. She swung her dark hair away from her face as she smiled.

'Happy days!' she said, raising her glass.

They soon gave up trying to yell a conversation and Andy nodded towards the room where people were dancing. He should have gone back to the children long before.

Lauren wailed when he said he was going out for a while. She was standing on one of the mattresses Andy had arranged for the children on his living room floor.

'Don't go, Daddy. I'm frightened in the dark.' She was only eight.

'Shut up, Lauren.' Tom, two years older, was looking brave and, at the same time, as if he wanted to cry.

All week Andy had eaten moussaka, ribs or chicken wings from foil trays in front of *EastEnders* or *Who Wants To Be A Millionaire?* promising himself that if any invitation came, any, to do anything at all, he'd accept.

'I won't be long, and anyway, you should be asleep by now. Evie in the flat downstairs will be listening out for you.'

'I want to go with you.' Lauren was holding on to his trousers with one hand, and patting a piece of scarf against her cheek with the other.

Tom sat up on his mattress. 'I'll tell Mummy you went out and left us by ourselves.'

What would Cathy say if she knew? Andy winced as he imagined her. 'Oh, Andy, I don't like the children spending the weekend with you, if you aren't even going to be there.'

Cathy always said he hadn't pulled his weight, but how much weight did he have to pull, anyway? In the past few years, it had been like heaving a boulder up a mountain.

All evening, as Andy stood by the drinks table, topping up his glass, he wondered why he had come. A group from the sports club did not see his wave and smile; they pushed past him as if he wasn't there or was so soft he could not be felt. But when he started to dance with

Dora, she locked her body on to his in the near darkness. He was aware of her breasts pressing up against him, and so here they were, in a minicab, heading for his flat.

When he opened the front door, the light from the bare bulb dazzled him for a moment, then he saw the children on the landing outside his flat, dropping plastic models through the banisters into the stairwell.

'Hello, Daddy. We're doing swimming lessons.' Lauren's face was covered in felt tip pen marks.

'Oh, what a poppet. Come here, you poor little darling.' Dora opened her bag and took out a tissue. She moistened a corner of it with her tongue and walked up the stairs towards Lauren. The child backed away, putting her hands over her face.

'Who's she?' Tom waved a cricket bat over his head. 'Evie said the bogeyman would come and get us if we didn't go to sleep. But there aren't really any bogeymen, except in stories, are there, Dad?'

Andy settled the children back on to their mattresses. They'd caught him out – late, drunk, with a woman – and that made him feel better, less guilty somehow. He sat in the darkened living room for a while, willing them to go to sleep.

How eagerly he and Cathy kissed before the children came along, when they did not need many words to understand each other. But as the years passed, the few words they used came to lose their meaning.

'Bye, darling.'

'Have a good day.'

'See you tonight.'

'See you then. Look forward to it.'

Late one afternoon at work, Gordon said, 'Let's go for a drink when I've sorted this screensaver. Kylie Minogue. Her bum's still great. The hot totty are going to The Hart. You up for it?'

Andy's instinct was to start back, alarmed, but he said, 'OK, I'll come for a quick one. I can't stay long. Cathy'll be expecting me.'

Gordon, who had stopped listening after 'OK', was already heading for the door, his crash helmet under his arm, the hood of his anorak on his head with the jacket and sleeves flying out behind like a cape.

The drinks after work habit happened so easily. All he had to do was buy a round or two of Bacardi Breezers and Stellas, and then sit back. The rum wound the girls up like clockwork dolls – their eyes sparkled, their tongues prattled and the metal in their piercings tinkled. He liked being there in the crowd, knowing he could go home when he'd had enough. He used to tell Cathy he was meeting business contacts.

With a start Andy remembered Dora was in his bedroom. He got two glasses and a bottle of Chardonnay from the kitchen. Dora had draped a scarf over the lamp and taken off her dress. She was smoking, squeezed into an armchair. Andy had never seen such a big bra before, and his eyes were drawn to the roll of fat bulging over the waistline of her tights.

She must be about fifty, he thought. What am I doing? He opened the wine and poured them both a glass.

'It's good to be here with you, Andy.' Dora gave a throaty little cough as she stubbed out her cigarette. 'I get lonely sometimes, don't you? Of course, you've got the kiddies, so it's different for you.'

'They're just here for the weekend.' Then Andy felt he had to ask, 'You haven't got any children, then?'

'Yes, but they're quite grown up now, in a manner of speaking. Ben's twenty-six and my little one, Amanda's twenty. But with Ben, it was a difficult birth and he's still like a baby really. We looked after him, did everything for him, me and Eddie, as much as we could, you know.'

Andy nodded, unsure where the conversation was going. Dora still had her shoes on, and he could see the straps cutting into her feet.

'It's hard for a man, isn't it, Andy?'

Was it hard for a man? Had it been hard for him? About a year ago, Cathy and he joined a sports and leisure club. Sometimes he went there early in the mornings as well as on Saturdays. It meant more time away from the family, and he knew he was drifting. He was comfortable in the gym or the aerobics class, nodding and waving at people he recognized.

A few months later, Cathy said, 'I'm cancelling my subscription at the club. I never have time to go there.'

Cathy was writing an MA dissertation for the Open University on the family life of Victorian women novelists, which she hoped to publish. Andy called it 'The Sex Lives of Dried Up Spinsters'.

'Give up the club?' said Andy. 'Why? You're only researching at the library on Mondays and Fridays. Why don't you go on a Tuesday or a Wednesday?'

'Oh, that would fit in with your little plans, would it? I'm allowed to go on days when there's no yoga, no Pilates, nothing I want to do, so you can go whenever you want to?' She pulled a load of clothes out of the washing machine and carried on before Andy thought of anything to say. 'Just because I'm not earning money at the moment doesn't mean I've forfeited the right to choose.'

Misjudged it there, thought Andy. He tried to smile a wanting-to-be-forgiven smile, but her back was turned as she bent over the tumble-dryer.

Should he have put his arms around her then, and looked into her eyes, once full of a brightness that he loved so much? But maybe her look would be cold and dead. He paused for a moment before wandering off towards the television.

In bed that night, when he put his hand on her breast under the duvet, she threw it off.

Months went by and he stayed drinking after work more and more often. Cathy put the children to bed early, so that she could settle down to write. Andy found it easier to get home much later, when Cathy was asleep, or pretending to be.

Andy filled Dora's glass again.

'Perhaps hard in a different way,' he said.

'It got Eddie down and in the end he'd had enough.'

'You split up, then?'

'No. It was pills, an overdose. He just couldn't go on. You know how it is sometimes. Happy-go-lucky type, he never expected a kid like Ben.'

Andy felt paralyzed, stuck in a dream. What had been wrong with his own life?

She sighed. 'I couldn't cope with Ben on my own, so I had to put him into care. He's such a big lad now.' She gestured with one arm, dimpled from shoulder to wrist as if fingers had left their imprints in her flesh.

One Saturday morning, Andy strolled into the kitchen, full of sleep, to see Cathy, silhouetted in the sunlight among shiny saucepans and gleaming worktops. He switched the kettle on and shook dark-roast coffee into the cafetière. Cathy was talking about Jane Austen – or was it Jane Eyre? – being the most interesting woman who had ever lived. Or was it the best creation in fiction? What did he think?

He poured boiling water on to the coffee, and inhaled the smell. Why had she got up so early? His feet and nose were cold, and the warmth of her body under the duvet would be –

'ANDY. You haven't been listening to a word I've been saying. You never do. Go on, what did I just say?'

'Oh, does it matter? I was thinking how –'

'Well, if you just don't care, I don't care about you any more either.'

He pressed the metal plunger down into the hot coffee, but the glass jug slipped and shot across the counter. A tidal wave of coffee and grounds erupted over most of the kitchen.

Cathy screamed. 'You could have scalded us both to death.'

'Trust you to exaggerate.' Andy's ear had taken a hit of the coffee and was searingly painful, but he did not mention it.

'I spent hours cleaning the kitchen this morning. Don't you have any respect at all for my time?'

'Look, I work, too, you know.'

'You. You've got the brain of an earthworm and you're about as interesting.'

'And what about you and your precious research? Don't you think you've become as dried up as the old bitches you waste all your time writing about?'

By the afternoon, they'd decided he should move out for a few months, but that was a year ago now. Andy hated telling the children he was leaving. Afterwards, he was numb, as if he'd been pushed on to a travelator, while his wife, his family, his life, all drifted past, out of reach. Gordon bought a house in Swindon and the rest of the work crowd moved on, into different jobs or exciting relationships.

Dora lit another cigarette.

'When I was a child, we put up with it all, the rough and the smooth. Is that how you're bringing up your kids?' She sipped the wine with a tiny appreciative smack of her lips.

'No, not really like that.'

'Oh, well, it takes all sorts. My Mandy's doing great at the university and I love her so much, Andy, I just love that girl.'

Andy loved his kids, he was sure of that. He loved Cathy. He had loved Cathy. He could see her now, her wavy hair against her face, which was still beautiful, after the years of marriage and children.

'You've got a nice place here.' Dora looked around the room. 'I nearly got burnt out three weeks ago. Left a scented candle on while I slipped out. Only gone about ten minutes, but when I got back, the telly had gone up. The smoke, the fire engines, you should have seen it. I still haven't got rid of all the soot.' She yawned. 'Let's go to bed now. You're a kind man.'

'No, that's one thing I'm not.'

'It's all in there, my love.'

'What you said, your life, I am sorry, you know, that you have had to put up with so much.'

She leaned forward and stroked his face. 'Don't worry. You don't have to do anything.'

She drained her glass, stubbed out her cigarette, unfastened her shoes and, easing them off with a sigh, slid under the duvet.

Andy changed into his pyjamas in the bathroom and brushed his teeth. He switched off the lamp in the bedroom and pulled back his side of the duvet. He did not want to touch Dora, so he lay on his back at the edge of the bed. She was asleep, her head resting on the only pillow.

As Andy lay there, thinking about Dora's life, images of suffering from TV news programmes flickered into his mind – people running from the Goma volcano with their clothes on fire, families in Jerusalem and Ramallah crying for their dead children, limbless orphans in Baghdad hospitals – everyone, everywhere burning, broken, blasted.

In a dream, through a mist, Andy saw Cathy and the children in the garden, picking red apples from a tree. Even in his dream, he thought, 'That tree never fruits.' They went into the house, without noticing that it was on fire. Andy could not move; his arms and legs were tied. From an upstairs window, Cathy, Tom and Lauren screamed for help. Andy twisted and turned in his bonds; he could feel the heat on his face. Black smoke puffed out of the doors and windows, and the roof was blazing.

As he struggled to free himself, he cried out aloud in his sleep, 'God, if there is a God, please save these ones I love.'

The sound of his voice woke him. Tears were running down his cheeks and he was tangled in the duvet, sweating in his pyjamas. Still half asleep, he saw it was a misty morning outside, as in his dream. He turned over. Dora was no longer there and the air in the room smelled fresh. He lay on his back, looking around. Dora's dress, shoes and bag were gone. She must have cleared away the wine glasses and ashtray, too. Stilling his own breathing, he listened, but there was no sound from the kitchen or the bathroom.

He opened the door into the living room. The children were awake, lying on their mattresses, watching cartoon programmes. Tom looked through into the bedroom.

'Has she gone?'

'Yes, yes, she's gone home.' Andy glanced into the kitchen and the bathroom to be certain.

Lauren turned away from *Rugrats* for a moment. 'I'm hungry. What can I eat that's nice and sweet?'

'Well, why don't we go out and buy some things for breakfast?'

'I'm hungry now.'

'The quicker you get dressed, the quicker we can get to a shop.'

He showered and dressed while the children started to pull on socks and underwear.

Andy remembered a day when he and Cathy were walking on Hampstead Heath, getting to know each other. Cathy was wearing a tan suede jacket and her hair shone. He needed to touch her, to be close to her. He wanted her and was almost faint with lust. He led her into a patch of woodland and he could feel desire and release in every nerve of his body. He fell in love with her as he made love to her.

Were the children always so slow to get ready, he wondered, or only if they were watching television at the same time? He coaxed them into clothes he thought Cathy might approve of.

'Let's go and have breakfast with Mummy,' he said.

'Yes, but I just want to watch the end of *Rugrats*.'

'It'll be on again later. Let's go now.'

Andy drove around the quiet inner-city streets to find a shop that was open. He bought four plain croissants and four filled with chocolate. As he was leaving the shop, he noticed a bunch of red roses in a bucket outside and, although they were not in their first freshness, he bought them, too. Then he turned and drove west, out to the suburbs. A haze hung in the air with a gleam of sun behind it.

Now he was driving past the houses he knew, full of people who had been his neighbours for eleven years. The children were bickering in the back of the car. The bag of croissants and the red roses were on the seat next to Andy. He stopped the car outside his old home. His heart was banging and he was aware of the blood pumping around his body.

'Whose car is that in the drive?' Andy said.

Tom looked up. 'I don't know.'

Andy parked at the kerbside and opened the doors for the children.

'Go in and tell Mummy we've come for breakfast. I'll be in the garden.'

He held the bag of croissants in one hand and the bunch of roses in the other and walked round to the back of the house. He stood under the apple tree, as the sun dissolved the mist, waiting to see if his life was burnt out or not.

MAQHA

LAMYA AL-KHRAISHA

MY FRIENDS AND I GO TO COFFEE SHOPS IN AMMAN. SOMETIMES it's a trendy place you'll find anywhere in the world: walls painted in primary colours, alternative rock, caffè lattes and macchiatos. Sometimes, like tonight, it's a place you'll only find in Amman. White brick walls, Bedouin rugs, Um Kalthoom and Abdel Halim singing songs our parents fell in love to when wars broke out and moulded our history and future. There are thick mattresses buffered and upholstered with distinct Jordanian patterns of embroidery. The colors are bold. Not the pastel blues, mauves, limes, and beiges that fill the expensive tourist shops where the wives of rich cats buy furniture for their quaint and small 'Arabic sitting rooms'. Rooms where the swords and trays hanging on walls are Ottoman or Persian. These patterns are stitched with thread that is blood red, black, orange, navy and old-tree green.

My friends and I sit at our table and a smiling man in a flowing white *thoab* and a red and white head-dress approaches us. In his hands are a gold pot with a spout like a long curving beak and a stack of small, thin porcelain cups with no handles. The man pours a shot of the unsweetened Bedouin coffee; he knows this hospitality must be accepted. He pours with his left hand and offers the cup with his right. The smell of cardamom brings back the countless Fridays I spent with my father in the village by the desert castles where he was born. He would let me sit with him and the men of our tribe in tents made out of camel hair. There I would drink the coffee offered to me like I saw the rough men in westerns drink their whisky. I wanted to be the son my mother hadn't given him yet. I'd snap my wrist upward and my head would go back, hot liquid sliding down my tongue and throat, burning. Baba would try not to smile and he'd ask if I was all right. I'd nod furiously. He knew but never said anything, just kept on treating me like his little *sheika*. I drink it properly now, swirling it around and sipping slowly, appreciating the flavour. When I'm finished I shake the cup with thumb and forefinger: no more.

As I hand the cup back to the man, I think that maybe I should just say 'thank you' but part of me wants to feel that the man has earned the *hatta* on his head, the tribal dagger at his waist.

'*Isht*,' I say to him.

I wait for him to reply, knowing that if it is anything other than the proper response, the old charm and comfort of this place will disappear for me and it will become nothing more than a cheap theme park.

'*T'eeshi*,' the man replies with a smile. His brown eyes are warm. I smile back; he knows.

In these coffee shops there are always hookahs: *argeeleh*. The flavours are like a fruit basket from Paradise: watermelon, apricot, cherry, melon, strawberry, apple, liquorice, grape. You can mix any two or ask for a cocktail. We choose and settle in. The friends sitting around me tonight are the ones who went through their childhood and adolescence alongside me. Although I haven't seen some of them properly in years, and although many lives around this table have been forged away from me, outside Jordan, somehow these are the people I still mean when I say 'my friends'. I look at their faces as they laugh and talk, eyes widening at remembered stories and almost-forgotten exploits. Lujain, Sagir, Rakan and Yaser. Tonight is the first time in a long time that we are all together. It is my thirtieth birthday and when I do the math the number I'm left with feels unbelievable: I have known these people for twenty-one years. I've gathered them here tonight for an important reason. I have something to tell them. I know the right moment will whisper to me; it always does.

My hookah arrives. The head, a small terracotta pot not unlike an eggcup, is stuffed with cherry-flavoured tobacco and covered with pinpricked tin foil. The man places the *argeeleh* by me and sucks on the metal mouthpiece at the end of a long tube as he adjusts two glowing coals on the head. The water in the delicate glass base gurgles as he draws. When he's satisfied he turns the *argeeleh* so it faces me and hands me a sealed plastic *mabsam* to use over the mouthpiece. He bangs his tongs together and smiles. I smile back and tell him not to forget about me and nod at the coals. His forefinger rests on his right cheek and he points at one eye and then the other: I'll serve you with my eyes. The tips of my fingers touch my forehead in a little salute: you are respected.

Fragrant *argeeleh* smoke wafts throughout the coffee shop, curling up walls to the ceiling in white plumes that dissipate on their way down. The smell of cumin and nutmeg sprinkled on lupine and fava beans blends with fruit-flavoured tobacco like familiar incense. My friends and I smoke and we talk. Of school days and school friends. Who's getting married, who's having babies, who's on drugs and who's an alcoholic. Rakan has been out of the country the longest; some of the updates make him cough on his *argeeleh*. He almost burns himself on the coals. Most of the gossip doesn't surprise me much. The country is changing fast. There is a young leadership that encourages modernity. Seventy-five per cent of our population is under the age of twenty-five; compliance in the capital is brisk. I don't know how I feel about all the changes: the nightclubs, the bars, the salsa parties held in ancient Islamic castles built on top of hills boiling with olive trees. These are things my friends and I complained we didn't have ten years ago, when we were still part of the seventy-five per cent. Now I, Sagir and Yaser sound like our parents did when we were growing up. 'We're losing touch with who we are, what matters. It's all too sudden. It's almost aggressive,' we say.

So we come here, Sagir, Yaser and I, while Rakan lives in London and Lujain lives in America. We come here to an old coffee shop in Jabal Amman, a road down from our old school, and we talk about work and cars and politics and scandals in our little country and we try not to think about how things are changing around us, how the country seems to be growing younger as we grow older.

Sometimes when we're feeling worldly we say that in the larger scheme of things we're a total of two monkeys and a watchman. In a rich family we're the poor relations. King Hussein once said: 'Our greatest asset, our richest resource is our people.' I look at my country, its streets, its rich, its poor, the old and new cars, the ancient roads and the modern ones they build obsessively every two years. I see its imperfections. I see the beggars by traffic lights and the children with runny noses trying to sell cheap chewing gum and newspapers to you as you wait for the light to turn green. I see the ratty yellow taxis driven by unshaven men with chronic road rage, CDs and prayer beads hanging from their rear-view mirrors twinkling, prayer carpets lining the back seats. I see the sloping hills with rough roads cut into them. I see the rickety pickup trucks, in their beds tens of gas cylinders, paint peeling, banging and clanking. They beep their way through the city, announcing their services. I see the tough-ass cats that live in the streets' big silver bins. I see the million-dinar houses in Abdoon and the broken-down cement ones in the south of the country. I feel the warm sun, look at the Amman sky and I can almost swear it saves that blue for us and shows it nowhere else. I see most of the good and most of the bad and some I can't make up my mind about. Except what I really see is home, the place I belong. But it hasn't always been that way. There are times I can tell you about. There were times when I wanted to be anywhere but there. When it was my prison, that sunny place with the yellow taxis and the cats living in dumpsters. When the only pinpricks of light that penetrated the darkness were these four people sitting around me tonight.

When I exhale, the smoke of my *argeeleh* feels like liquid silk on my lips and when I lick them I can taste cherry. If I let my eyelids drop a little, I can see Lujain without the long raven-black hair. It shrinks away from her shoulders, creeps up past her ears and there she is the day I walked into my new school. The thick hair is cut short, like a boy's, and a rat-tail spills halfway down her back. The dark brown eyes are intelligent and there is a softness in them. On that first day, I walked into class before the bell rang. I was wearing a navy dress, white socks and formal navy shoes, the only new student to fourth grade 'M'. Lujain was in a group of noisy boys when she looked up and saw me. They were all in well-worn trainers, faded jeans and white cotton shirts with long coloured sleeves. Baseball season at the Amman International School. Lujain recognized me and skipped up to say hello.

'Hi, Badia!' She grinned.

'Hi,' I replied, looking at my formal shoes.

'Your mom told Mama you'd be coming today.' She spoke English the way the people in *Three's Company* did on telly.

I didn't say anything.

'Come help me and my friends. We're building a tower out of bags. Bring yours.'

Lujain skipped away to the back of the classroom and I followed, a little hesitant. Yaser was there with his thick black glasses and frizzy hair. Sagir was holding the base of the tower of bags and giggling, his face red and puffy. And, of course, Rakan. He was leaning against a wall giving orders. He took in my outfit and flashed a grin that made my stomach feel funny.

'Guys, this is my friend Badia. She used to live in London,' Lujain said simply, hands on her hips. The boys nodded and told me their names. They seemed to wait for me to say or do something so I tossed my bag on top of theirs. Rakan clapped his hands once and rubbed his palms together.

'All right. How about we put a desk on top?'

And that was it. Lujain commandeered a desk and chair and put them next to her own and I was set. I was sure to come to school next day in jeans, trainers and a baseball shirt my mother had to scour Amman to find. I had met my friends. They weren't Heather and Fraser but they weren't pale girls in grey uniforms either and that was more than good enough for me.

I was four when my father was appointed to the Jordanian embassy in London. By the time we moved back to Amman I was eight and my life in London was all I knew. The huge family back in Jordan was something my sister Alia and I had acknowledged only superficially, despite the audio cassettes and videos my parents sent them of us. We arrived in the summer and stayed with my maternal grandmother who was divorced from my grandfather.

Back then Meme lived in the ground-floor apartment of the building she owned. Meme's of a generation of women who evaluate people by cleanliness. So when my father went to the Ministry of Foreign Affairs in the morning and my mother went to supervise the renovation of our apartment, my sister Alia watched Arabic cartoons and my grandmother cleaned. Meme would start with the kitchen. Everything on the heavy plastic green table was put aside and the table would be scrubbed and wiped down. While she did the washing-up I was allowed to put the permanent residents back: the bowl of *labaneh* balls, the twin bowls of dark olive oil and *za'tar*, the twin bowls of green and black olives, the plate of white cheese. It took me a while to get used to the food. The milk tasted like white water and the bread was different. But I took to the *labaneh* straight away even though it looked funny. Meme's *labaneh* looked like golf balls and she drowned them in a jar of olive oil by the kitchen window.

After the kitchen, the bedrooms and the toilets were cleaned came my favourite part. Chairs, waste-baskets, side tables, anything that could be moved, would go on top of sofas. The rugs were aired on the front veranda's metal handrails. Meme would roll up the cuffs of my trousers or tuck my skirt in my underwear and tell me to get the mops. Then she'd spill buckets and buckets of soapy water throughout the brick apartment. My grandmother would encourage me in Arabic as I slid barefoot in the suds, driving them out to the veranda with a long-handled squeegee, an *ashata*.

The afternoons at Meme's were devoted to Miss Adalat, the private tutor my parents hired to teach me to read and write classical Arabic, the vernacular in which I was improving with Meme's help being very different from the language used in school work and all forms of written material.

By the end of the summer my family and I moved into our apartment in Sweifiyyeh. It smelled of paint and paste and Dettol. When I got there I went to check out the room I'd be sharing with Alia. It was nice and in perfect order. My mum had bought a complete bedroom set from London: white hearts set in pink background. Deciding to wear something fresh I peeled off all my clothes, vest landing on a lampshade, and opened my new cupboard. Mama had packed all our winter clothes in separate suitcases so I hadn't seen them all summer; when I opened the cupboard I smelled my room in London. Lined on the floor I saw my red wellies and a row of shoes I had outgrown. They looked so familiar but they didn't feel like they belonged to me any more. My stomach cramped suddenly and I vomited. My mother walked in a moment later. I realized I hadn't seen her properly in a while. I wanted to tell her that I missed her, I missed

Playschool on telly, I missed bottled milk that tasted right, I missed the rain, I missed home and wanted to go back but my mother was shaking in the doorway, hair wild, a sponge in her hand. Eyes darting from the puddle of vomit to the clothes strewn all over the room she shouted: 'Look what you've done! I've spent all day trying to make this room nice for you! Look what you've done!' My mother had never shouted at me like that and looking at me she burst into tears.

Our apartment was always full of aunts and uncles who ruffled my hair and asked me to say things in English. They would gush about how cute my British accent was. They would ask me to say words I'd learned in Arabic and they would gush about how sweet my Arabic was. With these people came the cousins. We were always sent into the glassed veranda of our second-floor apartment to play and stay out of the grown-ups' way. There were some beating-up sessions where I was told I was nothing special just because I spoke funny. Often, I would hide in the bathroom by the sitting room and listen to the grown-ups. Meme would give Mama tips about which detergents to use and my aunt Ruwaida would give her tips about how to raise children properly without spoiling them.

By the time schools opened up in September my classical Arabic was good enough for me to be enrolled into third grade. My parents had done their research and found out that the Rosary School for Girls had the best record for the General Certificate of Education: *Tawjihi.* Also, Rosary girls graduated with impeccable French. My parents were sold. They were sold for about a year, until Alia's incident.

During my year at the Rosary School my Arabic, both colloquial and classical, improved and I learned new ways of saying things in English as I repeated with the rest of the girls in the class: 'Biskwits, biskwits, biskwits. I like to eat my biskwits with milk.' The French was interesting too; there was a certain 'Monique' in every sentence. The nuns who ran the school were extremely strict. When the muted grey lines of girls filed into the school building at twenty past seven each morning, the nuns would stand by the doors and scrutinize uniforms and hair. 'You, girl! Come here!' they would bark as they yanked girls out of the line if anything was wrong with their appearance.

Each day, after the bell rang announcing the end of the school day, I had to go and collect Alia from the kindergarten, a cold and cheerless place with crude-coloured drawings of Mickey Mouse and Donald Duck on the walls. The only pretty thing in the whole place was a framed piece of needlework hanging askew on a grey wall. It was a famous line from an Arabic poem that our teachers spat out at us if we displeased them: 'Stand up for your teacher and show him the respect he deserves; a teacher is almost a prophet.'

One day I got to the kindergarten to find Alia sitting on a chair in a corner, head down, one foot tucked behind the other, hands in her lap. Her soft sandy-brown hair was starting to loosen from the clips and hair-bands that kept it nice and tidy in the morning. I called her name and she looked up, most of her small face obscured by her thick rose-coloured glasses. She looked puffy and strange so I went to her. I told her to come on, Mama was waiting, but she just looked at me. I was tired, hungry and wanted to go home. I bent down to grab her red lunch-box and that's when I smelled it. It was sour and fresh and so *there*. I told her to get up and she did, quietly. I smelled it again and looked at her. Her right leg had a clean streak down it and there was half-dried shit on her white sock and on the heel of her black Start-rite shoe. 'I was too scared, Badia,' she mumbled, her head bent.

Getting out of the school was a five-minute odyssey. Go down the stairs from the kindergarten, cross the older girls' playground, pick either the steps or the long and steep concrete ramp, walk the long stretch that ends with the impossibly high gates. The ramp burned my feet as my shoes slapped against it and my toes gripped hard so Alia and I wouldn't slide all the way down. But the ramp was the fastest way to the gate beyond which hundreds of parents and cars waited, beeping impatiently. We were lucky that day. I spotted my mother almost immediately. She was parked close by. When I saw her, elbows on her silver Renault's steering wheel, chin resting on her palm, a giggle bubbled out before I realized it. Alia was clutching my hand, head down as she trudged beside me. Soon, my mother turned her head and saw us. In one hand I had my heavy school bag and Alia's lunch-box; Alia was clutching the other. My mother switched on the car and smiled at us distractedly; these days it seemed my mother looked through us rather than at us. I giggled again and suddenly the throngs of students, parents, teachers, the cars and buses and school bags, the dull grey uniforms, the beeping and bus drivers, the blazing Amman sun bouncing off car metal, my mother smiling vaguely behind her windscreen, and the smell of shit heavy in my nose was too much. The giggles bubbled up and out like a burping plughole.

By the time we reached the car I couldn't take deep breaths and my eyes hurt because I couldn't blink. I saw Alia's Start-rite shoe again and I was screaming and choking it was so funny. As I reached for the door handle my mother looked at me, questioning and a little amused. I had delivered Alia to her; now it was time to let this laughter out because if I didn't it was going to kill me right there by the car. Alia let go of my hand quickly, got in the back seat and smoothed her uniform self-consciously. It made me laugh harder; I couldn't see through the tears to open the door.

'What is it, Badia?' my mother asked, now more annoyed than interested.

The narrow road by the Rosary School was a monster sea of traffic, beeping and drivers hugging their doors with one arm as their heads poked out of their windows. I let go of the door handle, dropped my bag and Alia's lunch-box, put my hands on my knees and let it out.

'Badia, get in the car now! Stop being silly and tell me what's going on!' My mother's nervous voice.

I wiped my eyes and nose with the back of my hand, tried to breathe normally and opened the door. I collapsed into the car and dragged my bag and my sister's lunch-box behind me. I was quiet for a moment, trying to catch my breath and then my mother asked what happened in her most rational let's-talk-calmly voice. That started me off again; I hadn't heard that voice since we had left London; it was like hearing the voice of a ghost. In my head I could see Scooby Doo jumping into Shaggy's arms and crying, 'Yikes! A ghost!' I missed Scooby and Shaggy; I was never going to see them again. My head against the dashboard I heehawed hysterically, thinking of all the Arabic cartoons I now knew. My mother screamed at me then.

'You've upset your sister, Badia! Look! Now she's crying. Stop it! You're being silly!'

I sighed and leaned back into my seat, too tired to wipe my streaming face. The muscles in my stomach hurt and my eyes felt like whole white eggs, too dry for my sockets.

My mother was trying to get out of her parking spot and manoeuvre her way into the glittering river of traffic and blaring car horns. A father in a shiny black BMW cut in on us; we jerked to a halt as the man edged his way through. My mother shoved the base of her hand on to the centre of her steering wheel and kept it there. '*Haywan!*' my mother spat, her face red. Yanking her hand off the horn she snapped her head around and burst out, 'And what the bloody hell is that smell?' Air blew through my lips and I was gone. Mama's face seemed to crumble on itself as Alia sobbed that she was sorry but she was too afraid to tell Miss Suhair that she needed the bathroom, that the toilets smelled bad, that a hundred different things. My mother shook as she dried the tears on Alia's miserable face and told her it was all right, that they'd get her cleaned up in no time. I wanted to cry too; I just couldn't.

My mother raised merry hell with the school and by the time the next semester rolled around Alia and I were in the AIS. I came to my new school not quite trusting it to be different from my old one. But the teachers were friendly and the sound of children allowed to be children as they ran around in bright clothes and tossed books and balls around helped me. It didn't take long for me to make friends and forge alliances. Lujain, Rakan, Yaser and Sagir were just some of the friends I made there. At the AIS I was a kid again and I had a home again. My friends made me think of London and my friends there less and less as I learned how to play baseball, collect marbles, trade comics and make spitballs. I even started speaking English like the people from *Three's Company* too.

That's how I met my friends. Lots has happened between then and now. I look at them in the coffee shop tonight: Lujain with her pharaonic tattoo screaming blackly from the skin of her right hand, the hand she is supposed to use first for any deed. When she first got it she used to get looks; tattoos are *haraam* in Islam. But today she is just another young woman with a tattoo. Yaser is here and the heavy black glasses I keep expecting to see resting on his nose have been replaced by a slim Gucci design. He is the youngest partner at the largest auditing firm in Amman and he most certainly looks the part in his expensive grey suit. And of course Rakan, the boy I believed was The One for so long. Sagir, the friend I see the most, is looking at me with a question in his eyes. He opens his mouth and a soft cloud of smoke hides him and drifts towards me, lapping at my face, making it feel wet. I close my eyes and smell apples. Sagir knows something is going on with me. We still call him The Mouth but I think I might be the only one who knows that there's nothing wrong with his ears or his head. I smile at him and turn away, calling to the man to put fresh coals on my *argeeleh*. I need to be ready when I tell them. I'm not ready yet, but the night is young.

'Maqha' is an extract from the novel *Badia*

JACK & THE LAD

MICHAEL MAYHEW

'*The make-up of make-up artists.*'

'What?!'

David swatted his brow. 'Max Factor!! *The make-up of make-up artists!*'

Jack nodded. 'Right. Are you sure no one's looking?'

'So what if they are? This isn't some Eastern Bloc country, you know. This is London. I'm a man, of sorts, and I'll buy make-up if I want to. I was in Prague once and I tried to buy pressed powder and the woman refused to serve me. She actually refused to serve me!'

Jack shifted uneasily. 'Don't they have a shop in London especially for drag queens? I don't think you realize the looks we're getting. If we're attacked I won't try and save you, you know. I just feel that's worth telling. I won't try and save you. I'll leg it out of here to save my own skin. I gave up on the gay community years ago.'

David sighed. 'Does this shade suit my skin? You know, that's the problem with pressed powder when you're a man: unless you shave as closely as possible, the granules stick to your beard and you're fucked. Not that I'm going for that full hermaphrodite look, mind you. I'm well aware that even in drag I'm plainly a man. I'm a female impersonator. And I mean, I don't have that bad a beard, but I have to shave, like, every day. You're lucky, you're naturally blond. I bet you hardly have to shave at all.'

'Let me stand in front of you,' Jack said. 'Then no one can see what you're doing.' He propped himself against the Clinique counter, randomly winking and shrugging apologetically at the white-coated women wandering to and fro in their guises as on-site 'skin surgeons'.

'I don't care if they can see. Are you always this jittery?'

'Not usually, but if you start applying the 'curl'n'twirl' mascara I may leg it.'

David straightened up, a finger full of foundation firmly flattened on to his face. 'There. How do I look?'

'Like you've been embalmed.'

'Shit. Too pale?'

'Yeah.'

'Thing is I don't want too dark either, not really going for that Dale Winton look, like a kipper that just fell through the stratosphere. *Maybe it's Maybelline?*'

'I don't know.'

David sighed. 'This is no good. I need to shop with a girl. No offence. I tried shopping with my brother Josh once, and that was even worse. And yes, he's straight.'

'You took a straight boy shopping for make-up?!'

'I took him for protection. He's a bit of a lad but he'd cheerfully kick the head in of anyone who threw me the kind of glance you say people are throwing us right now. Am I embarrassing you, Czech boy?'

'Well, you called me up.' Jack was running his finger in concentric circles around his own sunny stubble. 'Hey . . . you can see my beard though, can't you? I don't look like a girl, do I?'

'No, you kind of look like a very pretty Czech boy, Czech boy. Now to the matter at hand: do you dabble?'

Jack frowned. 'I've been known to . . .' He slapped his brow in disbelief. 'Charlotte! Got to get her a valentine's card!' He set off towards the stationery section, David dawdling behind.

'You buy a valentine for your fag hag?!'

The selection was sparse, but sweet.

'It's a ritual,' Jack explained. 'We kind of love each other. Like that bloke off *Queer as Folk* said, "in an alternate reality I think I just met my wife". And yeah, I met her on a black magic forum in case you were trying to establish something.'

David finished rubbing his rouge off. 'Is she fag hag type 1, or fag hag type 2?'

'Sorry?!'

'Type 1 fag hag is a woman so ugly she hangs around with gay men because it's the only male contact she gets. Type 2 is the kind who hangs around with gay men because she's so beautiful it's the only peace she can get from simpering straight men. So, type 1 or type 2?'

'Oh, definitely type 2. She's slim, pretty in a Rosanna Arquette kind of way, and she laughs at all my jokes. She works here, too, but it's her day off. She wants me to get a job here but I'm like, get to fuck, I'm not working with all these Selfridges queens. Anyway, she still thinks I'm the bee's knees.'

David grinned, that kind of grin he did so well, a kind of rictus ear-to-ear epidermal elongation. 'You're quite sweet really, Jack. Don't look so frosty, 'coz it really doesn't suit you. Now, take a look at this.' He reached inside his DKNY duffel bag and pulled out a volume the size of a trade paperback. It was browning, the spine was peeling and, as David was so proud to point out, it didn't even have an ISBN number.

'What is it?'

'A grimoire! You know, like a real deal-type magic book. It's an under-the-counter job. It's my baby.'

Jack held it, turned it over in his hands. It felt leathery, and smelled of cheap incense. 'Where'd you get it?'

'You don't need to know that, Czech boy. Shall we go up to the fourth floor and get a cappuccino?'

'Tea. Cappuccino is so gay.'

'Tea it is.' David shrugged, and headed for the escalator. 'My treat. Selfridges do the most wonderful hot chocolate. They stick a dollop of the ice cream of your choice on the top and you just spoon it in. Divine. I was going to use that as my stage name, you know, the "divine David", but there already is one, so it's going to be "David Deluxe". I envision myself doing turns at the Vauxhall Tavern within weeks of hitting the circuit.'

Jack caught up with him, vacating the escalator and making a sharp right through menswear. 'This grimoire . . . Is it for real?'

'What do you think, Czech boy?'

'OK. And I can help because . . .?'

'Because you're interested in that sort of stuff, like I am. You're like me, Jack: we're not like other poofs, you and me.' David stopped, and sidestepped, framing Jack's profile in the fake photographic lens of his hands. 'Good profile. You know you're very handsome, Jack. I could fall for you in a big way.'

'Well, you have a nice dimpled chin going on yourself, but still . . . not really rough trade with all that rouge, are you?'

'It's a gay grimoire,' David said delightedly. He ushered Jack into the café and selected a seat far from prying eyes and eager ears. 'A gay grimoire, to conjure up gay ghosts.'

'Demons with disco tits?!'

'You're so droll. No, rough trade actually.'

Jack opened the book at a random page. 'God, it really doesn't have an ISBN, does it? Handwritten, too. Someone loved this book, didn't they? Someone took the time and attention to write out every single page, legibly even.'

'Page forty-two. Read about Adam. It's all about the Vicarage Fields shopping centre in Barking.'

'Heard of it.' Jack nodded.

As their beverages were brought over, Jack proceeded to feast on the felt-tipped text. 'Lot of stuff needed, so it says here anyhow: a Jeff Stryker dildo, a rusty nipple ring, bottle of poppers . . .'

'Poof paraphernalia.' David waved a hand dismissively. 'I'm thinking of it as a birthday present for my best friend, Ben. No more fucked up fairies for Ben. I'll get him a custom-made boyfriend.'

Jack wasn't even jarred. 'One of the conduits is a porn video, but it doesn't even tell you if it has to be straight or gay. I'm guessing gay.'

'He's lovely, Ben is. So cute. Real genuine cockney boy, and there aren't many of them around, I can tell you. He's looking for a boyfriend and I reckon this is something I can do for him.'

'OK . . .' Jack grasped the grimoire to his chest. It felt warm and solid against him. 'And I should help you with this because . . .?'

'Because read the fine text. I never said we had to give the present to Ben straight away. Gauge the goods and all that, if you know what I mean. And you read about Adam. He was a barrow boy, and that's just for starters. He's kind of hyper-masculine. So I take it that you're interested?'

Jack leant back, twirling his silver spoon in the raspberry ice cream. 'Yup. Real poofs are just too fucked up for me.'

'Spectacular. Now if you read the fine print you'll see we can't do it alone. But this is not the kind of thing I want any of those cheap occultist groups we may or may not have frequented in the past getting involved in. So do you have anyone in mind who's as socially warped and morally malformed as we two so obviously are?'

Jack opened his wallet and ran his thumb over the smeared picture behind the plastic cache: on the dance-floor at Benjy's, several Sundays previous, himself, Elliot and Jason – the three of them shoulder to shoulder, sweaty and in their regulation Reebok tops and trainers, beaming blatantly for the sudden photo op. 'Oh yeah,' he nodded. 'I think I got us a queer quartet.'

'Jason, someone is gonna twat you any second now.'

The lights went up, giving form to four boys on a sloping floor, tiled gold in its heyday but now downtrodden to a dowdy sort of yellow. Ahead of them the parade of shops veered off to the right, and the slope rose further still.

'There!' Elliot stepped back. 'We have light. See, I'm not just a thoroughly wholesome individual after all. I can do stuff. Now, who wants to twat Jason?'

David was ruminating over his reflection in a battered beige compact. He clicked it shut under Jason's nose with the kind of sleight of hand that took hours of practice in front of various larger, strategically placed reflective surfaces. 'I'd happily twat him, but pus stains are such a dog to wash out of good fibres.'

Up at the back, Jack winced. 'Ow, Jase. You've been cussed, man.'

Jason shambled up the slope first, leaving him licence to vent the Mong expression without further comebacks. 'Do they call drag queens that because they are like, such a drag?'

'I'm not a drag queen,' David declared. 'I'm a female impersonator.'

'You're just female,' Jason called back.

The floor tapered into a point, and then blew outwards to cover an expanse of some twenty metres or so in all directions, leading to various walkways and cold drink stands. Subtle shadows slid along the ceiling above them, edging down the escalators that led to a badly lit basement area. The shops were shut, the security arrangements scant. Morelli's coffee counter hadn't been mopped. Elliot ran his finger along it and licked up the sticky sugar.

'I could make us all a coffee,' he offered. 'I reckon I know how to do it. We had a machine like this in that office I worked in near St Paul's. Remember that, Jack? When I nearly flooded the first floor? God, I was such a twat.'

They all turned and looked at Jack. He was standing at the bottom of the left-side escalator, neck craned back, gazing up at the rafters. Of course he wasn't listening. He hugged himself. Jason crept up behind him and blew in his ear, beaming. 'You're not gonna cry, are you? That would be so gay. We all know how much you want a bit of rough trade.'

Jack wasn't jolted. 'You're such a prick, Jase. You do know that, don't you?'

Jason stepped back. ''Course I do. And against just such a spirit I feel that I should say something really poignant, something that encapsulates the gritty realism of this moment. Something about how insufferably banal it is here in Barking. Something that means something! Because this means something, doesn't it? What we're about to do?'

David set the pillowcase down in the centre of the floor. 'We need to clear these chairs and tables away,' he said. 'If things get spooky I don't want to be hit in the face by a flying salt shaker or something.'

'You said nothing like that would happen,' Elliot said. 'A straightforward séance, that's what you said.'

'Ask him!' David nodded at Jack. 'It's him who goes all autistic over this place, and it was my idea to start off with. Maybe not such a good one at that. My *Carry On* collection is calling me, right about now.'

This seemed to jolt Jack. 'I thought this was for your friend Ben?'

'It is. For Ben later, and for all of us right now. Now are you gonna stand there looking all Czech boy, or are you gonna help clear the space?'

'Who's Ben, anyway?' Elliot asked.

'My best mate,' David replied. 'Jack, you did tell them, didn't you?'

'Yeah, I told them.' Jack took the other end of the table and helped him heft it aside. 'I don't want to "sample" Adam anyway. I want to talk to him. There's something I want to know. Something about myself.'

'Can you imagine talking to a ghost?' Jason said, scratching his chin, zapping a zit. 'We're blasé about it now but if this works, man . . . I'll bet we'll freak. We'll fucking freak.' The others just looked at him, so he shrugged. 'Well, I will anyway.'

David nodded to the pillowcase. 'Empty that, someone.'

Elliot began sorting the various items that plopped out of the pillowcase: a pair of white Calvin Klein briefs; a Jeff Stryker cock'n'balls; a trendy rucksack; eau de toilette; designer sunglasses; a Kylie CD single (*Can't Get You Out Of My Head*); a picture of Judy Garland as Dorothy, doggedly defaced; a gram of speed, flawed with flour; a bottle of poppers; moisturizer (Clinique); a porno (*Power Tool 2*); a ribbed top (red); and finally a stainless steel nipple-ring, rusted.

'It's like the opening gambit of a straight-to-video Milwaukee teen-slasher flick,' Jason sighed. 'Four teens –'

'We're not teens,' Jack snapped.

'Four *queens* dabbling in forces they don't really understand, a well characterized quartet, which makes it all the more shocking when their staggering naïvety causes forces of unimaginable horror to leap forth and slaughter the lot of them within the first five minutes of said flick.'

'Do the things have to be arranged in any particular way?' Elliot asked. 'Like a pentagram?'

Jack was gazing at the picture of Judy Garland, momentarily mesmerized. He lowered it slowly so it allowed him a clear view of Jason's rather pock-marked face. 'Jase . . . you know what I'm gonna say, don't you?'

Jason was reading the blurb on the back of *Power Tool 2*. He grinned cheekily. 'Don't tell you'll be stuck on the scene for the rest of your life?'

'Don't call me a queen. It's almost as bad as being called a nonce.'

'The cock and balls should be in the centre.' David was in the process of distributing the dildo to the centre of the space cleared. 'And it should be pointing skyward. It's the conduit. I hope you washed it.'

'But is it art?' Jason raised an eyebrow. 'If no one wants this *Power Tool 2* video after we're done can I have it?'

'You're welcome to it.' David took a thin nib of blue chalk from his pocket and began tracing a pentagram, roughly ten feet by eight. 'We each need to sit at one corner of this, and it says' – he consulted the browning volume Elliot held aloft for him – 'it says we all need to make a little statement about why we want to call on "him".'

The four boys collected themselves at equal and opposing ends of the pentagram. The Jeff Stryker dildo took pride of place in the centre of the piece, with the other 'objets d'arse' arranged around in an order that seemed baffling to anybody not reading directly over David's shoulder.

'Who's going to start?' Elliot asked. 'You want me to?'

David closed the book and shoved it under his arse. 'It doesn't matter, as it goes.'

Elliot made a steeple from his fingers, and sucked in air between his pursed lips. The others waited. David was clearly pissed off with him, but that much had been obvious from the moment they'd met. It took a great deal of tact not to leave Elliot out of any given situation totally.

'I guess I'm just here for Jack,' Elliot said, nodding to the aforementioned. 'He's my best mate and all. I'd jump into a pit of queens in crop tops if he asked me to.'

David nodded; clearly this had gone entirely over his head. 'Jason?'

Jason stopped picking his ingrowing hairs. 'Well, I'm here for me, mainly. I've always been interested in this sort of stuff, you know, purely from a new age perspective. It beats another Friday night in Comptons, right?'

'Jack?'

They all turned and looked at Jack. Again, he wasn't with them. His fingers were strumming on the floor and he was nodding his head; a beat in the brain.

'You all know why I'm here,' he said. He didn't even look up; distracted wasn't even the word.

'You need to say it,' David said, 'or it won't work.'

'I'm here because they don't make rough trade like him any more; since it was legalized; undiluted, pure straight-acting lad. Only it isn't an act.'

'That's nice,' David nodded. 'And as for me . . . well, I'm here for Ben, like I said. Because if this works then maybe I can procure for him the perfect boyfriend. No one deserves it more.'

Jack kissed his lips, kind of. 'Of course.'

David exhaled slowly, with intent. 'OK. Now this is the bit Jack may or may not have mentioned to the pair of you.' He looked at Jack, and for the first time the entire evening, he cracked a smile. 'You want to tell them, or shall I?'

Elliot and Jason pivoted on their arses, gazing fearfully at Jack. 'Don't worry,' he said to them. 'It's not human sacrifice or anything.'

'I thought you were going to say we had to kill a queen or something.' Jason beamed. 'That could've been fun.'

'We need to wank,' Jack said simply, straight-faced. 'Coming as close together as possible. The cum-shots have to hit the dildo. Like, dead centre. Think "the biscuit game", but at least the last one to come doesn't have to eat it.'

Jason stopped picking. 'And that's it?'

Both David and Jack nodded. 'That's it,' David declared. 'Don't worry. Jack checked the rota. There's no one around this way for hours.'

Jack nodded. 'It's almost midnight – the witching hour. So let's make like Myra Gulch.'

They all waited.

'Oh, for fuck's sake!' David slapped his brow in disbelief. 'OK, I'll get the balls rolling, so to speak . . .' He unzipped his jeans and pulled his cock out. The others were surprised by how long it was; for some reason they didn't expect a drag queen to have a dong like that. They watched him wank for about forty seconds before Jack caught on and unzipped his combats. Elliot was the last to comply, and he tried to hide his penis inside his fist.

'What are you all staring at?' David asked.

'Your cock,' Jason said simply. 'It's . . . well, it's big, man!'

'Don't you get any ideas about sucking it.'

'I won't. And don't you try and suck mine either.'

'If it's as scabby as your face then no fear.'

'Shut the fuck up,' Jack said slowly, emphasizing each word in turn. He was one of those lads who reached his tongue out of his mouth as he wanked, and kind of curled it around the edge of his mouth in the way that some people seem inclined to do in moments of deep concentration.

A matter of masturbatory moments later . . .

'God, even I can't do it,' Jason sighed, tucking his tackle away. 'It's just so . . . gay. Gay in the worst possible way.'

'Jack, are you absolutely sure the security cameras aren't on?' David asked. 'I can see the little green light on that one above us, I swear it!'

'Can't we do it separately?' Jason asked. 'One at a time, while the others wait upstairs?'

'It has to be together.' Jack was almost there, flicking the pre-cum off his fingers. What Jack thought about to get him going, well, none of them knew the answer to that one. 'What's wrong, Jase? You're not usually this backward about coming forward.'

'I can't think of anyone who gives me a sufficient boner.' Jason let his cock drop on to his zipper. 'I'm getting friction burns.'

As things began to reach their inevitable climax, David became increasingly agitated, fumbling for something in his back pocket. 'This is for you, Ben,' he whispered, kissing it. He tossed the object into the circle. It hit the Jeff Stryker cock'n'balls but didn't topple it.

'What was that?!' Jack gasped.

'A surprise ingredient.' David was rocking back and forth. 'Oh, shit, I'm gonna come in a sec . . .'

'Let's have a look . . .' Jason pushed his cock back into his kecks and crawled forward on his hands and knees. 'I want to see what it was . . .'

'Jason, no!!' David screamed. 'Don't stop now!! And don't touch the display!'

Jack came. His spunk struck the dildo dead centre, and the whole thing went up like a match to spilt poppers. Jason screamed, falling on to his arse. Elliot turned and ran. David tried desperately to finish himself off.

The pain of a lacerated limb brought him to.

Jack had spilled out of the Ripple Road exit, in the process trapping his arm in one of those revolving doors that encapsulates a crowd of ten punters per revolution. He fell on his back on to the pavement, barely feeling it through the fur lining of his Fred Perry zip-up. He wasn't entirely sure whether the shock of what he'd just seen had knocked him out, or the shock of watching his own arm slowly dislocated by a grinding mechanical cog that whirred in time to the background beat of Baltimora's *Tarzan Boy*. The sky above was the bold unbroken blue of night-time. His breath came out in a thin, clear stream and he watched it evaporate against the smattering of stars staring down at him.

A moment more and he crawled to the cashpoint and pulled himself up via Barclays, which had to be something of a first given the sorry state of his bank balance. He smiled, despite the pain of garrotted bone and tendon. Maybe he could write David's stage stuff after all. There was a caustic quip in every queer, even a self-styled 'anti queer'.

Speaking of 'anti queers', he was suddenly clouted with clarity and a rare sense of concern for the welfare of others. David wasn't with him, neither was Jason or Elliot. He foraged in the mire of his recent memory; none of them had run out with him. Elliot had run first, which kind of disappointed Jack, as he'd always been able to count on him in the past. Elliot was like that, stable and dependable. Boring, too, but at least the cliché was comforting. You couldn't be stable, dependable *and* interesting; it was simply far too attractive, such a person, such a proposition.

Sirens sounded in the distance. Obviously one of them had tripped a silent alarm, something that Jack hadn't foreseen in his painstaking planning. Shopping centres in Essex didn't have silent alarms, surely. They had security guards and recycled fire alarms doubling as crime-prevention kits, but not silent alarms. Silent alarms meant lasers, and lasers meant sophistication, and that kind of destroyed the whole rough trade image that had lured the four of them there in the first place.

With his good arm Jack pulled a printout from his back pocket, and unfolded it. A rather more untarnished image of rough trade stared proudly back at him. 'Adam . . .' he said sadly, and promptly passed out from the pain.

Someone stepped over him, a shadow that gave a shrug of the shoulders, a cockney accent.

'Sorry, Jack,' someone said, 'but a lad doesn't wait thirty-seven years and then end up with a bitter old queen like you.'

'Jack & the Lad' is an extract from the novel of the same title

MISFIRE

CATHY WASSON

WHEN I WENT HUNTING WITH DADDY TWO WEEKS AGO, HE shot the truck. It was Saturday, the last day of deer season. Daddy had called earlier that week and said, 'Come go with me.' I figured it was on account of Bob, my sister's husband. Bob and his son Junior have been on us to go and I guess Daddy finally gave in. Daddy doesn't hunt much any more and I can count on one hand how many times I've been, but Bob goes most weekends, trawling a strip of forest Daddy owns on the other side of town. Bob says Daddy's land is eat up with deer but I've never seen one. As far as I know, Daddy hasn't shot one, but Bob got one last year and the year before that.

Daddy and I left early, the sun just coming up when we got to the field. Daddy had cleared that patch years ago and we ploughed it up every spring to plant corn and potatoes. Now it's hard and rutted and covered in yellow grass a foot high. Bob and Junior were already there, waiting beside their truck. Daddy pulled off the road and we rode towards them, bumping up and down across the field.

'Afternoon!' Bob shouted when we got out. He had a crooked grin on his face and made a point of checking his watch. He's ten years older than my sister but doesn't look it, with a wide, soft face and loose blond hair he lets fall in his eyes. When they got married two years ago, Bob asked me to be best man; he doesn't have many friends.

Leaning against his truck, Bob drank from a thermos, his cheeks red and full. The frosty air stung our skin and cold seeped up from the ground through our boots.

Junior rubbed his hands together and took his rifle from the truck. He's Bob's son from his first marriage.

'What you got there, bud?' Daddy asked him, knowing Bob had given him a new scope for his birthday the week before, when he turned fifteen.

'It's a Bushnell 3200.' He grinned, handing the rifle to Daddy. 'Forty-four millimetre.' He's scrawny, with a bony face and eyes too big for his head. 'You can pick a fly off a leaf at a hundred yards with that!' Bob had told us he'd given Junior his first rifle when he turned seven, though he had pellet guns before that. We all did.

Daddy held the scope to his eye and aimed toward the trees. 'Yeah,' he said. 'That's all right,' and passed it to me. Junior bounced on his toes while I cradled the butt against my shoulder. I held it there for a long time, picking out knots on tree trunks knowing he couldn't wait for me to hand it back.

'Let me see it,' he said.

'That's nice,' I said and handed it back to him. Bob has always given Junior the top of the line in everything – clothes, electronics – it doesn't matter, he gets what he wants. When I was his age I worked part-time at Texas Pete's flipping burgers and scrubbing down the grill. I don't know what Junior does. He was asking me about paintball.

'What kind of gun you got?' he said, his jaw trembling. I imagined he was cold. Daddy says he doesn't have an ounce of fat on him; he's all skin and bones. He wore a big camouflage jacket with so much stuff in the pockets it looked like he was carrying rocks.

'Tippman A-5,' I said, putting on my gloves.

Junior wet his lips. 'Is it standard or has it got the response trigger? How much you give for it?'

I didn't have time to answer before Bob was talking to me.

'How about taking Junior with you next time you go?'

'You got to be eighteen,' I said, breathing out like I was smoking.

'Hell, that's a load of bull,' Bob said, folding his arms across his chest and smiling at Daddy. 'We know better than that, don't we, Will?'

'I don't know,' Daddy said. Daddy's never cared much for Bob, though he wouldn't say so. Bob and my sister met one day right after he moved to town, when he was working as a mechanic across the street from her beauty salon, A Cut Above. When she finished work that day, her car wouldn't start. So after trying for a while, she went to the garage where Bob worked. She said he'd been standing there the whole time, watching her and smiling. He said they could hear her all the way from here to Buck's county, flooding the engine. After that he called her 'Leadfoot'.

'They're real strict,' I told them. The air was filled with the smell of wood smoke and dead, wet leaves.

Junior was quiet. He shifted his weight back and forth between his legs.

'I'll bet they'll take him if a grown-up goes with him. You could sign for him,' Bob told me.

I didn't answer.

'When you going next?' he asked me.

'We're talking about going in two weeks,' I said, 'the Saturday after Thanksgiving.' I turned to Daddy. 'But I don't know for sure.' The boys I go with I've known since high school. Of the four of us, I'm the only one who's married. We don't go that often any more; my wife thinks it's childish and two of the others go to state college, a couple of hours away. We'd been planning since September to go Thanksgiving weekend and I knew they wouldn't like me bringing a kid along.

Daddy kicked the tyre of his truck and asked Bob where they were headed. My guess was that we'd split up; they'd go in the woods one way and Daddy and I would go another. Daddy's tall, with wide shoulders and a thick chest like those wrestlers on TV. His face and arms are brown from the sun, but the rest of him is as white as a sheet. I favour him in the face, and I got his black hair, but I'm a head shorter and probably weigh half what he does.

Bob pointed to the trees, explaining where they'd built their stands. Then we all went to take a leak and get our guns.

Daddy told them, 'Go ahead. I'm going to go get warm in the truck first.'

'Me too,' I said and got in. Daddy turned the heat on full blast. We watched Bob and Junior high-step through the grass towards the woods, their rifles pointing to the ground.

'I'll let them get in there first,' Daddy said. 'I don't care if I get a deer or not.'

I didn't much care either. I'd like to be known to have killed a deer, have its rack hanging in our trailer, but I wasn't sure I could shoot one. What if I hit him and he ran off? Or went down but didn't die? Would I have to shoot him again?

'You thinking about going back to school?' Daddy said. The orange vests disappeared through the trees.

I nodded. My feet were cold.

'You only got two courses left,' he said. 'Now would be the best time, before y'all start having kids.'

He was looking at me, I could tell, but I stared out the windshield and didn't say anything. Before we left, my wife had taken one of those at-home pregnancy tests. Two blue lines had appeared in the window – pregnant.

'It'll be hard, I know,' he said, 'with you working. But you can do it.' Bob and Junior were out of sight. The sun had come up and golden light bounced off the field. 'There are harder things,' he said.

When we were little Daddy worked two jobs – swinging shifts at the glass plant and laying brick in between. Nowadays he drives a dozer for the vermiculite mine.

'You got it easy now,' I kidded him, 'sitting around all day.'

He smiled and cut the engine. 'It's easy all right.'

Waiting in the cab had knocked off the chill but my foot had gone to sleep. I started to shake the feeling back into it, not in any hurry to get to the woods. The thought crossed my mind that one of them might shoot us by mistake. I remembered Bob's thermos, how there wasn't any steam coming off of it. I would have just as soon gone back home, but we were already there; we couldn't turn around without waiting a couple of hours. We probably wouldn't even see a deer.

Paintball's better. You see the target; you get lots of good shots at them. Usually you get more than a few hits; it's a blast. The balls are the expensive part, that and the gun. But once you've got the gun, all you need are the balls. I got mine second hand – my gun I mean. It's one of the best, though they make better ones nowadays.

Daddy said he was just gonna load his rifle. He has a 35 Remington, with a six-bullet magazine. He opened the box of twenty beside him and started to slide them in. They're bronze with a lead tip. I heard the last one lock in place then POW YOW! The ringing in my ears was so loud, I thought for a second I'd lost my hearing, wondering, was my foot shot? I couldn't feel my leg; I looked down; I didn't see any blood. I looked at Daddy and he was sitting still, all white in his face. I looked at him all over, for blood, in case I hadn't seen it before because he still wasn't moving.

'Good God!' he finally said. Then we heard the hissing sound. We looked at one another and I could tell what he was thinking. We jumped out of the truck real quick and, for some reason, ran far away from it, though that was stupid because we both realized if it'd hit the tank, it would have blown us up instantly. I saw the truck sag a little to one side but I didn't know what it was, so I walked way out around it to Daddy's side and saw what he was looking at. The bullet must have gone through the floorboard and hit the tyre. It was going flat. 'Shit,' Daddy said.

I died laughing. 'Daddy, you shot your truck!' Daddy laughed too. We were both laughing and shaking. Daddy found the jack and we started to change the tyre.

'Bob and Junior won't ever let us hear the end of this,' I said, handing him the lug wrench.

'You're right about that,' he said.

Then last week, my wife and I came home to find Daddy's truck parked in front of our place, him sitting behind the wheel. We live in one of the nicer trailer parks in town, though we don't plan on being there long – we're saving to build. We pulled up beside him and I walked over but he didn't open the door or get out. That's when I knew something was wrong.

'How 'bout riding with me over to pick up your sister's car?' he said. He didn't say where it was. I got in and he backed all the way down the drive and into the road.

I said, 'Where we going?'

But he didn't answer. His right arm lay across the wheel and he steered with his wrist. At the railroad tracks we waited on a train with two engines. He said he'd had to pick my sister up from the sheriff's office and leave her car there, because she was afraid she wouldn't be able to drive herself home.

'What happened?'

'She called and said "Junior's been in an accident",' he said, drawing out the last word. 'He didn't get hurt. Your sister was with them at the sheriff's office but Bob and Junior had to stay behind and answer questions.'

'What kind of accident?' The first red light in town stopped us. We sat there, the only car at the intersection, waiting for the light to turn green.

Daddy stared straight ahead and didn't say anything. The town was dead; there weren't any other cars, just one stopped for gas at Speedy's. The next light caught us and we waited to turn left. Daddy put on his signal and let it click on and off. We watched an old man on a moped sputter by, a milk crate strapped to the back. By the time we got to the sheriff's office, I'd managed to get three sentences out of Daddy, but I knew better than to ask for more.

My sister's old Maverick smelled of stale cigarettes, and the roof lining that had come loose long ago was still hanging down, brushing my hair every time I turned my head. I cursed Bob for not having fixed it.

Their house was dark except for a light on in the back. We knocked and knocked but couldn't get anybody to the door. I told Daddy to ring the doorbell, that maybe they didn't hear us. He knocked again. Every now and then a car passed. I was fixing to go around to the back when Bob's voice came through the door: *who is it?*

'It's us,' Daddy said. 'We brought the car back.'

The deadbolt turned and Bob appeared in the doorway. His collar was standing up and his hair was all over the place. I asked if we'd woken him up and he shook his head and said no.

'But it's late,' he said, stepping aside, 'they're both sleeping.' We waited while he locked the door then followed him through the house to the kitchen. It's one of those eat-in kitchens with a dining area off to the side. Daddy took off his coat and sat down. I did too. It was hot. Bob told us the heater was busted; he couldn't get it to shut off. He said he'd have to look at it tomorrow. He pointed to the table and a glass of melting ice and said, 'Either one of you want something to drink?'

We shook our heads and said no thank you.

'She's better,' Bob said. 'They're both doing fine.'

'That's good,' Daddy said. 'You want to tell us what happened?'

Bob took a clean glass and dropped in a handful of ice from the refrigerator. From over the cabinet he brought down a bottle of whisky and filled his glass. He put on the top and set the bottle back. It was nearly empty. When he crossed the room he raised the glass to his lips. 'What you want to know?' he said, sitting down.

'How it happened.' Daddy slumped in his chair and picked at some dead skin around his fingernail.

Bob let out a long breath. He raised his head to the ceiling and clasped his hands in front of him. 'This morning Junior asked if he could have a friend over,' he started. 'I've met the boy before and he's a good boy. He wasn't one of those who got expelled with Junior that time. He came over around two and they watched TV and played video games. I left to go pick up some brackets and when I got back, they were still inside, sitting in front of the TV. I said, "You ought to be outside doing something. It's a beautiful day." They got up and said they wanted to shoot targets.'

Bob has a log set up in the field where they do target practice.

'I helped them gather up some cans and let Junior use my rifle so they each would have one. I heard them down there shooting.' Bob took a long drink from his glass. 'A little while later, Junior came up and asked if he could show the boy my gun.' Bob's got a 357 Magnum. Daddy and I looked at one another. 'He's shot it before,' he said, taking another drink.

A click, click, click sound came from the wall. Mounted over the buffet was a small grandfather-style clock with little gold chains and a brass pendulum that swung from side to side.

'You keep it locked up?' Daddy asked him.

Bob shook his head. 'It wouldn't have mattered if I did. I was the one that let them have it.'

Daddy nodded. He took out his pocket knife and cleaned the dirt under his nails.

'Well,' Bob said, pinching the bridge of his nose, 'Junior took it and a box of bullets down with him to the field. I thought about going with him, I did. I don't know why I didn't. Guess I just thought they were big enough, you know?' He drained his glass and set it down. Reaching to the counter, he grabbed a pack of cigarettes and lit one.

'I walked around outside for a bit,' he said, 'listening. I heard the first shot and just stopped and waited. Then I heard another one. Everything seemed OK. Still,' he said, 'I wanted to be outside, so I thought I'd wash my car. I walked in the house and, as I was coming through the door, I heard the gun go off again. I got the bucket, squirted some soap in the bottom, set it in the sink and turned on the hot water. That's when I looked up. Out the window I saw Junior coming. He had the boy in his arms, stumbling up the hill, his knees buckling under him. All I could see was that they were bleeding.' Bob blew smoke across the table.

'I ran. I ran out there. Junior dropped to the ground when I reached them. He fell over on top of him. I thought they both were shot. I couldn't tell. I pushed Junior off of him.' Bob's chin started to quiver. 'Then I saw.' Bob put one hand to his face and covered his eyes. Red hairs curled off the backs of his fingers. He lowered his hand then thumped off ashes in the ashtray I'd fetched. He took another drag then crushed it out.

'Junior was trying to say something, but I couldn't tell,' he continued.

'What do you think it was?' Daddy asked.

'He said, "The gun went off. He was handing it to me and it went off."'

'What did you do?' I asked him.

'I yanked off my shirt and wadded it up and laid it on his chest. It . . .' He shook his head. 'It . . . I didn't know what to do, if I should press it, or . . . if . . . I held it there and pushed just a little, but the blood . . . I yelled at Junior to run. "Run!" I said. "Run! Get help!" He jumped up and ran to the house. I don't know how hard I was pressing or if that was the right thing to do. I didn't know. I looked at him, at his head. It was . . . it was . . . I moved it back a little so his neck would lay straight. His eyes were open . . . and his mouth. The shirt . . . the shirt was wet. I tried to . . .' Bob put his face in his hands. 'But he wasn't . . . he wasn't . . . his heart wasn't beating. The blood wasn't pumping. It was just . . . He wasn't breathing.'

Daddy put his elbows on his knees and leaned over. He let his head hang down and roll from side to side.

Bob uncovered his face. His eyes were fixed on the floor. The skin under one eye quivered.

'What happened then?' Daddy's voice was dry and even.

'Junior called out, "They're on their way." That's when I lost it. I just lost it. I couldn't get up. I couldn't move from where I had him, so I just shouted. I just yelled at him. I couldn't stop. I yelled and yelled.' Bob reached for the glass but it was empty. Just ice left.

We all sat there; nobody said anything.

'I shouted at him. I couldn't help it,' he said.

'What did you say?' I asked him.

Bob turned his eyes to me. 'I don't know what I said. I don't want to know.' He looked down and pressed his lips together to stop the tremor in his chin. 'He didn't say anything,' he mumbled. 'He just stood there. He just stood there and took it.' Bob rubbed his face and said, 'He didn't mean to . . . it wasn't . . . it was just that . . .' He took the glass and held it in his hand, rubbing its side with his thumb. 'I'd give anything to bring that boy back.'

Daddy sat up. 'Have you seen his folks?'

Bob shook his head.

'You got to see his folks,' Daddy said, his head tilted to one side. He stared at Bob.

Bob shook his head. 'They don't want to see me,' he whispered.

Slowly Daddy said, 'You have to see his folks.'

Bob took a deep breath and looked at Daddy. 'I don't have to.' His eyes glistened.

The clock clicked from the wall and the two men stared at one another.

Daddy said, 'Their boy's dead.'

Finally Bob said, 'I know what you're saying,' his head bobbing up and down. 'I know exactly what you're saying. But it's not like that. It was an accident. And if anybody's to blame, it's not him. Because *my* boy . . .' he said, lifting his arm and pointing to the hall, '*my* boy . . .'

All at once we looked in the direction he pointed: Junior stood in the doorway, wearing boxer shorts and a T-shirt. Wiry muscles ran up and down his arms and legs. One hand was on his hip and one foot rested on top of the other. His eyes glowed at Bob.

'You all right?' Daddy asked him.

He didn't look at Daddy. 'That's what *you* think,' he said, scowling at his father.

Bob lowered his head and said, 'No. No, I don't.'

'Yes you do. You think it's my fault *too*.'

Bob stood up and said softly, 'Come sit down.'

Junior turned on his heel and disappeared down the hall. Bob flopped back down in his chair.

Daddy got up and walked to the sink and ran himself a glass of water from the tap. He stood there and drank it, looking out the window.

Bob had a finger in his glass and swirled the ice round and round. He took it out and wiped it on the leg of his pants. 'You know,' he said, 'it could've been me.' He turned to me. 'It could've been you.' He raised his voice until it filled the room. 'It could've been any one of us, right here.' He cut his eyes towards Daddy. 'You know that, don't you?'

Daddy walked back to the table and motioned for me to get up.

'We're going to go, let you get some rest,' he said. 'We'll talk later.'

I followed Daddy down the hall. From the doorway we could hear Bob.

'He carried him back, you know. He carried him all the way back to the house.'

Bob and Junior didn't go to Daddy's for Thanksgiving. My sister came, but didn't stay long. Then yesterday, Saturday morning, the phone rang. We had just finished breakfast and were still in our pyjamas. I picked it up to hear somebody say: 'I'm not going to be able to go play paintball today.' For a minute I couldn't think of who it was. He said, 'Chuck?'

Junior. It was Junior. I had to think of what he was saying. For a second I thought I had forgotten to do something or that I was supposed to be somewhere else. Then I remembered. We had talked about it the day we went hunting. I held the phone to my ear and thought for a second. He asked if I'd heard him.

'Yeah,' I said. 'OK.'

COOKED

HEIDI AMSINCK

OTTO KAISER, MY MENTOR, SIXTEEN YEARS DEAD, STANDS IN THE doorway of the kitchen, as bright and alive as if he's just walked in from his morning constitutional.

It's not a good time. We're fighting fire, high on adrenalin and with the smell of burning flesh stinging in our nostrils. The runners keep filing through with their empty trays, ready to carry plates of food upstairs to Basilic's waiting diners. My team has been cooking for one and a half hours flat. They spent the whole afternoon prepping vegetables, meat, fish, sauces and garnishes, after which we shared some pasta, bread, tomatoes and olives around a couple of tables in the back of the dining room. Contrary to popular belief, chefs do not eat well themselves; the frugal meal sticks in my gullet. Besides, I have something on my mind: Jenny Silver, a food critic for one of the Sundays, is in the restaurant tonight. Recently, she wrote something which has ruined my concentration, disturbed my sleep and made me even more foul-tempered than usual.

I close my eyes, but when I open them again, Otto is still there. I know this should not be happening. Otto passed away in 1988 after a massive heart attack. His funeral was the last time I visited Denmark.

I try to concentrate on the work in hand: plating the salted duck with the orange and ginger sauce and caramelized endive. It is my favourite dish on the menu because it is the most beautiful, the colour of naked skin and sunsets and seashells freshly washed onto the beach. The duck rests perfectly blushed on its pond of golden sauce, and the aroma steaming off the plate brings to mind the mouth-watering bitter-sweet flavour of the meat.

But it is no good. How can you ignore a dead man staring at you across the room?

I'm supposed to be in charge. This means that, apart from a little work on presentation as with the duck, I don't do any actual cooking; rather I keep everyone on their toes and check that each dish that goes out to the dining room has a quality I am happy to lend my name to. So far this evening I have sent back two dishes: a truffle and Parmesan-crusted turbot because it was too cold and a fillet of Highland beef, because it wasn't rare enough. The cooks responsible have been castigated and the atmosphere in my kitchen is now sufficiently scary to ensure a smooth running of things for the rest of the evening. I have just about been holding everything together, until now. Otto's appearance throws me off track, which is no good, no good at all. Not tonight when that bitch Jenny Silver is waiting in the dining room, looking to find fault.

Yet things start going wrong, fast. Restaurant kitchens are small spaces: when chefs work they have to become a single, multi-limbed organism, relying on adroitness and telepathy in equal measure to stay out of each other's way. Getting it wrong can mean being scalded, knifed, burnt, drenched or pinched and I am getting it wrong now: a pan of scallops lands on the floor, splattering hot fat across my legs, when an unfortunate Spanish trainee chef crosses my blind path.

'Get a fucking grip, butterfingers, or you can piss off back to Barcelona,' I spit, pointlessly wiping grease off my whites.

'*Oui*, chef,' the Spaniard replies, smartish, as he bends down to pick up the pan and its contents.

'You dunce,' I say, standing over him.

But my weakening grip on reality is becoming a problem. A restaurant kitchen works only on a clear line of command. The minute the juniors start questioning chef's behaviour – and I sense the Spaniard looking quizzically at me now – order disintegrates with anarchy and disaster the predictable outcome. Vince, my sous-chef, who knows me better than most, senses that something is up and steps silently into my place. He is both competent and dependable, good enough to be running his own kitchen. Perhaps I have been selfish and kept him too long. I know that he has started to resent my superiority over him, and a couple of times lately I have caught him going over one of my plates when he thinks I am not looking. I watch him now, as he bends keenly under the hot lamps, poking at the plated food like a surgeon at the operating table.

Then I feel something behind me, and turn to find that Otto has traversed the room in a split second. Guilt, mixed with terror, washes over me. I am a boy chef again, trembling before my master's wrath.

Otto is dressed for work in his chef's jacket with 'Kaiser' stitched over his heart. A long, pristinely white apron reaches the knees of his black and white check trousers. A rag hangs from his waistband with the pincers he used for frying pieces of meat and fish, when not substituting his cut and calloused fingers. My mentor was a man of stature who when wearing his chef's whites seemed to attain an imposing one and a half human size. He hardly ever raised his voice; there was no need, as all the cooks, myself included, feared him more than their own deaths. From being dragged at regular intervals across the great gas stoves in the kitchen, his arms were permanently singed free of hair, leaving the skin as ruddy and leathery as a pig's arse. Sweat was always streaming off him and running into his eyes and moustache, and he had to wipe his face at regular intervals with the back of his trotter-like hands.

My kitchen is so hot that the cooks sometimes go to cool down in the walk-in fridge. Yet Otto's hand feels like a block of ice on my shoulder. His lips are as blue as herring fillets.

Otto once had me cook a Sauce Espagnole nineteen times before he was satisfied. This took the better part of a fortnight as each version of the sauce required several hours of simmering, skimming and straining. I would start in the classic way making a brown roux to which I added a mirepoix of very finely chopped celery, carrot and onion, some mushroom trimmings and chopped tomatoes and finally the brown stock that was made fresh every day in Møllergården's kitchen. The first batch was dismissed by Otto as 'snuff spit'. After the third and fourth had been similarly written off, I considered jacking in the chef's profession altogether.

'It's nothing to me whether you stay or go,' Otto said, not lifting his eyes from the evening paper.

After the fifth batch, described by Otto as 'horse diarrhoea', something new inside me took over, something I didn't know I had. More than a wish to prove myself to Otto, it was stubbornness, a yearning to take control. Night after night I stayed in the kitchen, watching over my stock and even sleeping on the floor next to the stove. It wasn't a simple matter of following a recipe, I soon learnt. It was about using one's intuition to make subtle changes along the way, until the flavour of the browned meat and vegetables was invested into each molecule. Otto ignored me. Batch number fifteen received the note 'Average'. When I got it right, he withheld his praise. 'Now go and do that again tomorrow,' was all he said.

No one cooks Espagnole anymore. It is considered old-fashioned.

I shade my eyes against the apparition beside me.

'What?' he says, his voice booming in his great barrel chest. 'You don't recognize me now? What the hell has happened to you, boy?'

No one but me appears able to see Otto. All the chefs de partie are busy; they are not looking at us. Neither is Vince, who is shouting at them, his voice resounding between the stainless steel cookers. The young cooks are keeping their skull-capped heads down, bending over the pots and pans like old men. I consider poking a finger into Otto's gut to see if he is real, but think better of it: he wasn't the sort of person you messed around with.

'What's the matter? Cat got your tongue?'

'I . . . I don't know what you mean,' I stammer. The Danish words emerge, rusty, from deep within my memory. I must have spoken them out loud, because Vince is frowning at me. The Frenchman has straightened up and is wiping his brow. 'Hey, Adam. Who are you talking to?' He touches my arm. 'What is it?'

I flinch. 'It's nothing. Nothing, OK?' I rub my face with my hands and shake my head vigorously to snap out of the strange spell that has come over me. Then one of the boys comes up to Vince to ask him something and I'm off the hook, though not with Otto. The big man folds his arms on top of his massive bulk and tuts, slowly shaking his head.

'Look at you, son,' he says. 'Kitchen is a shambles. You've got your sous-chef wondering if his boss has lost his senses. He'll be thinking his boat's come in, if you don't start pulling your rank on him and pronto. Look, they're laughing at you, boy.' He nods in the direction of a couple of the juniors sharing a joke. I feel my cheeks start to burn as I storm over to them. 'Fucking concentrate on your work. Couple of wankers,' I thunder down their necks. 'Can you hear me?'

'*Oui*, chef,' they reply in unison.

'That's it,' says Otto, beside me. 'That will do.'

I am filled with anger and confusion. Otto is right that things have been slipping somewhat of late, but none of it is my fault. It's that woman, Jenny Silver, and the niggling, snide comments in that column of hers. If not for those, I would have been just fine. 'They are out to get me, Otto,' I say. 'They are waiting for me to fail, to lose my Michelin stars.'

We walk through the kitchen, past the various cooking stations: hot starters, sauce, meat, fish, larder, pastry. There are bits of food on the floor, splurges of sauce. I notice a cherry tomato that has split open, like a heart.

Basilic's kitchen is in the windowless basement of the building. The ground floor is reached via a peeling back staircase. Otto and I walk up the stairs and stand behind the windowed double doors to the restaurant. I press my nose against the glass. The customers, mostly dark-suited men, are seated to attention on high-backed wooden chairs at round tables decked to the floor in thick white damask. At the centre of each table a small candle, flickering inside a crystal ball, casts a ghostly light over the scenes of culinary worship. There's a muted calm in the room, in stark contrast to the roaring furnace of the kitchen below.

Quickly I find the person whose poisoned pen has robbed me of my peace. Jenny Silver is seated at the other end of the room with her back to the floor-to-ceiling frosted window that screens the diners from the street. She is wearing a black silk shirt and around her neck a short string of bright red pearls, as though her head has been severed from her body. (I wish it had.) Suitably, for someone with her name, Jenny

Silver's shoulder-length hair is as white as snow, though, like me, she is barely out of her thirties. She is studying the menu; Raoul, the greying Egyptian head waiter, is bent over her, servile and nodding.

A few minutes later the door swings open with great force and Raoul barges through, almost knocking me off my feet. Raoul likes nothing more than intrigue: he will locate and exploit any weakness in a matter of seconds and is obviously amused by my state of distress.

'Jeez, Addie, didn't see you there,' he says, stepping back theatrically. It's clear that he can't see Otto either.

'That Miss Silver's not a happy bunny, is she? Jeez,' Raoul says, waving his order pad and drawing one nicotine-stained finger across his throat. 'She actually wanted to know if the scallops were fresh. She thinks we use frozen? Jeez.' Raoul laughs heartily, showing all of his yellowed teeth. But his mirth evaporates when he sees my expression and he backs off, mouthing and gesturing to one of the other waiters. 'What the hell is the matter with him?'

The scallops become the final straw. Jenny Silver's question, recounted by Raoul, finally detaches me from sanity, and months of too little sleep and too many amphetamines send me into a professional tailspin that will change the course of my future. When I wrench myself free of Otto's freezing grasp I have only one thing on my mind to say to Jenny Silver and damn her and anyone who dares to stand in my way: 'You want me to give my all? Well, here you are.'

I walk back down to the kitchen, my stride full of purpose. Vince is there. 'Ah, Adam. Nice to see you. Would you . . .' He starts towards me, but I brush him aside with a sweep of my hand.

'Hold Miss Silver's starter!' I shout as I grab a plate and head for the walk-in fridge and close the door. I feel inspired; something beautiful is happening to me. On my way back towards the dining room I pick up one of the domed silver lids with the gold ball handles that we use for serving and walk ceremoniously with the plate held up high. The young cooks stop what they are doing. Vince waves his hands in the air and says something, but I cannot be stopped now; each of my steps is predestined. I am pulled as if by gravity into my own fall. Only a sideways glance at Otto who is still standing by the double doors to the dining room makes me doubt myself just a little. He is shaking his head again and looking glum.

'You don't want to do that, son,' he says. 'You'll be sorry' is the last thing I hear the old chef say as I step over the threshold and out of the only life I know.

Jenny Silver's table has by now been set up for her starter, the damask neatly swept by Raoul and her glass filled. She meets my eyes as I place the plate in front of her.

'Miss Silver.'

'Mr Sand,' she says, almost regretfully.

I slowly remove the lid. It is a credit to the woman that she doesn't scream or create a scene, but merely sits there looking at her plate and the perfectly rounded human turd in its centre.

'I made it for you specially,' I say. Then I bow deeply and walk away backwards. I can just about hear one of the guests whispering 'Shit' behind his hand, which under different circumstances might have been funny.

Sometime later, perhaps hours, perhaps only a few seconds, I feel a pat on my shoulder and hear a voice that says: 'I think it's time you went home.'

'Cooked' is an extract from the novel *Cooking for Arabel*

FIRST

DUNCAN LAWRENCE

'GO SOUTH,' I TELL A NECK AND THINNING HAIR, AND WE'RE OFF. We rollercoaster down the avenue, the seat coughing as the cab bounces over the cross-streets. Ten minutes later we've arrived, and I get the driver to circle the block twice before I step on to the cold street. I walk past what looks like an entrance then decide to take a brisk tour of the area with its faded lettering, forgotten pubs, windows smeared with torn posters, mud. The employees of a cab company watch me, their faces yellow then soapy white as the sign on their wall glares 'TAXIS & CAB CARS'. As I pass I hear the dull clicks of a cerise neon tube spelling out 'OPEN 24 – 7'.

Before long I'm back where I started, staring at the black entrance. Is this it? By the time I locate the door in the shadows, a dull studded affair that is quick and heavy, I am ready to stop my expedition and continue on home. My sexual drive dissolves as I pull open the door.

The lobby is worn and apologetic, my idea of an abortionist's cramped waiting room (damp magazines, wicker table). Before me sits the gatekeeper, snug behind his scratched plastic barrier, long grey hair sticking to his forehead like a lacquered wig; the man's fingers scuff the page of an exercise book with four inked columns. What am I doing here?

'Name,' he says.

'Jesus Pambal,' comes out of my mouth and I watch him hesitate then misspell the words; his pen continues erratically beyond the final letter, finishing with a dismal paraph.

'Thirty-five,' he says, pointing an elbow to a rate-sheet taped to the aqua wall. *30 single entrance + 5 deposit (refund when KEY IS RETURNED!!!) NO key = NO deposit. comeon guys lets work TOGETHER!!!!* He hands me two warm towels and a delicate key bound with a loop of elastic.

I kick into autopilot and watch myself removing my clothes in a corridor lined with gym lockers that smell of damp bread – no, musty cucumber. My hand grabs a towel, then locks the door and snaps the jangling key to my left wrist.

Beyond the locker area is an empty gym, the equipment old and incomplete. I walk past these forgotten weights and trudge up a flight of wooden stairs into a busy pool area. All the men are naked and wear white towels around their waists. As I watch I see an occasional hand reaching down to secure a moist knot.

I sit on the plastic ribs of a deckchair. My toes are fluffy and wet on the cool tiles. I stare at hazy images on a squat television bolted high above the row of men lounging against the opposite wall. My closest companion has a large hairless rectangular head, his skin florid with rash and heat. He removes his glasses and gives them a brisk rub with the corner of his towel. Nestling behind each ear is a thin imprint of a spectacle arm and some bristles he missed while shaving.

Three things: there appears to be a holding pattern around the pool – men circle and pass through an archway painted with too-ripe grapes into what must be the steam rooms and showers; most of the men are in their late twenties; none look at me.

I can sense that the man on my left is eager to start a conversation so I focus my attention on the reds and greens on the screen. He reaches across to touch me.

'No.' I rise, and then realize that he's merely steadying himself on my chair. I ignore him and walk past the unwholesome pool, then through the archway and down a wide passage lined with dripping opaque doors. A door on my right opens and an elderly man steps out, his broiled skin hanging from his back and legs. The skin on his gawping face pulls down from his eyes, leaving the exposed flesh tender and steaky. Disorientated, he steps towards me with a bald calf, then turns to the showers at the end of the passage and stumbles away, his heavy towel slapping against his arse. I follow him to the noise of the showers and watch as he manoeuvres past their younger occupants. He secures a dripping nozzle and hits out at the two pressure valves. I leave him soaping up behind me.

All the thinking I've done about this place is sexier than actually being here. I noticed the ads in the city's gay rags, groups of Adonises fresh from the gym, flash smiles, welcoming eyes. The truth is that these places thrive on youth and rejection. This promise of youth makes me feel unsexy and fat. Rejected, unsexy, *old* and fat.

The steam room door bangs closed behind me, and when my eyes become accustomed to the medicinal haze I can make out shapes of men sitting against the walls, their legs snug against each another. Even here most of the towels appear to be firmly bound about waists. The atmosphere is of restrained primness, decadent little convent girls waiting for their turn on the dance-floor. We all watch each other; there are a few glances in my direction but my boring search for a place to sit soon loses my audience. I manage to encourage some men to make space near the door.

There are a few whispers, but for the most part everyone just sits and waits. Nothing happens. I thought gay men were fabulous, horny bastards. More nothing happens. The smallest bit of movement seems to create excitement. We are on the lookout for a lethargic wrist or an extravagantly rearranged towel. The amount of activity appears to be inversely proportional to the age and beauty of the mover: the young and pretty remain motionless, bored with the attention; the older trolls are spry and willing to flash and fondle.

I'm shivering in the breeze from that fucking door which is being propped open by a party of whispering teenagers. A few of my fellow observers jump up to investigate; some return, some leave the room. In walks my red-faced companion from the pool and he insists on squeezing in next to me, his leg pulling against mine.

I look at the men around me. Lichen stains grow across the grout. The vent pumps out a dull cloud of steam and hot spluttering water. I feel my companion pressing against my thigh.

'No,' I mutter, refusing to look at him.

No reply. His severed hand floats into view, all slippery fingers and strong ivory nails tripping on the ceramic. He holds his hand above the tips of his fingers. It looks like a little person walking across the tiles toward me, index and middle fingers taking a stroll. The fingers continue to march the hand beside my leg before one points to the steam room door, towards the glassy pruinose barrier. I shake my head. Then the hand twists and the thumb produces a sachet of thickly foiled condom which he rocks between his fingers.

Action in the corner. One young man crouches before another, some observers scrum around and after a few minutes I give up trying to look through this circle of men. I'm yawning. Time to leave.

'Stay and watch,' I say as I pass my companion. 'More fun than me.'

'Oh, you can be fun.'

'No. Stay and watch.'

The showers are not much warmer, and after a quick visit to the remaining steam rooms I spend a few minutes in a sauna watching a dusky child sleeping in the dry heat. The towel clings to my legs and my eyes burn. There are no clocks in this Bates' motel whorehouse, though I can't have been here for more than an hour. No one gives me so much as a second glance. Even the pretty boys with feet dangling in the pool don't seem to get any attention. Everyone waits for someone else to make the first move.

I have to get out of here. This was a mistake. I return to the stairs and then find myself walking up to the next floor, away from the lockers, further away from the exit.

At the top of the landing is a dark corridor with yet more doors, perhaps a dozen or so, all leading off to the fuck rooms. I step into an empty room and take in the dusty light-bulb, the taut plastic sheeting pulled over the worn foam mattress. On my way back to the corridor I accidentally kick a grey roll of toilet paper placed on the floor. Most of the rooms are occupied. I feel an adrenal kick as I think about the flaccid bodies, chests thick with hair, legs, arms scarred by the folds of the Kevlar sheeting. From behind the closed doors I'm only able to make out the noise of standard, buff Hollywood porn. I pass a few men in the corridor who are all too serious, too focused.

I feel I'm doing it again. When I should simply draw a line from A through B, lay out the puzzle and wrap it up with a swift conclusion, I find myself snagging on the details. Instead of presenting the events and letting the story get on with itself I'm focusing on toes, dribbled water and hairline cracks. I suppose it's because I know that once I'm past this *foreplay* description of my unconsummated night out with the boys I'll have to get on with the real story. I have to try and deal with Henry and Delores First, my truth and their lies.

From the pool area below me I hear a dropped glass smash on the tiles. As I look down at my bare feet the gentle throb of my heartbeat grows in my ears. Time to leave this passage with its flimsy wooden doors and gentle black bolts.

I head for the stairway (perhaps I'll stop off for another quick walk around the soupy pool!) when a door is pulled open and out steps Jesus Pambal. The real Jesus Pambal. The Jesus Pambal I work with. The Jesus Pambal whose name I've stolen. He's still looking into the room, saying something over his shoulder. I wait for him to turn, wait for him to look up at me, wait to be recognized. Instead his conversation continues and I somehow manage to hurry past him down the stairs. As I cross the first landing I catch sight of a man stranded in the centre of a misshapen pool of blood – homosexual *en meurette*. He lifts his foot, the underside sliced by glass lying shattered on the tiles. And at the edge of this inky blood an attendant motions for him to remain still, waving both hands as if shooing away chickens. I turn the corner cutting off this tableau and run down the remaining stairs to the lockers.

Here I change quickly, my legs and crotch difficult and wet as I pull on my trousers. Twice I step on the saturated towel with my sock.

I perspire in the early morning as I head for the cab-hire company around the corner. For once the streets are empty. The office is open though unable to supply any cars.

'Yes, next time I'll book,' I say as I step back on to the street. I need to head south towards the arched lights reflecting off the river.

'First' is an extract from the novel *Henry First*

JOHNNY & LULA

ALESSANDRA SARTORE

A N INTAKE OF BREATH LATER I GASP, 'DON'T KNOW WHEN I LAST hoovered the carpet on the stairs . . . but I should do it very soon.'

'What are you talking about?' says Jeremy, taking his jacket off and letting it drop, a thud as his mobile phone hits the red-varnished floorboards.

'Didn't you notice I was a bit unresponsive when you were fucking me from behind? I had to keep my mouth shut so I wouldn't choke on the dust balls. You had my face pushed right into the steps. They are filthy.'

He laughs heartily. 'Sorry, sweetheart, I had no idea.'

I give him a mock *duh* look. 'You didn't notice I didn't grab you much? Like when you stuck your dick in my mouth I didn't use my hand? I took my chewing gum out but I couldn't think of where to put it. I was trying to reach the wall but you didn't let me – bit gross I know.'

His face creases into a wider smile. 'Ingrid, remind me to book an appointment next time you want a surprise fuck, so you can sort all these little things out.'

'Oh gosh no, it's not like that, but I heard this story recently. Friend of mine's boyfriend got chewing gum tangled into his pubic hair. I tell you it wasn't pleasant.'

'She had it in her mouth? Trashy girl . . .'

'No, I mean she did, but it got lost in the bed and he woke up thinking, "Christ, what's this?"'

'Oh come on,' says Jeremy, smoothing down his shirt.

'No, it's true, they were both crying with laughter when they told me, and you know the best part? They weren't even together that long when it happened. I think it's a good sign. That relationship will last, I tell you.'

'God, some of your friends are mad.'

'They're not mad, and she's a lawyer!' I say, on the defensive.

I throw my coat on the nearest chair and as I turn to open the fridge he grabs me by the hips and pulls me to him.

'Hey, wait, can't we open a bottle of wine first?'

'No, I want you over here,' he says, playfully twisting one of my arms behind my back.

He positions me in front of the large mirror in the living room, pulls my skirt up and in one smooth movement hooks his hand inside my tights and knickers. In two yanks they are down around my ankles. I don't think this is a very attractive look, so I reach down and remove them completely.

'I should have worn hold ups. Sorry I had no time, but managed at least to change into a short skirt. Do you like it?'

Running his hand over the fabric he says, 'Yes, I do, especially the feel of it. What is it?'

'Satin I believe. You should have seen me with the teenagers in Top Shop where I bought it. Felt a bit of a fraud and even thought the music was too loud. Me!'

Jeremy's not listening. Swiftly hitching me up on his hips he slides me over his hard cock. I let out a quick scream and he freezes for a second.

'Am I hurting you?' he asks, concerned.

'No, no, but the curtains are open.'

'Oh leave them,' he says, resuming his pushing. I know he can't keep this position up for long, but I appreciate he's trying and it's so pretty to watch.

'No, no, it's bad enough I nearly died when the light went off in the hall earlier. What would we have done if the neighbours had come in then?'

'Nothing, we'd have heard them turning keys in the door and stuff first.'

'You might have. I wouldn't. I was trying not to eat dust, remember? It's bad enough you grabbed me in the car earlier.'

'You shouldn't bend like that to get the shopping.'

'Back door doesn't open, and you put the stuff on the back seat,' I say feebly.

'Anyway, it's quiet around here,' he replies.

'Agreed, but it's only seven o'clock. There's people coming back from work.'

'Oh, Ingrid, stop it now.' He pulls out and dropping me on my knees thrusts his cock in my mouth again. I register that it tastes clean, a mixture of me, with just a faint hint of that body lotion he uses after the gym.

We catch each other both looking sideways at our reflections. I know he's thinking 'movies' – after all, I tell him often enough that he's nearly as big as that super-porn hero I like, the Italian one, Rocco. I am vain, too, but I think other movies, box office stuff. The light is dim and in this halfway position I sort of look like that woman in *Star Wars*, not the first one, the latest one, what's her name? Natalie Portman. I think of her as French but the name is not entirely. Jeremy looks good too. My mouth is sliding effortlessly up and down on his cock. His hair is still brown here, not grey like on his head and the forest on his chest. He has a hint of a tan, but maybe again it's the light. He didn't go with us to Formentera this year. I can still remember the argument we had and the kids got very upset. I felt like some sad divorcee and of course none of my single friends wanted to come with us – wouldn't have been much fun going to bed early and being all responsible. Mirelle likes her cocktails, so does Hannah, though now that she's pregnant perhaps not; Maxine was busy working. Oh never mind. He didn't come with us and we managed, end of story.

Jeremy lifts me up and turns me to face the table. Just as well I haven't set it yet as I'm soon holding the edges while he keeps fucking me. This is a good height for both of us. We are not going to come, not now I don't think. We are just finding out that our bodies are the same as the last time, that it feels good this way or that way. I try to kiss him – I always do – but he's not in that mood. I am not sure he ever was. I think of a much younger lover I had once. We used to kiss all the time. Maybe you don't kiss so much when you are older or just not so in love perhaps.

After a few last harder thrusts he pulls out. I move away. My heels gets caught in the cracks between the floorboards. 'Damn this floor. It drives me nuts.'

'Take your shoes off then. I know you don't like being short, but it's fine by me.'

'No, it rather ruins the outfit. Wait, I'll go find different ones and some hold-up stockings. Feel naked without them.' I return from the bedroom with an even higher, but less spiky pair.

I reach for the bags from Marks & Spencer and start opening packets and getting pans out of cupboards, but Jeremy says he's got us a surprise starter. And it is: paté de foie gras. In his excitement he's forgotten I don't eat meat. In my excitement I say I'll have some. Why the hell not? I was never a veggie for the sake of the animals, and if I were, this would be really the wrong sort of meat to eat. I allow myself a little, just in case a stomach upset by long-forgotten protein ends up ruining our evening. The wine he's brought to go with it has the consistency of an intoxicating liqueur. I wonder if I'll ever stop associating anything French with his ex-girlfriend. It was long ago, but moments later as if on cue he says, 'I've been talking to my dad and really, you know that spare cash I saved? Well, it can't buy much here – in fact, nothing in London and nothing much in Devon. I was thinking of northern France. What do you think?'

'Don't know, Jez, I think if you are planning to drive it's still a long way there and back, depends how often you'll do it.'

'Every couple of weeks, if I get the contract I want,' he says, savouring his baguette.

I am not sure I like France at all – Italy suits me better – but he does. I hold back criticizing his plan; it could take months to find the property and sort out the admin, so I beam him a smile and ask, 'Can we have dogs there?'

'Sure, why not? We can bring them back and forth now,' he answers in his best indulgent voice.

'But they'll be confused by the language and where do we keep them here? This flat's too small.'

'Let's start with just one dog. OK?'

'Fine, but we'll have to fight the kids for who gets to name him. If we are not careful we'll end up with something out of a Pokemon sticker pack.'

I turn away to get my starter. It's come out well too: Thai prawns on a bed of noodles, just a little as there's tuna steaks and vegetables and dessert – all easy. Dessert is one of my favourites, couldn't be simpler: slices of panettone dipped in brandy. Jeremy doesn't do coffee, which is an inconceivable flaw. Maybe that's why the French girl left him. I could have some, but it feels wrong. I could definitely do with a cigarette though, but those are totally out of bounds. He hates smokers, says watching his mother slowly die of emphysema was agony for him. I am not sure that has anything to do with me making an effort to give up; it's more likely those ads about prematurely ageing skin speak to me more strongly.

I see Jeremy looking at some of the Christmas presents still unopened under the tree, and that reminds me: 'Lula wants to go climbing with you. "Real mountains" – she said it again yesterday. You have to take her. You promised.'

'I mean to. I want her to get a taste for it but it needs planning. It has to be somewhere safe, and it's too cold now. Shall I call them? What time is it?'

'No, my mum will be putting them to bed shortly. Best not to get them excited again. Johnny was a bit fractious anyway – he's still dragging that flu with him.'

We feed each other some more panettone on the sofa and there's a movie on. We watch it for a while. It's near the end, but it's boring and I want to switch off but Jeremy says, 'Wait, there's more.'

'When did you see this?' I ask, absent-mindedly picking up some of Johnny's Playstation2 discs from the floor.

'When it came out,' he replies.

I do the maths quickly. 'Not with me you didn't,' I say, turning sharply to face him.

'I was probably away working in Southampton then,' comes the measured reply.

Changing the subject I add, 'You must really help me to get Johnny understand he can't just leave his stuff wherever it suits him. It turns into chaos in here and you know he listens to you.'

'I will talk to him,' says Jeremy, not really paying attention, 'but you have to cut him some slack. His school reports are rather good aren't they?'

'Yes, they are, but even Lula picks up after him and I don't want her to. She's got years of that to come when she grows up, believe me.'

When the movie ends I get up to get some more wine and say, 'Hey, I found some footage of me in a mini-kilt, just like in one of your fantasies. Wanna watch?'

He sits straighter on the sofa and takes a sip from his glass. He looks a bit unsure, and I can read his thoughts so clearly: 'Who filmed you then?' But he's too cool for that and he controls it.

'Sure, show me,' he says, and lies back.

I press Play. I lined it up earlier, and we see these two children in matching red tartan skirts. They are gathering snowballs on a pavement by some black iron gates. The colours are saturated bright; it was a sunny day.

'Which one are you?' asks Jeremy, smiling as my little trick is revealed.

'I'm the one on the left, in the little white boots. How cute are they? The other one is my cousin Susan.'

'How old were you there?'

I nestle on his lap and kiss his neck. 'Two and a half, nearly three. My mum is not pregnant with my sister here yet – must have been the following year.' She's nice, my mum. I take in the stylish sixties' coat casually on her shoulders, fox on the collar with a silver brooch, and her black hair, lacquered high. The images fizz out to static.

'Such a pity there was no money to shoot hours of Super 8, only a few minutes here and there,' I remark.

'Super 8 films only came in rolls of a few minutes each,' Jeremy says.

'They did? You know everything, darling.' I've lost interest already and am pulling at his belt. 'Take it off,' I say.

'No, you take it off for me, then maybe if you are good . . .'

'Oh,' I say, a touch too quickly, 'you'll go down on me? You haven't done that yet. You seem a bit cock centred tonight.'

I pull his jeans down and now comes the awkward moment – you never get over it. What to do when they are blocking his movements, halfway down his thighs, his knees? But he moves away and takes his shoes and socks off like you don't even notice, and the jeans come off pretty fast. He's great Jez, he never fears losing his erection for one second. Not even after a bottle of wine on his own. All is done so fast. I imagine him arriving in the operating theatre and just thrusting his hands into the sleeves of the gown, which a nurse is holding ready for him. Someone will put the mask on him, hand him the gloves. Like dressers do for actors. He fucks me for a while then pulls out and kneels on the floor and starts to lick me, very slowly. I forgot how good he is. When he does it, I get the full edit. I make sure he's got a cushion under his knees. I want this to last as long as possible but I am too excited and he knows it. He moves his tongue faster then slows down and faster again and I come clutching his shoulders and burying his face into me. As I go limp he lifts me and carries me to the bedroom. I like this part; my weight is easy on him. Though I am aware it's not a great distance to go, I know he'd carry me to safety if our home was washed away in a flood. He'd walk for miles. I like holding on to him, breathing in the creases of his neck. He throws me on the bed and I reach to turn the small fairy lights on. In this light you can't see I haven't had time to tidy up in here. Not that it makes any difference to him.

Turning around I knock a pile of books from under the window and they scatter around.

'You've got too many books in here,' he says.

'I know, mean to read them but who's got the time? Shall I read you a story now?' I ask teasingly, picking up a hefty novel.

'No, I have brought back a little something, a toy,' he says.

'Oh yeah?' I look up, eyes I am sure glimmering with anticipation. 'What is it?'

He goes into the living room and comes back with his hands behind his back. I can't see what it is, but I want to be helpful. 'Shall I get a blindfold?'

'Yes, but first I want you to wear this,' he says handing me a . . . 'A hospital gown?' I screech. 'Honey, this rather defeats all my efforts with the "turning on" underwear, but whatever does it for you, does it for me – I think. Can I keep my stockings on and my heels?'

'No, I want you to take everything off.'

I do, and put on the soft cotton robe with the silly fastening at the back, and then the blindfold. Thank god this one doesn't have an airline logo on it, but it's white so it goes with the theme. I lie back and can't stop squeezing my legs together as I feel the excitement building up in my womb. His hands pull my knees apart gently and I barely feel he's inserted something and it's not his hot cock. The hospital gown rather gave it away I think and it's one of those gynaecological gizmos, the ones that seemed so frightening when you first went for your swabs as a teenager. Now it's not such a scary thing; the cold metal feels fantastic as it cools the temperature in my body. I want to touch it and hold it, but I hear the noise it makes when it gets screwed into place. I can only guess Jez is looking at me, deep inside me, as he's not touching me, just saying 'Very nice' in a hypnotized sort of rhythm.

'Is everything OK with my womb, doctor?' I ask in my best tremulous voice.

'Yes,' he replies, 'you've done a great job with the shaving.'

'Mmm yes, I knew you'd appreciate it.' I hear the noise of his hand rubbing himself. I instantly want to participate, but in this game tonight I don't necessarily make the rules, though my co-operation is required soon after. As he frees me from the implement he loses the faraway look and says, 'You know I wouldn't ever think of this when I am with patients, don't you?'

'I know, honey, and thank god you are not a gynaecologist. And I'd ask for a woman anyway. But it can be very erotic. We know it, you know it.'

I consider for a moment whether this is bizarre. It is not the most bizarre thing I can think of. You use what you know. If Jez was a barber he'd give me the most erotic haircut ever. If he was an accountant he'd make me write figures very precisely in a big ledger, murmuring numbers in my ears as I sit on his knees and concentrate. We'd be wearing suits of course and he would spank me if I added up wrong. But he's not a fetishist and never requests anything kinky and there are no obscenities either. Now there's a word . . . I wish there was some kind of evolution in the language available to us for all this: throbbing, pulsing, rubbing, pumping, cock, cunt – it's all so basic. I specifically hate 'juicy'.

He strokes the back of my neck and I feel like a sort of Bambi going doe-eyed and sleepy, but he's not ready for that. He moves his hand to the front and gently presses on my windpipe. There's an exercise that feels like this in yoga class: you compress the thyroid and when you let go, your blood courses faster around your veins and you get a small rush. He knows I get off on my throat being constricted, but is ever so careful and never presses that hard. We fuck again like this till I come as the usual 'Oh gods' try to make their way out of my mouth. Then it's his turn, and then he's lost to me. I lie next to him and watch him regain his breath. I twine my legs with his and rest. A few moments later he moves over and holds me in a tight embrace, his heart still beating fast. He kisses my hair, my head, my neck. I burrow further into his chest and squeeze his shoulders, my palms flat on his blades. I wish I could press him into my body as one and for him to say 'I love you' but he doesn't. So I don't say it either. We fall asleep instantly.

I shift and wake up. I am very thirsty and slowly and awkwardly reach on the floor to find the bottle of water. I sense Jeremy's not asleep because he's not snoring. He speaks first, quietly.

'Are you awake?' he asks.

'Yes.'

'Wide awake?'

'Think so,' I reply.

'You know why, don't you?' he says, turning to me and gently tugging at my hair.

'Aw, but that was such a tiny line and it was hours ago,' I say, regretting how it was me who suggested it.

'Yes, but we're not used to it any more,' he chuckles in the dark.

'Either that or it's gone off, I've kept it such a long time. Do drugs go off?'

'Not really. It was in the fridge wasn't it?'

'Yes, do you think that's off limits enough for the children? It's in one of my eye drops packets.'

'Oh no, that won't do, Ingy. You better put it somewhere more difficult to reach.'

'OK. Talk to me, I am definitely awake now,' I say, hearing weariness creep into my voice. He tells me about this book he's nearly finished reading, the third part of *His Dark Materials*. I don't know how he manages such long novels. Then again, it's hardly a taxing one and anyway, I no longer think he's fucking nurses every time he's on call. You've got to get bored of it after twenty-odd years, not counting medical school, I reason to myself.

'There's a drama version on at the National Theatre. Got great reviews – want me to get tickets?' I ask.

'Not sure what my schedule is and the new guy at Médecins Sans Frontières wants me to go to Iran – there's a lot of follow-up work to do on the earthquake.'

I tense. 'Oh, Jeremy, no, the kids won't like it at all. They never get used to it, and neither do I. We haven't discussed this properly – you can't just keep making all the decisions without us.'

'Ingy come on, you know I want to. It's just been too long since I've been in that situation. I have to keep my skills up.'

'For what? So that next time you can go even further away? I know, I know, but it's just . . . For a start I inherit the swimming pool run, the ballet school run and – everything really. We need to organize this properly. We can't just rely on Alisha all the time – it gets to be very expensive.'

'We'll talk about it. I won't have to go till next week. And I hope my phone will work there – I'll call every night, I'll send pictures. They won't miss me that much and it's good for them to know what goes on in the world.'

'They won't care. What do death and destruction mean to a five- and a nine-year-old? They just want their daddy, here.' I can sense this is going nowhere at this time. I haven't got the energy and I always lose, so I add in my sternest pleading voice, 'You make sure you find a satellite link and you call. Every day, OK?'

I make to turn away from him, but his hand slides under my belly and he starts playing with me. The rhythm is wrong and I am a bit dry and too tired. I know I won't come now so I just lie there. I hear the noise of his other hand on his cock and I lift my head.

'Darling, surely you don't want more? You're just so greedy, there's no way you have more sperm now.'

'I know, but I like falling asleep doing this, you know that.'

An image of him as a child tugging at his penis for comfort pops into my head and I feel very protective.

At six thirty I wake up again without the alarm. He likes the radio but I won't have it – if something wrong comes on like that bore, Dido, I end up having a bad day. Jez is breathing deeply now. I get up to have a cup of coffee in peace. I look in the bathroom mirror and Princess Leia is staring back, only it's the Carrie Fisher version this time – worse, as she is now, a near pensioner. Where did these lines come from? I have a quick bath and go back and get under the covers again. My breath must feel cool on his cock as he stirs and immediately pushes his hips up. I go up and down for a while as the taste of toothpaste gradually disappears from my mouth, then I stop.

'Come on, Jeremy, it's seven o'clock and if you want to be at your meeting at eight we've got to go. Like, now. And I've got a bunch of Asian bankers flying in this morning. I can't be late.'

I start pulling clothes out of the wardrobe. He's looking at me and I wonder how sexy he'll find me now with my office uniform of black trousers and jacket and sensible shirt. There's no time for fancy hosiery, but I grab some lacy underwear. He slaps my ass as he stands behind me one last time, limp cock nestling tightly on my bum cheeks. I turn around and scold him. 'Don't you dare – black shows up everything.'

Inside the train carriage Jez stands too close to me and occasionally leans down to kiss me. You never see teenagers at this time of the morning so we make a passable impression. I feel slightly embarrassed, so I push him away, though I am pleased. It takes a few hours for his tenderness to surface after sex, but it always does.

He gets off first. I carry on to the City.

When I arrive home in the evening all is still and dark. I hesitate over the first flight of stairs and feel my chest tightening. Something black in the corner gives me a fright. I lean and pick up the glove. 'That's where you went then,' I say to no one. Inside, I survey the debris of the night before. It's a mess, though I remembered to soak the pans and thanks to M&S there aren't really that many, though the congealing fat from the paté jar floating in the sink gives me a sudden squeeze of guilt in my guts. I forgot we drank brandy too, but I find the small glasses in the bedroom. There are clothes everywhere. For a while I hold on to Jez's Gap shirt, the collar so clean still. Lula helped me pick it for him. I hear her little voice in the shop saying 'blue like Daddy's eyes'. I find the gown – 'Property of St Thomas' Hospital' says the tag – and then the implement, I forget what it's called. I wash it in very hot water in the sink. I've never held one in my hands before. It looks like a bird's head and it's heavy. Not sure where to put it – it belongs to the cutlery drawer in a sense, but I end up sticking it in a shoe box. I must tidy up properly before Alisha comes tomorrow. I put a CD on, old Brian Eno for comfort. Then I run a bath and soak. It's only when I am in it that I remember I didn't pick up matches for the candles. I hate the light in this bathroom. We have to change it, and the noisy extractor fan too. I think about where Jez is now. Not sure if I want to wash my hair, wanting to hang on to his smell for as long as possible. He's texted a couple of times during the day, nothing serious, just the usual banter: 'Next time, young lady, prepare to feel my firm hands on your ass. You should tremble.' I replied with some other standard script: 'Oh, I am so wet right now, sir.' Wet doesn't really do it justice, I think. The weather is wet, the clothes out of the washing machine are wet. My cunt is something else, but I am lost for words.

He won't be back tonight. I hope there's no pile up on the M25, no train crashes, no real carnage. He's the senior consultant there. They only wake him up for the unmanageable stuff and I can't bear to think of him with his hands deep inside someone's ribcage. My uncle was a fishmonger and my auntie said that had to be worse. At least Jez never carries any smell back from the theatre. Once I asked him: 'If I turned up in casualty with a massive wound or as a train crash victim, would you operate yourself? Would you trust your hand to be steady if it was me?'

'Yes, I think I could handle it,' he replied.

'But what if it was one of the kids?' I challenged him, thrusting my face close to his.

He hesitated then. 'What's with the morbid questions? No, I don't think I could, not with them, I'd go to pieces.'

Shit! The kids. I forgot about picking up Johnny and Lula. Then again Mum hasn't rung to say 'Come and get them off my hands, they are tearing the house down as usual and your dad's had enough already.'

Granted, I am a bad mother, I think as I turn the hot water tap back on, but it's OK to forget the kids really. Because, you see, they don't actually exist. I made them up one time and Jeremy went along with it. He's got his fantasies and I've got mine. To tell the truth, we are not married either. Oh come on, you'd picked up on that hadn't you? There was something that didn't quite ring true. For a start you don't really have sex like that on a weekday with your husband, do you? Or maybe you do? If so, I don't want to know, as this is what I tell myself to make sense of Jeremy's absence: that it's more fun this way and that we like it like this. But ask me again next week, when he's gone.

I lean out of the bath and pick up Lula's favourite doll from the floor. She's blond and curly haired, like I was when I was little.

PROFILE OF JONATHAN COE

SUE TYLEY

IN A NUTSHELL

Jonathan Coe has received excellent reviews for his latest book, *Like a Fiery Elephant: The Story of B. S. Johnson*. The biography was described as 'marvellous . . . moving and superbly researched' (*Sunday Times*); 'so wonderful, so compelling, so finger-tinglingly exciting' (*Observer*); 'lively, important and very thorough' (*Guardian*). Such praise is perhaps surprising given Coe's distrust of literary biography and that his subject – a writer of novels to an exacting aesthetic and of poetry, plays, films, sports reports and much else besides, whose career spanned the 1960s and early '70s – is, as Coe acknowledges in the Introduction, 'unknown nowadays to most British readers under forty'. It is less surprising when you discover that Coe took the same approach to this work of non-fiction as has made his novels increasingly, award-winningly successful, and written a book which explores and develops form; is concerned with finding, shaping and telling stories, truthfully imagined; and above all aims to give pleasure to the reader.

IN THE BEGINNING

To begin at the literary beginning: like Michael Owen, the protagonist of *What a Carve Up!*, Coe had written his first fiction, episodes from the casebook of a Victorian detective named Jason Rudd, by the time he was eight. He has described its style as a cross between Sir Arthur Conan Doyle and P. G. Wodehouse, authors to whom he was introduced, in a household in which books didn't figure prominently, by his grandfather.[1]

By fifteen he had written his first novel, which he sent to Spike Milligan's publisher. He had devoured Milligan's *Puckoon* a few years previously and thought his own novel similar; he now thinks it was dreadful, and has also described his writing at that time as an attempt to write like Evelyn Waugh which ended up like Kingsley Amis, of whom he's never been a great fan. The novel was rejected, and is the only piece of work Coe has ever burned.

It was Henry Fielding, whom Coe discovered at sixteen in the form of *Joseph Andrews*, who changed the direction of his writing. Fielding introduced him to the architectural potential of the novel, to the possibilities of multiple plots and complex inter-relationships on a large scale. The epiphany and continuing interest led Coe to select Fielding as the subject of this Ph.D. thesis – 'Satire and sympathy: some consequences of intrusive narration in *Tom Jones* and other comic novels' – nearly ten years later.

IN SEQUENCE

While working on his thesis, Coe wrote what was to be his first published novel, *The Accidental Woman*, a story of chance, relationships and indifference by an intrusive narrator who suggests in a footnote that readers may be better off listening to Prokofiev. He had written three novels by the time he was twenty-five, all of them, to his mind, publishable (the figure excludes the bonfire-destined

---

1 Getting his grandson to like Wodehouse was his great crusade but he never quite managed it and Coe's knowledge of his grandfather's favourite remains slight. Winning the 2001 Bollinger Everyman Wodehouse prize for *The Rotters' Club* nearly provided him with the means to resume his education, since he should have received a set of Wodehouse's complete works as part of the award, but it has never arrived. (What's more, Coe saw neither hide nor bristle of the pig with whom he was supposed to have his photograph taken, both pig and photo op falling victim to the chaos of security surrounding President Clinton, who presented the prize that year.)

Milliganesque one) and, having tried unsuccessfully to place them for five years, was ready to pack it in if *The Accidental Woman* too failed to find a publisher. Happily, *The Accidental Woman* was accepted by Duckworth (Coe says 'luckily' and doesn't know if he really would have given up if it hadn't been), for an advance of £200 and a suicidal contract, which Coe was advised not to sign by an agent who said she didn't like his work enough to want to represent him. A mixed blessing, then, but after sixteen rejection letters the acceptance was enough to make Coe literally jump for joy. He reflects that life was perhaps easier for the unpublished aspiring writer in those days (1986) and wonders whether such a start would be possible now in the climate of unapproachable publishing conglomerates rather than directly approachable intimate independents. (Duckworth was run by the husband-and-wife team of Colin and Anna – pen name: Alice Thomas Ellis – Haycraft.)

A Touch of Love, several stories of chance, relationships and frustration, four of them by one of the characters,[2] was published (also by Duckworth but for a £300 advance this time) in 1989, *The Dwarves of Death*, a story of chance, relationships and murder scored for percussion and piano, in 1990, but sales of all three books proved 'very very small, kind of off the scale really', and Coe again told himself that he would give up if his next novel, *What a Carve Up!*, were to sink without trace in the same way. 'But I was lucky, and it was quite successful, and it didn't happen.' In fact, *What a Carve Up!*, multiple interwoven stories of chance, murder and 1980s' Britain refracted through a writer and multiple forms of writing, won the 1995 *Mail on Sunday* / John Llewellyn Rhys Prize and the French Prix du Meilleur Livre Etranger, though Coe assesses the effect of these awards as minimal.

Like *What a Carve Up!*, *The Rotters' Club* (2001), a story of chance, relationships and adolescence in 1970s' Britain refracted through music and multiple forms of writing, was a 'serio-comic novel with a big public dimension as well as a private dimension'. In between – and Coe has commented on how each of his novels tends to be a reaction against the one before, so that those with a large political and social canvas are followed by something more contained and inward-looking – came *The House of Sleep* (1997), a story of chance, relationships and the eponymous sleep with two timeframes and several film frames. *The Closed Circle*, a story of chance, relationships and middle-age in

---

2 Despite possible appearances, these summaries are intended neither dismissively nor disrespectfully. On the contrary. It's just that the Reduced Shakespeare Company method can prove a salutary way of revealing essence and pattern, provided you're content to leave nuance and detail for another day.

1990s' Britain refracted through fewer forms of writing (an informed guess), due out later this year, is part two[3] of *The Rotters' Club* rather than a completely new novel, which explains why it bucks the alternating trend.

On form

All Coe's fiction, to a greater or lesser degree, explores and develops the form of the novel, though the current trajectory – with which Coe is comfortable – is towards the more conventional. His most recent novel, *The Closed Circle*, is told mainly in an omniscient third-person narrative voice and has caused one friend to observe that he has started to write like Trollope, a comparison which initially filled him with dismay as he finds Trollope rather a dull writer. Coe downplays the letters and emails with which the novel is punctuated ('that's hardly radical – the epistolary novel has been around for centuries'), though like *The House of Sleep*, it also contains poetry: four poems presented as though written by the character Benjamin Trotter. This from a starting point (albeit a slightly dodgy one made possible by 'the art of the sweeping, uninformed dismissal' and 'a thriving, unshakeable contempt' for twentieth century writers, both learned at Cambridge) of agreement with B. S. Johnson that the novelist's duty is to pass on the baton of innovation, and to build on the phenomenal legs of the relay run earlier in the century by Joyce and Beckett, a duty in which, Johnson thought, the vast majority of British novelists were failing or, worse, of which they were unaware.

Even though he describes Johnson as setting himself the not inconsiderable task of re-inventing the novel with every book he wrote, Coe also points out that there is nothing new under the sun, and that many of Johnson's formal devices were borrowed from writers such as Laurence Sterne, Marc Saporta and Philip Toynbee. For himself, time and experience have modified his conviction regarding the obligation to innovate, but while he maintains that none of his novels are very experimental, he doesn't take the form of any new novel for granted: there is a period at the start of the writing process where he consciously decides on the appropriate form for that particular book. The one that interests him most in retrospect is *The House of Sleep*, whose alternating timeframes, he says, opened lots of avenues which wouldn't have been available to him otherwise. (The Author's note to the novel advises the reader that 'The odd-numbered

---

3 Originally, it was going to be part six, but Coe decided not to write volumes two to five.

chapters . . . are set mainly in the years 1983-4. The even-numbered chapters are set in the last two weeks of June, 1996.')

Other formal variations in Coe's work include narratives within the narrative (*A Touch of Love*, which contains four stories written by one of the characters); following the structure of a song (*The Dwarves of Death*, whose section headings include Intro, Theme One, Middle Eight, Solo, Key Change and Fade); the integral use of a film and a kaleidoscope of different forms of writing (*What a Carve Up!*, which features the real-life film of the same name and, among other forms, newspaper columns, magazine articles, meeting minutes, diary entries, TV programme transcripts, footnotes, letters, including spoof ones, agricultural research notes, juvenilia, an internal title page and a Preface, which appears at the end though it returns to the beginning); and sections with different timeframes (*The Rotters' Club*, which ends with a thirty-six page sentence celebrating a moment). Coe has also noticed his predilection for circularity: *What a Carve Up!* begins and ends with the same sentence, and *The Closed Circle* ends in Berlin with the same conversation which opens *The Rotters' Club*.

While he refers to this aspect of his technique as 'playing games with form', Coe maintains that there is a serious intention behind it, 'to convey reality more tellingly', and not simply to make a joke. He also cautions, 'I don't think you can afford to do any of these things unless you've got the reader

ON-SIDE

on-side', and getting the reader on-side, drawing him in by attending to his wants, needs and pleasure, is one of Coe's distinguishing and quality-assuring hallmarks.

Humour is perhaps the most conspicuous of the features through which Coe aims to give the reader pleasure, but he doesn't will or force it, he says: 'it's just how I write, although I'm always relieved when it happens' – relieved because as well as entertaining the reader as self-prescribed, it also serves to secure his allegiance for the next fifty or so pages as he carries on in the expectation of being given something like that again. As well as moving his readers to laughter, Coe also aims to move them to tears: 'emotionality, of which these are two sides of the same coin, is the important thing. And,' he continues, 'I'm more and more becoming reconciled to the idea that readers want – are entitled to want – some kind of thrill of recognition from a book . . . to have [their] instincts confirmed about something, to feel the shock . . . and the thrill of recognizing something [they] haven't seen before.'

Then there are the traditional novelistic virtues such as plot, which Coe (inter)weaves to a labyrinthine degree; character, both three-dimensional psychologically realized ones and two-dimensional caricatures; vivid dialogue; distinctive voice; thought-provokingly relevant themes . . . And throughout the novels there is, for the vigilant reader, a rewarding sprinkling of intertextual and autobiographical references: to a band called The Unfortunates, the title of a B. S. Johnson novel, in *The Dwarves of Death*, for example, or to Coe's own early novels in the titles of those written by the protagonist of *What a Carve Up! – Accidents Will Happen / The Accidental Woman* and *The Loving Touch / A Touch of Love*.

It has to be said, though, that Coe livens up his fiction as much for his own sake as for the reader's: he has confessed to getting bored easily while writing, to changing voices frequently because of losing confidence in them, and to breaking out of a conventional narrative line into email, letter or unpunctuated dialogue as much because he can't bear to do another chapter in the third person as because the subject matter requires it.

INTERVENTION

Coe has said that he is bemused by the expectation, given voice in phone calls from journalists, that writers are qualified to solve the world's problems: he's never really seen why making up stories and inventing characters necessarily gives you an insight into the conflict in the Middle East, say; he knows no more than anyone else who watches the six o'clock news. Yet he has also said that a novelist should 'achieve a universal truth', which implies a degree of moral responsibility and insight, and in his choice and treatment of social and political subjects in some of his novels (1980s' Thatcherite Britain in *What a Carve Up!*, 1970s' industrial relations in *The Rotters' Club*) he engages critically with big issues. Again, in *Like a Fiery Elephant*, he describes writing novels as 'an intervention . . . an act of lunatic faith in the notion that by adding something to the world we might somehow be improving it'. Asked about this aspect of the writer's role, he begins tentatively: 'I wish I had an articulate answer to this . . . I just want to feel that my time hasn't been wasted, that I've written something that's true, not in the B. S. Johnson sense of having actually happened but true in the sense of plausible, true in the sense of being accurately and properly imagined.' And the fact that Coe knows from his correspondence that *The Rotters' Club* struck a chord with, among others, a nineteen-year-old Italian woman who grew up in Verona as well as with contemporaries who shared his experience of growing up in Birmingham in the 1970s, demonstrates that it hasn't, and that he has.

INVASION EVASION

And what does the writer get out of writing? In *Like a Fiery Elephant*, Coe quotes B. S. Johnson as saying that he wrote novels 'to exorcise, to remove from myself, from my mind, the burden [of] having to bear some pain, the hurt of some experience: in order that it may be over there, in a book, and not here in my mind.' At the end of the book, he states his own view that novel writing 'is not a hobby (although we're allowed to find it enjoyable); it is not a form of therapy (although it can be therapeutic)'. Reminded of these two positions, Coe acknowledges the personal aspects of enjoyment and therapy, but returns (was he evading the admittedly invasive question or was it set up too obscurely?) to the novelist's public role, to satisfy the reader, and says (well out of reach now) that he thinks the reading public is currently ill served by the literary establishment, in the form of publicity and prizes, with regard to providing guidance about what to read. To illustrate how out of step that establishment is with public taste, he cites a survey conducted at Hay by the organizers of the Orange prize, in which five hundred festival-goers were asked to nominate their essential contemporary novel; the list of the top fifty included only three Booker prize winners and, a little better, eight Orange shortlisted titles. *What a Carve Up!* was on the list, but that wouldn't have been Coe's reason for mentioning it.

IN HARNESS

On the subject of prizes, Coe doesn't think that the awards he has won in this country made much difference to his career, although the two French prizes did have an effect in France; they have to be of the order of the Booker, Whitbread or Orange prize to have a significant impact on sales and success. As for the importance of a good agent to the management of a writer's career, it depends, says Coe, on how you define 'a good agent'. His definition is someone who is a perceptively critical reader of his books, and who places them with publishers intelligently and attentively. Which is why he ignores anyone who asks why he isn't with a huge agency which (cl)aims regularly to secure megabuck deals in America and is happily settled with Tony Peake, whom he describes as 'wonderful, the best [agent] in London as far as I'm concerned' and to whom he feels married; they have in fact been together for longer than Coe's actual marriage. For the first two years of his career, though, Coe didn't have an agent at all; probably not a viable option nowadays.

Up to and including *The Rotters' Club*, Coe had a group of friends from university to whom, in addition to his agent, he would send early versions of his novels for comment. His latest novel, *The Closed Circle*, however, was only read by his agent, his editor and two or three friends chosen because they had expertise in particular areas addressed by the book which he wanted checked. This was partly because it was written quickly and there wasn't time, and partly because it's not a brand new novel, it's part two of *The Rotters' Club*, and he has known for a long time what was going to happen and what the tone was going to be like. He says he hasn't missed the wider feedback: 'I finally feel after seven novels that I trust my instincts enough to know when I've written a dog and when I've written one that's going to work.'

INTERESTS AND INFLUENCES

Books read at school (the emphasis is 'books he was *made* to read at school') of which Coe has a vivid memory include *Animal Farm* and *Lord of the Flies*, but they didn't excite him in quite the same way as the extra-curricular work of Flann O'Brien and Conan Doyle. His other enthusiasms around this time were non-literary, and included 'rather esoteric, not-quite-prog-rock groups' – though the first record he remembers buying, at the age of eleven, is a Bill Haley and the Comets album, probably his grandfather's influence again.[4] Then there were television programmes such as *Monty Python*, *Marty Feldman* and *The Goodies*, and he lists the TV script writers Dick Clement and Ian La Frenais among his heroes as well as his influences.

Other acknowledged influences? Fielding, Dickens, Flann O'Brien, Rosamond Lehmann, Hermann Hesse, David Nobbs,[5] Ealing

---

4 Coe would later become the pianist and composer for a cabaret group called 'Wanda and the Willy Warmers'. What he mainly remembers about their material is how filthy it was, while his music was tuneful and melancholic. They made, he says, an interesting combination of which, regrettably, no recording survives. Coe also played in and composed for a jazz quintet, which shrank to a quartet, and plans to reacquaint himself with the piano when he takes a break from writing next year.

5 Some facts about the one I had to look up: David Nobbs is a novelist and TV script writer and the creator of Reginald Perrin. He has worked with comedy, B. S. Johnson, Robert Musil and Bohumil Hrabal (for multi-page sentences among other aspects of *The Rotters' Club*).

And, for the record, since everyone asks though Coe's answers vary, contemporary novelists he admires include (the order is Coe's) Alasdair Gray, Andrew Crumey, Nicholas Royle, Julie Myerson, Suzannah Dunn, Helen Dunmore – to name just a few.

IN CONTEXT

Many aspects of Coe's fiction tie in with contemporary thinking about culture, literature and critical theory. For example: the themes of chance and identity; the questioning of, and breaking up/down perspectives on, meta-narratives such as history and narrative itself; its features of intertextuality, pastiche, self-consciousness, discontinuity and permutation; not to mention Lacanian psychoanalysis. And in laying bare the process and problems of literary biography, and borrowing techniques from another form, *Like a Fiery Elephant*, too, is quintessentially post-modern. But Coe is not conscious of working within these parameters or of reflecting these shared concerns; his creative decisions are instinctive and, he says, 'I think a novel's great strength, its great trump card, is its individuality and its freedom from movements . . . if I have any sense of [working within parameters] it's of a sort of novelistic tradition, a social-realist tradition weighing down on me and being quite hard to break out of. But then again, I think realism is the great strength of the . . . British novel.'

IN ADDITION

In addition to his post-modern, serio-comic, social-realist novels and the Johnson biography, Coe has written biographies of two screen actors: *Humphrey Bogart: Take It and Like It* and *James Stewart: Leading Man*. But he has said that he has no talent for non-fiction, once describing a period of writing it as like wading through quicksand compared to writing fiction, while for Michael Owen in *What a Carve Up!*, the commission to write a history of the Winshaws soon begins to pall.

Or compared to writing screenplays, which offers the same joy of being able to make up dialogue and have characters do what you want

virtually all the major figures in comedy since the '50s, and has adapted *What a Carve Up!* for the small screen. Coe interviewed Nobbs for the Summer 2000 issue of *The Idler*.

them to do. He worked on early drafts of *Five Seconds to Spare*, the 1999 film version of *The Dwarves of Death*,[6] and has written a screenplay of *The House of Sleep* (a novel in which film is featured, as it is also in *What a Carve Up!*) for which production funding remains outstanding.[7]

Coe has explained elsewhere that he doesn't write short stories because he invariably expands them, adding more characters and backstories, until they turn into novels.

The only poems he has written and published as an adult appear as intrinsic elements of *The House of Sleep* and *The Closed Circle*, but he says he would love to write more, and has recently started to read poetry again under the guidance of friends with discriminating taste who can direct him to 'the good stuff'.[8] He's reading Yevgeny Yevtushenko at the moment, whose combination of love, politics and pulling at the heartstrings is what he thinks good poetry should be.

Having had a five-year period early on in his career of writing lots of reviews, Coe does so now only if his arm has been twisted. During that time, he gradually – too gradually, he says – became uncomfortable with the idea of writers reviewing other writers' books. He also realized that sometimes he was only completing books because he had to write a review of them; he describes himself as 'a bad finisher of books' and on those occasions when the honest thing to say would have been 'I would not have finished this book', as a reviewer he didn't have that option.

---

6 Coe says the final version was beautifully photographed, but that audiences could make neither head nor tail of it, which he puts down to the novel itself having a messy plot that doesn't work. The film never went on general release and only came out on DVD, but it's still available.

7 To complete the picture (if only they would): *What a Carve Up!* has been under option for the last eleven years but remains unmade, and filming of *The Rotters' Club* begins in August for broadcast in three hour-long episodes on BBC2 some time next year. The screenplay is by Dick Clement and Ian La Frenais which, Coe says, 'I'm very excited about because they are heroes of mine'.

8 He taught English poetry for a year at Warwick while he was studying for his Ph.D., and describes the experience as a nightmare. Although Cambridge purported to give undergraduates an induction into the canon, he reckons he was ill-read in English poetry when he left, and survived teaching the course only by keeping one day ahead of his students; not a very fulfilling experience for them, he suspects, or him.

Fiery not white

Appropriately for a biography about someone who believed in the chaotic, untidy, untied nature of life, *Like a Fiery Elephant* represents a tangle of contradictions. In the Introduction, Coe describes his distrust of the assumptions that underpin the writing of – and public appetite for – literary biography. Acknowledging the apparent naïvety of his position in the face (picture a slavering maw) of a culture which has turned novels merely into one stage of a process devoted to 'the scrutiny and interrogation of writers' lives in the name of that insatiable curiosity which feeds on anyone reckless enough to set themselves up as a public figure', Coe believes that 'a work of literature should speak for itself' and regrets that 'No one retains any real sense of the novel itself . . . as a reliable model of human nature: we have lost all semblance of that kind of faith in literature, or in the trustworthiness of writers'. And he is aware, and wary, of the dangers of voyeurism, insensitivity and over-simplification inherent in the genre for both biographer and reader. Yet he confesses to being 'a bit cheeky' in stating his distrust, since he himself will read anything, including biographies, on those people – writers, composers, artists – about whom he feels passionately. Literary biography for its own sake, however, a book about someone who does not interest or move him (he cites George Eliot as an example) he cannot imagine himself sitting down and tackling – though he pre-emptively admits to the probable injustice of his view. And here is another acknowledged contradiction: he recognizes that most people have not even heard of B. S. Johnson, let alone have an interest in him, yet here he is, inviting them to learn more. This 'was always the challenge of the book, that most literary biography starts from the assumption that there is a general level of interest in the subject, which there hasn't been for B. S. Johnson. I had to do a certain amount of throat clearing to get myself primed and convinced that the book I was going to write was actually going to have any kind of audience.'

In circles

Which takes us back to where we started, although this isn't quite the end. What should guarantee the audience, and create the interest in B. S. Johnson and his work that wasn't there before, is Coe's handling of the material – a final paradox, since that handling is novelistic rather than traditionally biographical: 'In retrospect, I approached it exactly as I would one of my novels. Where it was necessary to change viewpoint, break out of the linearity, play games with the form, that's what I did, but I never sat down and thought, "B. S. Johnson was an experimental novelist so I have to write an experimental biography". And it started out as a very conventional, linear biography . . . but that didn't interest me really as a writer.' And so we have a distinctive, often humorous, self-deprecating, intelligent, acutely perceptive narrative voice self-consciously engaging in its task; the creating and shaping of the same but different (life) story out of Johnson's novels, documentary fragments and the voices of those who knew him. We have the variety of the fragments and (transcribed) voices themselves, the time shifts and the suspense of the delayed Fragment 46, which is flagged by the following footnote: 'You will notice, by the way, that Fragment 46 is missing. This is because it was almost the last thing that I found while going through Johnson's archive, so I think you should read it at the end of the book. (No flicking forward, by the way: this is a bound object, a work of "enforced consecutiveness", not some box full of loose sections to be shuffled and read in any order you choose!)' And we have intertextuality in those section headings that are taken from the chapter titles and body of *Christie Malry's Own Double-Entry*. And the whole is respectfully wrapped in Coe's admiration: for Johnson's 'command of language, his freshness, his formal ingenuity, the humanity that shines through even his most rigorous experiments, his bruising honesty. For all these, he remains one of my greatest literary heroes. And above all, I suppose, for the simple reason that he took himself, and his art – or craft, vocation, call it what you will – so seriously.'

So to quote again from the reviews (and it is to be hoped that the echo of *What a Carve Up!* is entirely intentional) 'it draws the reader in irresistibly, as Coe writes with brio and relevance' (*Sunday Times*).

IN INCONCLUSIVE CONCLUSION

This *is* the end, although that doesn't mean it's conclusive. Coe has said that he's not a writer who's comfortable with writing about periods that he can't remember first hand, and it's true that his novels to date often 'write out [his] own experience': the summer holidays at Porth Ceiriad in north Wales; being an authorityless prefect with a pretended penchant for a holdall; the bedsit in Coventry. But he also points out that he knew nothing about sleep clinics, factory farming, arms dealing or industrial unrest when he started writing, and that those parts of the novels are based on research rather than first-hand knowledge. But he thinks he's 'at the point that B. S. Johnson reached, which was a complete moment of crisis for him, when he ran out of experience to write about, or actually you find yourself writing about your present experience which is too close to get any kind of objectivity about.'[9] As a result, two of the 'very nebulous ideas' he currently has for future projects are 'a play set in the eighteenth century and a big novel set mainly in occupied France during the '40s'. He wants to use these vehicles 'to imagine and fictionalize' two more of his heroes (that word again), one a novelist and one a composer, and hopes to achieve the degree of intimacy with his subjects which was one of the things he most enjoyed about writing the B. S. Johnson biography. At the same time, he says 'You're still going to be writing your autobiography whatever period you write about, I think. I certainly am. I believe Johnson was right about that – that you only have your own story to tell really.'

But before Coe resumes his story in this way, there'll be a suspenseful pause – and you shouldn't hold your breath: 'I don't know if I'll do it. I'll probably do something completely different' – in which he spends more time with his family, perhaps succumbs to the temptation of invitations to overseas festivals in appealing locations, practises the piano and – who knows? – closes another circle by reconvening 'Wanda and the Willy Warmers'.

---

9 Two comments from a discussion at the Hay Festival involving Coe and John Updike are relevant here. Updike spoke of writing from life – but with a difference: there needs to be a gap for the spark to jump, a gap in which devices, distance and invention come in. And Coe remembered Updike once saying that what he saw through the eyes of his character Rabbit Angstrom was more worthwhile than what he saw through his own, even though the difference may be only slight. Coe said that what interests him is the nature of the imaginative freedom gained by doing this, by seeing through the eyes of others.

INCOMPLETE CHECKLIST

Born Birmingham 19 August 1961

EDUCATION

King Edward's School, Birmingham 1972-1979
BA Trinity College, Cambridge 1983
MA 1984 and PhD 1986 University of Warwick

BIBLIOGRAPHY

The Accidental Woman Gerald Duckworth and Co. Ltd 1987
A Touch of Love Gerald Duckworth and Co. Ltd 1989
The Dwarves of Death Fourth Estate Ltd 1990
Humphrey Bogart: Take It and Like It Bloomsbury 1991
James Stewart: Leading Man Bloomsbury 1994
What a Carve Up! Viking 1994
The House of Sleep Viking 1997
The Rotters' Club Viking 2001
Like a Fiery Elephant: The Story of B. S. Johnson Picador 2004
The Closed Circle Viking 2004

PRIZES AND AWARDS

1995 *Mail on Sunday* / John Llewellyn Rhys Prize (*What a Carve Up!*)
1995 Prix du Meilleur Livre Etranger – France (*What a Carve Up!*)
1997 Writers' Guild Award (Best Fiction) (*The House of Sleep*)
1998 Prix Médicis Etranger – France (*The House of Sleep*)
2001 Bollinger Everyman Wodehouse Prize (*The Rotters' Club*)
2004 Chevalier dans l'Ordre des Arts et des Lettres – France

NOTES ON CONTRIBUTORS

LAMYA TURKI HADEETHA AL-KHRAISHA is a Jordanian Bedouin of the Bani Sakher tribe. In 2002, aged twenty-five, she was awarded first place in the British Council's national creative writing competition held in Amman. Lamya has worked as a subtitler for *ShowTime* and as an interpreter / translator for the United Nations Development Program. She is currently working on her first novel, *Badia*.

HEIDI AMSINCK, a journalist born in Copenhagen, has covered Britain for the Danish press since 1992. Heidi has written numerous short stories and was shortlisted in 2003 for the Royal Society of Literature's V. S. Pritchett Memorial Prize. Living in North London with her husband and two young sons, Heidi is currently working on a novel.

JONATHAN CATHERALL has taught politics to undergraduates, poetry to children, and English as a Foreign Language. He now raises money for charity from grant-making trusts and foundations. He is working on a novel set in urban Indonesia.

TAMSIN COTTIS is a teacher and therapist and is the co-founder of Respond, a national charity supporting people with learning disabilities who have been sexually abused. 'Jude' is an extract from her novel, *Barefoot on Sharp Stones*. She lives in East London with her partner and three daughters.

PAUL DALY is originally from Wales but now lives in South London. He currently advises pharmaceutical and technology companies on Research & Development government incentives. He is working on a novel: a pharma thriller and not-quite-love story.

LIZ FREMANTLE's ambition, to be a Bunny Girl, was thwarted due to her tender age, so she embarked on a career in fashion journalism instead, becoming, eventually, Fashion Editor at *Vogue*. She has written for *The Erotic Review* and lives in London where she teaches yoga and is writing her first novel.

NADINE GRIEVE has worked as a radio and television producer for the BBC. She lives in London and is writing a novel about betrayal.

SALLY HINCHCLIFFE has recently returned to London after two years in Swaziland and currently works at Kew Gardens. She was shortlisted for the BBC2 Double Exposure Screenwriting competition and selected to read one of her stories at a Tales of the Decongested event. She is currently working on a novel, *The Year List*.

ALISON HUNTINGTON was born in South Wales. She works as a freelance copywriter and lives in North London with her partner and baby son. Alison is a second year Certificate student and is working on a novel about metamorphosis.

ANNE KOCH was born in Montreal to a Hungarian mother and a Dutch father, but has now lived in North London for more than twenty years. She has travelled extensively as a journalist and currently works for the BBC World Service. Anne is writing a novel about how the past can consume the present.

DUNCAN LAWRENCE was born in Johannesburg and is the youngest-ever recipient of the South African Amstel Playwright of the Year Award (in 1990 for *Modern Eating Habits*). Duncan currently lives in London where he works for an investment bank. He has written two screenplays and is writing a novel called *Henry First*.

MATTHEW LOUKES lives in East London with his wife, Jackie. Matthew was shortlisted for the 1998 CWA New Crime Writing competition and has had some sports writing published in magazines and national newspapers. He is working on a novel set in London.

MICHAEL MAYHEW was born in South East London and has had several short stories published in recent years. He has juggled a number of odd jobs in between abortive attempts to relocate to New Orleans and somehow managing to get a decent sociology degree. He is currently working on a novel, *Jack & the Lad*, in which the supernatural and the search for rough trade become entwined.

HELEN PIKE lives and works in London. 'Hellfire Corner' is an abridged extract from her novel, which is set in England and Belgium in 1919 and 2004. She is the recipient of an Arvon Jerwood Award.

ALESSANDRA SARTORE learnt English in her native Italy by listening to David Bowie records. She came to London to meet The Clash and wrote for *Rockstar* magazine. She travels extensively and maintains a flexible career. Alessandra has written a collection of short fiction, 'If I Was a Good Girl, Would I Write Such Wicked Stories?'. Her debut novel, *Trail*, features Cambodian refugees, drug smuggling and revenge.

AMANDA SCHIFF has lived in London all her life. She left school at sixteen to pursue a career in film, and is now a film producer and teacher of screenwriting. Amanda is working on her first novel, a contemporary story of love and supernatural possession set in Los Angeles. It has nothing to do with the film industry.

SUE TYLEY has a Ph.D. in English Literature and works as a freelance knowledge management consultant. Her job has taken her to the Royal Navy, a secure psychiatric unit and the City. Sue has written a collection of short stories and is now working on a novel.

SOPHIE WARNE lived in Brixton. She published several guidebooks – most recently *Gabon, São Tomé and Príncipe* (Bradt) and *Paris* (Footprint) – and wrote travel pieces for publications that include *The Times* and *Wanderlust* magazine. She was writing a novel, *John Angel*.

CATHY WASSON is American and lives in London with her husband and two children. She is working on her first novel, *Going to Graceland*.

WILLIAM WEINSTEIN was born in England but has spent much of his adult life in Europe and the States. He now lives in London with his wife and son. William has had several articles published in magazines and was shortlisted for the 2003 Fish Short Story Prize. 'All the Hard Ways' is an extract from his novel of the same title.

HEATHER WILLIAMS is American, lives in London, and will soon move to Berlin. She is working on a novel. 'Blind Friend Date' is her first published story.

RACHEL WRIGHT was born in Dallas, Texas. In 1999, she was named one of the state's student journalists of the year and was shortlisted for the Texas Young Playwright competition. Rachel has written a collection of short stories and is starting to plan her first novel.